THE END
OF PITY

Also by Robie Macauley
THE DISGUISES OF LOVE

THE
END
OF PITY

And Other Stories by ROBIE MACAULEY

McDOWELL, OBOLENSKY INC.

New York

Acknowledgment is here made to the following publications, in which all but one of the stories included in this volume first appeared: *Esquire*, "The Academic Style"; *Furioso*, "A Nest of Gentlefolk"; *New World Writing*, "The End of Pity"; *The Kenyon Review*, "The Thin Voice," "The Chevigny Man" and "Legend of the Two Swimmers"; *The Partisan Review Book of Modern Writing*, "The Mind Is Its Own Place"; *Tomorrow*, "The Invaders"; *The Sewanee Review*, "The Wishbone"; *Quixote*, "A Guide to the Muniment Room."

Manufactured in the United States of America by The Haddon Craftsmen, Inc., Scranton, Penna.

Designed by Stefan Salter

TO

GEORGE MACAULEY

EMMA MACAULEY

TABLE
OF CONTENTS

THE END
OF PITY

A NEST OF GENTLEFOLK

THERE was a man outside who said he knew where the fellow was hiding, but he had to wait until we could find Oscar's pipe. It turned out that the pipe was in a desk drawer just where Oscar had left it; the tension relaxed and everybody turned back to what he had been doing. "Let him in," Oscar said.

Oscar stood by the window putting some tobacco into the bowl of the pipe and the two of them stared at each other for a minute. The old German was thick in body and limb; he might have been built, not born, he was so riveted, so bolted, so bound, so ribbed, so keglike. You thought so until you saw his face, which was a tender raw color and delicately insane.

There was a long pinched nose, absolutely classic lips, fine white hair and for eyes two blueberries that slid around in their sockets of cream.

In whatever side street or second story we set up our office, the CIC sign hung out like a welcome to the whole European underworld of fantasy: a Salvation Army, a pawnbroker's, a confessional, a zoo, a second-hand dealer in fables. Those White Russian colonels, those Albanian slave laborers, Mongolian deserters from the German army, Dutch Communists, French spies, German anti-Nazis who had lived like ghosts for six years—all came through our door to deposit unbelievable specimens, bones, queer fish, curios. But we examined them all, assayed them all. Now and then, stuck to the bottom of some huge ugly fake Chinese-vase of a story we would find a genuine rare coin of truth and these were what kept us going, our margin of profit.

All this was quite unknown to Oscar, although he was the officer-in-charge. He smoked his pipe whenever he could find it, ate his dinner and filed reports with the G-2. He was a kind of proprietor who could not tell you what he bought and sold.

But I could see all of that change the moment he stared across his desk at the old German. I could see the sudden spark of imagination from freak to freak, for Oscar simply had never met one of his own kind before.

Oscar wore his air of junior-officer efficiency like some absurd garnish of camouflage; underneath it he was tallow, a fat gray candle without a wick. This strangeness the G-2 colonel (a nasty schoolmistress of a man) could not fail to notice and daily he would jab and jab Oscar with his sarcasm or, sometimes, thump him with fury when things went wrong. When Oscar returned from these meetings and sat at his desk his face looked like the face of a circus clown (the one that always gets hit) who has just stripped off the grease-paint smile and the cherry nose and sees his own naked misery in the mirror.

"Tell me about it," said Oscar to the old man, although

he knew only three words of German himself. The man began in a sludgy whisper that belonged more to the trunk than the head, *"Herr Hauptmann, Ich wollte . . ."* Larry Stein, who was sitting at one of the desks, began translating without even turning around.

I had been on such chases and I knew the story before it began. There was a castle on the hilltop, rather inaccessible; the mysterious comings and goings. There was the man with the moustache seen in the garden, the servant who got drunk in the Wirtshaus and said this and that, the people on the road who looked like SS men, the plane that came over one night just after the surrender, seemed to land and then to disappear.

None of us quite realized what was happening. John Short was sitting on the field safe cleaning his fingernails and reading a copy of *Stars and Stripes* spread out on the floor in front of him. Gillespie was leaning out of the window; Larry stared at the wall and translated; I tried to finish a letter to my aunt in Muskegon who sends me lidlike peanut-butter cookies. All was tranquil. But Oscar and the German stared at each other in a frenzy.

They had been kicking aside some trash in the attic and —suddenly! Yes! They were holding it up to the light. It *was* the philosopher's stone! "Men!" Oscar shouted in a choked voice. "Get ready to move!"

He had jerked up the field telephone and wrung its lever; he was calling, "Get me Thimbleful—you, Stein, get a jeep out right away. Gillespie, the M-3's. No, no, *this* is Thimbleful CIC, what I want is Thimbleful G-2—Mac, the maps, some rations . . ."

As it turned out finally there was something wrong with

the line and Oscar never got through. We had all been tramping aimlessly about, in and out of doors, up and down stairs, waiting for the moment when Oscar reached the colonel. Then after the flash of blue fire, the sudden electrocution, we would have applied artificial respiration, offered him a drink and said, "Well, after all, there *could* have been something in it."

But the colonel couldn't be reached, so here we were out in the courtyard beside the jeep—Stein, Gillespie, the German and I—loading in boxes of K-rations, field glasses, two M-3 submachine guns. Then Oscar appeared in the doorway; he was carrying a pair of handcuffs.

He turned around and yelled back to John Short inside, "Listen, Johnnie. Get through to him as soon as you can. Tell him the whole story and say that I'll send back the co-ordinates as soon as possible. Tell him to stand by; we may need some help." Full of such spirits, Oscar came banging down the steps and sprang into the jeep. The rest of us were quiet. It was as if three teetotaling Baptist deacons suddenly found themselves in a taxi with a wallowing drunk.

We were living in one end of a big sour-yellow building that somehow had the appearance of an immense stalled trolley car on which a black roof had been clapped. The yard was sleepy and dusty with sunlight; at the other end of it the German women were hanging up their wash. For three weeks the world had not believed in this bogey, this desperate runner, this wild refugee who now and then took hiding in the haunted house of a mind like Oscar's.

Larry drove and Oscar sat next to him. In the back seat I was crowded between Gillespie and the old man, who stared and worked his lips. We switched around the corner of the gateway and joggled down the street towards the end of town. We passed the Postamt, the Friseur, the Drogerie, through whose wavy greenish fishbowl windows people peered out at us. Three old women stood like stalks planted in the middle of the sidewalk staring at the carful, wondering why the old fellow was being carted off like that. A dangerous Nazi, probably, and no one had ever known!

"Little do they realize!" Gillespie whispered to me. I knew he loved this now that we had started because he got his greatest pleasure out of watching elaborate fireworks displays of folly that somebody else must pay for.

Oscar's face was raging calm; he studied the green map in its glassine case. A horse and wagon backed up to let us by, some kids sitting in the gutter shrieked at us, windows flashed in the sun, we ran into a big puddle of shadow and then passed through the gnawed stone arch at the town gate and headed due south.

The landscape we were now driving through was robbed from a copy of Grimm or Andersen; it was pure kindergarten legend. Under that childhood-blue sky, on that road winding among meadows green as first innocence, in those Hansel-and-Gretel woods, it was possible to believe in chasing dragons. In Bavaria.

But, on the other hand, the whole country had the atmosphere of a Potemkin village. The world had been carefully faked for our coming; the streams were colored a deeper blue, the grass and trees dyed a greener green, the buildings sprayed with artificial sunlight to give just the right antique effect, the papier-mâché hills covered with cardboard terraces, the people put into peasant costumes. A mile behind this quaint countryside was a dreary landscape where bodies

of dead Jews were stacked in camps, ruined munitions fac-
tories sprawled beside greasy rivers and sullen people in
ragged overcoats walked in the rain. Or that's how it seemed.

The old man looked bewitched as he sat beside me; the
wind caught his hair and made it a blaze of white fire around
his pink skull as he turned his sensitive face from side to side.

Larry Stein drove fast and I could see him turn toward
Oscar every now and then. He was an Iroquois right out of
Leatherstocking Tales with a profile like a chipped-flint
arrowhead and a savage pragmatism. In big cities he was
the world's best woodsman and guide; he had hunted and
fished that wilderness alone since one day in 1936 in Berlin
when he came home from school and heard that his father
had been dragged off. He was trying to get Oscar to stop
at another CIC detachment to pick up some help. He was
describing a fortress high as Gibraltar and packed with
SS men.

Oscar finally gave in. I knew Stein was hoping that someone, preferably a major, would point out what a wild-hare
chase this was. So we turned where the sign said *Calliope
CIC*, dipped through a hollow, passed a village with a chow
line in the square, dodged round a Signal Corps truck stalled
in the road, saw the village straggle, thicken again like a
meandering sentence and come to a stop with a tall house
like an exclamation point. On the door was written *Calliope
CIC* in chalk. The huge black arrows pointing down to the
cellar windows were still unerased but somebody had tried,
with thin blue paint, to change the street sign from *Hermann
Göring Strasse* to *George Patton Strasse,* but the point of the
joke was lost in dribbles. I went inside with Oscar.

Dust on the windows, flies, wall maps, field desks, empty
bottles, pfc. "Where's the C.O.?" Oscar asked. The man was

dissecting a Luger on the table and he waved at a door without unsquinting his eyes from the scattered steel bowels and vertebrae in front of him. Thumps, crashes from the other room. A paper skidded out of a desk, somersaulted, hid under a chair. A crossdraft of dust in the sunshine.

When we opened the door onto a big schoolroom, four were tossing a medicine ball around and about six of them were playing football in the middle of the floor. "Captain! Captain Berry!" Oscar shouted, but a lieutenant was carrying the ball, an old knit cap stuffed with rags, and nobody paid any attention. In a minute they were all spilled on the floor, laughing and yelling.

In time Oscar was able to make the captain listen to him. The captain sat on a table (holding the ball so the game wouldn't go on without him), brushed off his uniform and listened a little to what Oscar had to say. Some of the other players came over and stood brushing their clothes off, too. "Let's go," said one of them.

"It might be dangerous," Oscar was saying. "I could use maybe half a dozen men. You know how well the big shots are guarded." The captain picked a splinter out of his knee and shook his head. There was a squabble of laughing and pushing behind him. Finally a roosterish lieutenant said, "Where is this castle?" Then he added, "How do we know it's in our territory?" "Yes!" said the captain, smiling for the first time. "How do we even know it's in our territory?"

When we had all trooped into the other room Oscar found what he thought might be the location on the German 1/25,000 situation map, which was covered by a transparent sheet marked with flags and lines in grease pencil. "About here." He spotted it with his thumb.

The captain and the lieutenant almost bumped heads; the

lieutenant suddenly crowed, "Out of our territory! Six miles out of it." Straightening up, the captain assumed an orientation-lecture manner, faced Oscar and said, "That's right, Captain Hind. You can look right here at the map and you'll see that the dividing line between your divisional area and ours makes a little dip here, putting the place you're talking about definitely outside our territory."

As we went, he smiled again, his mouth the shape of a cookie cutter. "I'd give you some of my men but who knows? Something might break right here and then I'd be caught short." When Oscar was going out the door, the captain yelled, "I hope you get the old boy." Then we could hear him calling signals again in the schoolroom.

Larry was leaning forward, his arms folded over the wheel. Gillespie talked to some kids who wanted gum; the old man sat bolt upright in the back seat. "No dice?" asked Stein.

"No dice and no remarks. We're going to carry out this mission if—if—"

"We have to do it ourselves?"

"Yes," said Oscar as he climbed in. "If we have to do it ourselves."

Stein started for the main road; we traveled for over two hours. The old man kept directing Stein, leaning forward to exude his greasy whisper. Right, left there, now cross the bridge. At last we came to a little crossroads and the old man thought he'd missed a turn. We slammed to a stop. Stein turned around at him and said, "All right, you dumb bastard, you trot back and look at the sign again."

When he ran he cantered; he was like a barrel knocked end over end. He finally got to the crossroads, stared at the guidepost, came clattering back at us again *"Richtig!"* he yelled from twenty feet away, then scrambled for the jeep, all knees and elbows, as if we might jettison him yet. "These goddamn stupid Heinies," said Stein. "*Was?*" said the old man.

We had some low hills to cross, then the road took a sickle-blade slope into a village; we could see what had happened there from a long way off. It was one of those isolated spots where some local party member, some gray-haired Volksturm lieutenant had rounded up, perhaps, a few men from the town, a dozen farmers, a Russian slave laborer or two, served out some rifles and a *Panzerfaust* and told them to fight.

It was strange the way our artillery had smashed the near end of the town like a baseball bat swung down on a tray of tumblers. The rest of it, tall brown jugs, squat jars, fat bottles, seemed to have been barely jiggled.

Out in the street at the end of the hill there was a gang of prisoners in gray-green tunics shoveling up dirt and broken stone. Larry stepped on the gas and we headed for them as fast as we could. But at the last moment the bunch split up like figures in an old Harold Lloyd movie and went tumbling and diving into the rubbish on the side of the road.

The pfc. in charge of them yelled at us and Oscar, too late, said, "Slow up, slow up." Somebody told me once that Stein had killed a prisoner that way in Neustadt.

So we slowed up, we eased by the foundation-mouths surrounded by walls like broken molars with the wrecks of chimneys (shattered canines) sticking up here and there. Old women picked and searched about in these ruins and old men, ahead of us, pushed wheelbarrows of poor retrieved household stuff down the street. Stein drove on as if he would have spilled them, too, if he dared.

A block away I could see one strange place where shells had peeled away nine-tenths of a house and left the side wall standing there alone, an amazed white rind. Three feet of each floor had been preserved, and on the first story a little cupboard and a bowlegged table with a phonograph atop it huddled together like wooden children on that odd shelf.

Then I saw him; there he was. On the second story the white wallpaper with its juicy roses was quite unsmeared and in the corner stood a walnut washstand with a white towel on its arm. But in the middle of the wall staring out from behind a black frame square was our fugitive, with his shiny cap and his famous face.

It was there he was hiding, in full view yet out of reach, perched in the ruins quite safe after all, unviolated by the shell that had smashed his hosts flat into their cellars!

And it seemed that's where he would remain, until time itself obliterated him; perhaps the snow and rain would peel him off the wall like an old circus poster or eventually some wrecking crew would dynamite him down, I don't know. He watched us disappear as the jeep swung around a corner.

When the air-raid siren sounded and the iron shells (or bombs, perhaps) came down on the chinaware village, did he tremble on his wall, was he afraid? Did someone, after the family was all gathered in the air-raid shelter in the cellar, remember him and want to go back? And did somebody else viciously point out the obvious truth? What did he do when the shell hit?

Are the neighbors (if there were any afterwards) scandalized to see that he was left alive after the family was squashed by its own roof and tumbled walls? Or did they say, "Poor fellow" and wish the best for him? I wish we had stayed for the answers.

But instead we went on into the unwrecked part of town, jounced through the humpbacked streets and finally came out on a country road which we followed for three-quarters of an hour. At last the old man asked Stein to stop. He pointed ahead and to the left where the towers of a castle on a tall hill looked pink in the sun like wax candles on a birthday cake. He said he would wait for us until we brought the prisoner back. Then he would claim his reward. He sat down by the side of the road and even Oscar was glad to get rid of him.

In ten minutes we were on the road that squirmed upwards from the base of the hill towards the now unseen castle. The meadows gradually lowered themselves and became indistinct; after a long low-gear period, the road at last began to level off.

From there it crossed a bridge and lifted up across a little slope to a wide crested gate. All this in soft focus: colors were like paint smears; the air was full of dust and sun, three white geese wandered on the arched stone bridge, the trees wavered in the breeze, a white pompom of a cloud floated over the castle. In a moment Jeanette MacDonald, dressed in a peasant costume, might have stepped out to sing. But instead it was a tall old man in black, carrying a canvas case; we nearly ran him down.

The brakes agonized shrilly; we all bounced forward when the jeep's heels dug in, the geese ran in flop-winged panic, the old man staggered and dropped his little bag. Oscar swiveled the muzzle of a submachine gun at his stomach.

The dust settled for a minute. Now what? "Put down that gun," the old man said. His authority was native because you saw it in his face and eyes while Oscar had only his captain's bars, a poor ersatz at best, so Oscar lowered the M-3 back to its place beside the seat. The old man did not move out of his place in the road. He was very tall in a way both ministerial and military. He had white ogive eyebrows; he looked a little like Norman Thomas.

Now he was smiling; he picked up his canvas case again. "And who are you, sir?" he said, quite naturally taking the question that belonged to Oscar. Respectfully Oscar told him. (Oscar seemed to be reminding himself that, even though captured, he did not legally have to tell more than his name, rank and serial number.)

"And what do you want?"

Not one of us had ever imagined the moment of our being asked that awful, that ridiculous question. It was the trick cigar that blew up in Oscar's face (getting us all a little black). For the first time, I think, since the old man had stepped into the office, Oscar saw clear. But it was too late. All he could do was mumble and look at his hands.

After three or four minutes it was Stein who finally had to say it. We were all startled at last when the name came out. It sounded like an obscenity that has long since passed out of use.

The old man had picked up a caterpillar from a leaf in the meantime, but when he heard that name he was suddenly affected with humor. He dropped the caterpillar and staggered back against a tree, surrounding it with his black broadcloth arm and giving a pleasant andante laugh.

At last he saw how impolite he was being, for we all sat there frozen and Oscar's face was jerked out of shape with pain. He recovered, he straightened up, he tried to make it seem that he had never laughed at all.

"Gentlemen," he said with grace, "allow me to introduce myself. I am Adrien, the Comte de Montfort, and I am in charge of this property, which belongs to my relatives, the Hohenlohe. I shall be pleased to have you inspect it, by all means. I have several guests at present—refugees from other places—however, you may see for yourself that this person is not among them."

Then he came forward and sat down on the fender of the jeep. Stein started; we rolled across the bridge, up the incline and through the gate into a big bumpy courtyard paved with stone. The castle front that faced us was like a being partly dressed in armor, partly in knee breeches, wearing gaiters, a tuxedo coat and a tricornered hat. Victorian bay windows were cut into battlemented medieval towers and under stretches of mansard roof there were hints of baroque, rococo, the Greek revival.

As we got out of the jeep, the Count motioned toward a gate in a six-foot stone wall. "My friends are in the garden. Perhaps you would like to meet them first? To search there?" Oscar did not dare answer as he followed the Count like a newly captured burglar. But there was no patronizing sound in the Count's voice; it was all hospitality. He even made Oscar enter the gate first.

"This was in medieval times the castle refectory," the Count went on in his bland voice. "The roof was destroyed in a fire and never rebuilt. Later generations established here this delightful English garden."

And, in fact, it was delightful. There were flat little highways of gravel leading through the grass, seats, arbors, great cloudy green bushes, plots of flowers, low-swinging trees and even a fountain that could be heard far away.

There were people moving about near the other end; we

saw pastels of gowns and heard their voices. An old lady in a long lavender dress with a figure thin and upright as a twisted paper spill, with a hat like a full platter on her head, came sailing down the lane at us.

A few yards away she called in a delicate voice, "Oh, they are American soldiers, but are the Russians not coming then?" The Count answered. "Do not be afraid, Mathilde. The Russians are not coming. These American gentlemen have simply paid us a visit. They were—looking for a friend."

She had reached us now and the Count made introductions. The Countess Mathilde von Giech, he said. Her face seemed to be made of a fine gray crepe paper, its system of wrinkles was so minute and complex. She had no lips to speak of, a neat blade for a nose and clever buttonhole eyes. Her hands were like ancient ivory keepsakes.

"Do come," she said, selecting my arm, "and have some tea with us." And so we walked down the path towards the tea table, hearing the sound of water from the fountain and the even gentler tones of those noble voices as we came near.

The Count made a courtly occasion of our introduction, giving our full names and presenting each of the old ladies and the old men in the vicinity of the table by his or her title in French. Thus Graf von Hardenberg (cavalry moustaches, clipped white head) became le Comte de Hardenberg; Principe di Castagneto (bone-bald, a doggy, jowly face) became le Prince de Castagneto; and another Italian lady (an Alp for a bosom, a waterfall of double chins) became la Marquise de Soragne. We were lost in a snowstorm of names from the *Almanach de Gotha*. I heard Prince Boris Massalsky, le Chevalier de la Tour d'Auvergne, I heard Thurn-und-Taxis, Hohenlohe-Bartenstein, Ehrenreich, Plettenburg-Wittenstein, Wurmbrand, Durcheim and a dozen others, famous and ancient.

Some of the old men and a few of the old women looked haughty and stared, but only for a minute because most of them smiled, bowed a little and several of them began to talk to us all at once as the servant was giving us cups of tea and bread with cherry jam.

None of them was under sixty and most seemed to be nearer seventy or eighty. Their clothes denied any change in fashion since the turn of the century. Their conversation, as it began again, was a concert; their voices rose and fell like virginals and harpsichords, antique but in good tune yet. Here and there among the faded colors of faces and clothes stood out the brilliance of a dyed waxed moustache, a ribbon in a buttonhole, or the glint of a precious stone. But generally everything was subdued, polite and gently obscure; the direct sunlight was never invited here. After the introductions everyone turned to the business of tea.

The Countess Mathilde had drawn me to one side and we were sitting in a little arbor forested on three sides by cool leaves.

"Do you know," she said, "that we have been anxiously listening to the wireless and awaiting you for several weeks?" She smiled into my eyes with just a shred of flirtation.

"Anticipating your coming? Oh my, yes. We talked about it often and the Principe even said that we should repel you with halberds—he was joking, of course. Then when the first of your Americans arrived we could hardly believe that they were soldiers! Such innocents, such smooth-cheeked young boys!" She sat next to me as if she were riding sidesaddle:

balanced, alert, always carrying the reins of conversation lightly in her hand.

"They drove up in your little military automobiles and spoke to Count Adrien—we were all here in the garden. They insisted on searching the Schloss—for hidden Nazis, I suppose.

"And what do you think they did then, sir? None of us would believe it! Somewhere among the goods stored in the cellar they discovered a bag of golf clubs and several balls. So they took them and drove down to the meadow just below the Schloss there and we could see them all afternoon knocking those little golf balls about!" She laughed her pretty canary-bird laugh, pitched at the right gentleness so as not to offend me and ceasing soon enough to avoid all hint of excess.

"My great-grandfather was one of the generals who defeated Napoleon Buonaparte, you know," she said. "He would not have surrendered so easily! I think he would have tried to shoot your soldiers. He might easily have done so too, they were so unaware." She stopped for a moment and considered the toe of her shoe.

"But then, I suppose you would have dropped a bomb on him long before he had a chance to do any harm."

The Count had led Oscar off down a garden path to an aperture in the wall that overlooked the countryside; and there they stood, peering through our field glasses, the Count pointing to certain spots on the plain now and then. Gillespie sat on a long wooden seat with Prince Boris Massalsky, the Chevalier de la Tour d'Auvergne and a small German lady whose veins ran under her transparent skin like blue silk threads. They were speaking rapid French: four violins all going at top speed.

I looked around for Stein and suddenly I saw him. Full of smiles he was approaching the group of old men and ladies seated around the tea table. He was speaking to the Graf von Durcheim, offering a pen and a notebook and I heard him say in a candy voice, *"Entschuldigen, Herr Graf, ich möchte Ihre Unterschrift haben . . ."* He was getting all their autographs.

The Countess Mathilde began to talk again. "In any case, we were overjoyed to see the Americans when they arrived. I was so afraid that it would be the Russians who got here first. Prince Boris has described to us how barbarous the Bolsheviks are—worse than savages or cannibal islanders, he says, and quite capable of killing us all."

"But weren't you sorry to see your country defeated?" I asked.

"My country?"

She looked surprised. "Oh, you must mean Germany. No, I don't think so." There was an old lady in a garden chair who was signaling to her with a handkerchief.

"Our wars were won and lost a long time ago, you know," she said. Then she excused herself to go to her friend.

I talked to the gentleman on my left for a while (his English was not nearly so good); then I looked up to see Oscar, the Count, the Countess Mathilde and Stein together by the entrance to the castle. Oscar was motioning. Gillespie and I excused ourselves and went toward them.

Oscar was trying to get away now and the Count was urging us to tour the castle with him. "It is of a certain historical interest," he was saying, "although it dates from a rather late medieval period."

The Countess drew me aside to say good-bye. She whispered, "The Count has told me whom you are looking for.

My dear boy (please don't mind my calling you that), do not believe for a single minute that we would tolerate such a creature here! It's quite impossible!"

She drew herself up straighter than ever and the flora of her hat seemed to tremble with invisible storms. "Not for a minute!" Her whisper was sharper than a saw blade. "You have no idea how ill-bred and vulgar that man is said to be!"

When we had finally said good-bye, the Count took us through the castle. Part was made up of enormous echoing halls, panoplies, rooms with thickets of antlers on the walls, vast stone floors and blackened paneling. We had a look into the other part—the apartments where the guests lived, which were nondescript, Victorian and comfortable. The Count took us up in a tower, showed us a suit of armor an ancestor had been killed in and finally offered to take us through the cellars. Oscar impatiently refused. He kept saying, "Well, it's getting a little late now, I'm afraid . . ." But the Count always had one more wonder.

Finally Oscar said flatly that we must go. The Count raised his hand, smiling around at all of us. "But not yet, gentlemen. I have saved the best for the last. Here is something you must not miss. I should consider myself most ungracious if I allowed you to depart without having seen it." He led us down a hall, unlocked a door and brought us into a large sunny room, lined all around the walls with tall wooden cabinets and having a long trestle table running down the center.

The Count went across to a cabinet by the window and drew from it a shallow wooden tray; he then laid it on the table. The sun struck it and for a moment I thought it was filled with great jeweled brooches and buckles of a shining blue. They were butterflies.

"For, gentlemen," said the Count, "this is one of the finest collections of *Lepidoptera* in the whole world. Here you see an exhibit of *genus morpho,* the beautiful South American creatures—these are the *Didius* and the *Menelaus*." He was bringing out more of the glass-topped trays. "The *Venus* and the *Cacique*," he said. One was a deep blue with two white dotted lines and the other was patterned in blue with white and deep-yellow rings. "Here is the *Sulkowsky*," the Count said, putting another tray on the table, "and the *ega*."

We went on to cases of The Great Peacock Moth, the *Apollo* butterfly (his were the best he knew of) and a great display of bird-winged butterflies that the Count, as a young man, had captured in Asia—the *Croesus, D'Urville's, Priam's,* the *Pegasus*.

As we went around the table we spent exactly the correct time admiring each tray. If we showed a tendency to move away too fast, the Count's long hand would go out and he would commandingly point out this or that unusual marking or some specimen exceptionally rare.

Our impatience grew and grew until it took all of the Count's control to suppress Oscar's long sighs and obvious fidgets. The tide of shadow rose in the room and even the gleam of the bright wings began to be obscured. The Count talked on and on, telling long stories of the hunt and pointing out the beauty of the game. "I associate them with the beauty and glory of the past," he said.

Oscar finally spoke up, rebelled against the soft tyranny. We must leave immediately. He had an appointment this evening. But the Count had been expecting it. "Now!" he said. "The final thing. The dessert, as it were. Five more minutes, gentlemen." He led us over to the far corner of the room, wiped his fingers on his handkerchief and slowly and ceremoniously drew a black frame, narrow and longer than the others, from a drawer.

At first all we could make out underneath the glass was a black tangle of lines, a huge arabesque. The Count waited a moment before he explained.

"This," he said, "was presented to me by an admirer, a Swiss schoolteacher to whom I once showed my collection and who, in gratitude, constructed this unusual memento."

"But what is it?" asked Stein.

The Count smiled in his satiric way at Oscar. But I think he was really smiling at all of us.

"Don't you see?" he asked. "It is my initials—A, small d, M—written out in flowing script by means of a splendidly matched series of marching earwigs and stag beetles."

THE MIND IS
ITS OWN PLACE

KIDDER was a small man with drunken eyes and a red
nose like a buoy that floated in the middle of his face.
He was an old-time crime reporter, from way back, he said,
and the shifting tides of his profession had left his features a
kind of littoral of dishonesty. At ebb you could see the sad
boulders and mud banks of his failure. At high tide he was
full of a salty self-importance: a "prominent foreign corre-
spondent." He seemed to brim. "Remember the Lindbergh
trial?" he would ask. "You probably read my stories on it.
That was my biggest thrill." Then: North Africa, Italy and
France, mostly anecdotes about whores and black markets.
Once an Arab sniper had nearly shot him out of a jeep. They
all grew to lament that bungler's eyesight.

That autumn they were living at the Mampei Hotel, town
of Karuizawa, Nagano Province, Japan. All around them
were the beautiful mountains. Out of his second-story window Gamble could see them rising in the distance and imi-
tating, without any self-consciousness, the clean lines of a
Japanese print. Three-quarters up they were furred with the

23

little brush strokes of forest, but higher they grew sharp against the sky. His neighbor was the great white-headed, peaceful smoker, Asama, who seemed to rest all day and exhale occasional clouds from some enormous hookah in his belly. "Asama-san." Gamble liked the way the Japanese called them; as if they were old gentlemen (his own queer pun in a language he didn't know).

Going down to dinner, he met Kidder in the lobby. The sun and moon were in conjunction with him. He had on his his pink pants, a forest-green officer's shirt and around his turkey throat was a white silk scarf like a dead gull floating in the shallows. "Mac," he said, taking Gamble's arm, "I've got a great feature story here and I want you to help me develop it."

"Oh?" Gamble said, going on down the hall toward the dining room. "I'm pretty busy."

"No. Wait a minute." They stopped outside the leather-covered doors. "I won't tell you what it is, Mac. I'll let you judge for yourself, but take it from me it would be a fine thing. It wouldn't do you any harm, either. All I'm going to tell you right now is that we've got a couple of visiting officers —air corps guys from Tokyo. Now one of 'em don't matter. The other's what I'm interested in. I'll bet you can spot the difference—you're an intelligent man, Mac." The last phrase was one of his verbal counterfeits, false twenties for lavish tipping.

Karuizawa had been put off limits for American troops. It was a special place in Japan, a summer resort town where the Japanese had interned a good many foreigners, diplomatic staffs and others, during the war. On the Machi you passed German business offices, branches of Hamburg or Leipzig firms. Swedish girls with butter-colored hair rode bicycles in the middle of the street; in the doorway of the post office an Italian third secretary talked with a Vichy Frenchman while a Jew from Vienna, a refugee, edged coldly by. They were all restricted here, waiting. A fortuneteller on a back street did a good business, but each of them was always telling his own fortune and the crystal ball of imagination gave each one back his own hope or his own anxiety—prison camp, home, South America, Palestine, a thousand others.

In the meantime Karuizawa had been put off limits, which meant that a general and his staff were usually spending the week-end there and all higher officers who could manage to get special passes relaxed at the Mampei. Brave with their ribbons and jovial in their condescension, they appeared at Gamble's mess. Gamble was in charge of the small Counter-Intelligence detachment assigned to the town and he had work to do.

Behind a platoon of beer bottles the two officers sat. Major Campora, Captain Lamb—Kidder introduced them. They did not get up or shake hands, they nodded. "Talk about hot," said the major, "did you ever see that woman Fuller picked up in Manila? Hey, Mac," he turned to Gamble, "how are the geishas in this town?"

He was a big man; he had an acre of face. It was a boy's face in which something had made a difference—old-young or young-old, it was hard to judge the distinction. He delivered himself as if he were the juvenile lead, but something had gone wrong with his make-up. Behind the quick flare of his smile, the aging eyes centered on you, somewhat apprehensive, a little aggrieved.

The captain was a dark young man of about twenty-six and

he could be spelled out much more easily, it seemed: Delta Kappa Epsilon and R.O.T.C. Gamble barely glanced at him and Kidder took the chair at his left and began to talk about some party in Tokyo where they had met.

One by one the CIC men drifted in and sat down. Terry, the Nisei interpreter; Henty, the North Carolina lawyer; Jim Carpenter, the fat man. Carpenter was a great reader and quoter of Dickens and he exaggerated life into a kind of illustrated endless edition of *Pickwick Papers*.

Carpenter had been appointed to bully Matsuda-san. Matsuda was their waiter, the only waiter. In his despondent face were all the doles and sorrows of a world of coolies and with Carpenter he played an eternal vaudeville act of oppressor and oppressed. He was a master of every shade of gloom from merely that of a man whose pocket has been picked to that of a martyr impaled on white-hot irons. Matsuda adored Carpenter and followed him around. Carpenter knew quite well that all of Matsuda's relatives had recently moved in with him to share the CIC rations, but all he did was try to keep the losses to a minimum.

"*Maat suu daa!*" Carpenter yelled, and in a few moments he arrived on his silent straw sandals with the air of a dozen funerals about his bowed shoulders and his long face. "Cook late," he said.

"Cook late!" yelled Carpenter. "What a specious invention of the oriental mind! He's been there since five o'clock. I saw him. You've been stealing the sugar again, Matsuda-san."

Matsuda's comprehension of English suddenly sank to the vanishing point. During the argument that followed, Kidder took Gamble aside, over to the window that looked out on the garden.

"He's a great guy, isn't he?" Kidder said with his false smile. Kidder's habit was to estimate personality by its most deplorable tendencies and Gamble began to be aware that he was intended as the subject for some experimental lie. But Kidder's next words surprised him. He leaned close to the window and spoke in a confidential half voice. "I knew you'd like him, Mac. Here's the pitch. That man is a very unusual personage—nobody here knows it but me and maybe he don't know I know it, but that man was bombardier on the plane that *dropped the atomic bomb on Nagasaki!*"

He turned quickly and put his hand on Gamble's shoulder as if he expected him to bolt or yell. "Now keep that quiet, Mac. Let me tell you my idea."

Gamble was trying to recall the newspaper stories of last August, blurred now in his memory. He could remember some descriptions of the mission and the explosion, but the names of the crewmen and their pictures (or had there been pictures?) were lost to him. The mushroom cloud had dwarfed everything else. Perhaps Kidder was telling the truth.

"So what?" asked Gamble distrustfully. He knew that in a moment he would be knee-deep in the quicksand of Kidder's persuasion and he wanted to turn his back and walk off. But the men at the table were paying no attention to them, laughing and arguing about something; he felt a little afraid of Kidder's malice.

"Now take this guy," said Kidder in a low fast-moving voice, "who was personally instrumental in ending the war, delivered the death blow, you might say, to Japanese aggression. He's a kind of symbol of all the men in the service—young, carefree. He don't know what a great part he is playing in the destiny of the whole world." Kidder dropped easily into his Sunday-supplement style.

"He comes here on his first leave from Tinian after dropping the bomb. Now what's the most important thing in the world today, Mac?" Kidder did not pause for the answer. "It's world peace, isn't it? Well, here we see this American boy in contact with the Jap people for the first time. We get together a little party—and here's where you come in, Mac —and we watch his reactions when they come face to face. What's the result going to be?" Kidder spread his hands melodramatically in front of him.

"I think I can tell you the answer right now. He don't hold any hard feelings. He's just an American kid out for a good time. Live and let live, that's our motto now that the Japs have been taught a lesson in history." His voice sank to an auspicious rustle. "We got to have understanding, see, that's the only way to world peace."

Kidder's face looked becalmed and distant; his eyes stared over Gamble's shoulder into space. His treacherous shoals and deceptive shoreline seemed hidden and Gamble felt oddly confused.

"Isn't that a hell of a good story?" Kidder said. "I got one of the big slicks in mind to sell it to."

You discounted Kidder immediately, that was the trouble. You looked at the insignificant body and the bar-fly face and you realized by his look that he had summed himself up long ago, just as you were doing, and that the result had been a handful of small change of doubtful currency. What you never realized was the infinite cocoon of his craft and guile. One deceit enveloped another like some exasperating eternal puzzle and the more you did to expose his motive, the less you accomplished. He was of no importance. Gamble told himself that, yet he was never sure. He always wondered, as a kind of academic question, if underneath all these false protective covers of his life Kidder had not got hold of some malignant truth that he cherished like a secret virus while it ate him out.

Gamble was using the telephone an hour later while he thought of this. The telephone in Karuizawa is an inexplicable oriental demon, capable of long sinister silences, pitiful sobbing sounds and sudden wrong numbers. He was trying to call Fumi Shiga. In the last five minutes he had progressed from the distant noise of two pieces of sandpaper being ground together to the wailing of a newborn child to a muted snorting of some animals in a zoo. *"Moshi-mosh!"* he shouted.

Kidder had got around him. He realized it even as the process was going on. "I was thinking of Kay and Fumi Shiga," he had said. "I heard they got a nice place and I bet you could persuade them to have a little party tonight. Naturally we don't tell anybody what we're up to." Gamble had refused strongly at first. Gamble had come to Japan with a hatred of all Japanese and a resolve to be cold and correct. Without knowing how it had happened, he discovered that he had made several friends. Kay and Fumi were sisters, daughters of a once wealthy family. Their father had been killed in the Philippines and their house in Tokyo had been burned in a raid. Their mother, a worn-out genteel-looking woman, worked for some Military Government office in Tokyo while the girls stayed in their former summer house here.

"Why don't you give a party up in your room?" Gamble had

asked. "There's Miss Suzuki and that other girl, that friend of hers."

Kidder had looked pained. "Not *that* kind of a party, Mac. I didn't mean that kind of a party."

In the end Kidder had managed him. He had offered to furnish some food and some beer. He had subtly introduced Major Richter's name and brought to Gamble's mind that bullfrog face and that parade-ground tone as the major told him, "Now I want you to co-operate with Kidder up here. He represents one of the big newspapers in the States and we want our work to get full coverage. Remember, Gamble. Kidder's an excellent man [Gamble knew the major despised him] and I know you'll get along."

Then an afterthought as he turned away: "Don't let him find out how to get hold of that Japanese gin though."

And Gamble had finally given in half-heartedly. "*Moshi-mosh! Dozo, Shiga. Ichi-san-roku-ju.*" he said. Then, with shocking immediacy, it worked.

Yes, said Fumi, as if speaking from the bottom of a lake, they'd be delighted to have a party. They hadn't invited anyone over for a long time. She'd invite Hiro and his brother and perhaps the Naguchis would come. And—Gamble was hurriedly trying to explain something of the situation when the connection broke; then he couldn't recover it. The system, which seemed to work on metaphysical lines, anyway, went into a deep trance. Then there was the faint animal snuffling at the end of the line again and that was all. Gamble banged the receiver down.

At about eight o'clock Gamble met Carpenter and Terry out by the jeeps. The air was frosty but not actually cold and as the light retreated things seemed strangely to take on sharper edges. Gamble wondered if it could be a trick of his own mind. The bushes in the garden beyond the auto stand looked like intricate, crisp black pastries and Carpenter's suddenly lifted profile with its glowing cigarette seemed suddenly pared and sharpened. Kidder and the other two were not there yet and as Gamble stepped on the gravel he remembered them from dinner.

The conversation had been desultory and joking. From watching the major closely, Gamble had not learned much. Or at least he had not learned the answer to a question that existed only nebulously somewhere out of reach. He had collected some trash of obvious appearances: that the major had a thunderclap laugh and a bully manner, that his eyes could look a little crazy and fugitive even in the middle of his talk (or did Gamble imagine that, superimpose it on the moving picture?), that his stories always involved or dragged in a passionate woman, no matter how extraneous she was.

Kidder had wormed through the conversation leaving a thread of himself behind; there were suggestions as to his close friendship with generals, hints of past accomplishments, concealed admonitions to Gamble and insinuations as to what he might be in a position to do some day for those who remained his friends. The captain seemed to have talked a lot but Gamble could not remember a word he said.

At last they came thumping across the porch, carrying packages and stretching the tail of a poor joke that must have begun somewhere far back in the corridor. Things were piled in and Gamble took one jeep, Terry the other.

They drove down the lane, turned once into a road, then again into the Machi, the main street, where the shops were already blank and shuttered for the night and where only a late cyclist or two went on down the street with the continual sharp singing of the little bell on the handlebars. In one direction the town frayed away toward the railway station; in the other it climbed like an unnatural staircase on the road that led past the Empress Dowager's villa (thick set about with palisades, dark pine groves and truculent-looking guards) to the top of Mount Yagasaki. The sky bloomed with stars and the curved moon looked like a dazzling delicate night-shoot.

They made their turn past one of the dark shops, rattled across a small bridge and finally came to the by-road among the tented trees. They could see lights through the branches and when they came down the path to the door, Fumi was standing under the glass lantern. The light sifted down over her black hair, her shoulders and the lilac bushes on either side of the step. As Gamble introduced the strangers, she ducked her head shyly. She was wearing a white woolly sweater, a gray skirt and saddle shoes. In the drift of diffused light her face looked both young and antique, like the face of a princess on an ancient worn silver coin. The major had nothing to say, for once, and the captain only mumbled. Gamble could sense in the air the soundless exclamation point of their surprise. "Come on," said Fumi, leading the way. "The party's begun."

In the broad living room half lighted by the fireplace and one squat lamp, Kay was arranging some plates and glasses on a table. She smiled and nodded at the introductions but at first, in accordance with a little unconscious habit of hers, said nothing. She was not at all like Fumi; her sharp good looks were completely fashionable and they were impossible to localize for they had no clue of nationality about them. All that was oriental about her was a vague sense, some slight accent of her person or features like an almost imperceptible variation in the tones of a musical voice speaking your own language perfectly. Gamble was always newly surprised when he saw her again; but this time he was not the only one.

Lamb, the air corps captain, was standing in the middle of the room staring at her. "You sisters?" he asked in an abrupt hoarse voice, and when nobody answered him for a minute, "Speak English?" Carpenter laughed sarcastically.

It seemed impossible that he could have forgotten Fumi's words or missed the appearance of the room with its modern furniture, its range of bookcases full of French and English novels, the Remington portable on the desk.

But Gamble noticed that he was staring at her with a kind of rigidity, a look of sudden anxiety that seemed to pull taut all the rigging of muscles in his careless face. Gamble himself was startled. What strange witness had the man seen? What chance explosion of knowledge had occurred? But all the others were simply looking amused or uninterested. The captain's lips looked actually white and Gamble could sense but not define some obscure violent struggle in him. He seemed as if trying to reject some perilous certainty.

"Oh, passably," said Kay, smiling. "Better than I speak Japanese, at any rate."

"You go to American school here?" the captain asked in his strained voice.

At first Kay had seemed a little perplexed and amused. Perhaps this same thing had happened before. But now she seemed to perceive that it was not the same thing and Gamble sensed that she was becoming both a little baffled and a little angry. As a kind of curious parenthesis, it occurred to Gamble that it was the captain's flat midwestern voice that sounded foreign to him and Kay's easy one that sounded germane and congruous.

"No," she said, "Fumi and I went to a Sacred Heart school in New York. We both graduated from the University of California and we've been in Japan only since 1940. I hope our broken English doesn't offend you?"

Suddenly the major snorted; he tried to cover up by pretending to cough into his handkerchief and turning to inspect the books on the shelves. The captain began to turn red and Gamble watched the muscles in his throat clenching and unclenching. Then all at once everybody made some kind of noise or movement. "How about some music?" Terry said loudly and went over to put "St. Louis Blues" on the turntable. Kidder started to explain to Fumi what he had brought in the paper bags and Carpenter began walking around, humming loudly to himself. The captain actually hung his head. With a look of horrible embarrassment, he went over to the window and stared out, his fingers picking absently at one of the blind-cords. Gamble wanted to laugh, but not because he had seen something funny.

When Hiro and his brother arrived with the Naguchis a few minutes later it all seemed forgotten and the party, like a machine that has been quickly repaired, got under way. Hiro organized the rolling up of the carpet, drank two glasses of beer very quickly and got the dancing started. "You remember my brother, don't you?" he said to Gamble. "I think he would like to argue with you. He comes to parties to argue, you know, the way I come to drink beer."

They looked like a team; they were almost interchangeable. Both of them wore the same immaculate clothes—sports jackets and gray flannel slacks. They both spoke with the same

English accent, danced flawlessly and they went everywhere together. It was thought that they detested each other.

Hiro had been in the navy, but he had seen little of the war. Kyo was a former pilot who was almost a local legend. He cultivated his elegant look and intellectual manner as a kind of ambush and he was the hero of a dozen hairbreadth stories—always told by somebody else. He had been shot down in the sea near a jungle island, had nearly died of burns on his body, had persuaded some natives to take him off to another island, had been captured, escaped, and at last by a devious process of hitch-hike had made his way back to Japan before the war ended. There was a story that he had nearly committed suicide when he heard of the surrender but that Hiro had saved him. He smiled and spoke to Gamble, said that he had promised not to argue tonight and then moved away.

Gamble watched the major dancing with Fumi. He was holding her closely and talking in a low voice. As they turned, Fumi was smiling and replying. They looked perfectly natural; they were having a good time. This was Kidder's prediction and Gamble felt irritated with himself—not because he himself had had any preconception of what was going to happen, but because he expected that Kidder had. And it was not the perfectly obvious one that Kidder had handed him like a free coupon. Gamble could not help but believe that Kidder had rehearsed some subtle and malevolent effect in the labyrinthine turns of his secret mind. But what? Why?

Kyo was now by the fireplace, laughing his cock-crow laugh and pouring beer out of the pitcher. Gamble, avoiding the dancers, walked over just in time to hear Kidder finishing a story that Gamble had heard before.

Kidder, an old rigger of all the journalistic clichés, soon after his arrival in Japan had set out to interview "the man in the street." Only it was the man-in-the-mud, he explained, because he had finally found what he wanted in the person of a farmer, knee-deep in the mud of his odorous rice paddy. Through his interpreter Kidder had asked the questions and Gamble could almost see him with his spectacles (assumed for the occasion), peering forward with a kind of faked zoological zeal at his dirty specimen of public opinion. What did he think of the end of the war, Kidder had asked.

All very well, the Japanese had thought.

But didn't it come as a surprise to him that Japan had lost? Hadn't they been telling him all along that Japan was winning? The interpreter passed it on.

Japan lost? The man mumbled for a while over it.

Finally with a pleasant smile: But Japan hadn't lost. And —with a sudden polite inspiration—he himself thought it excellent that the Emperor had been pleased to invite so many of the American soldiers as his guests to Japan.

Kyo was still laughing when Gamble came up and he handed him a glass full of beer. On the other side, leaning against the mantelpiece, Captain Lamb frowned at the story.

"Well," said Kyo finally. "I'm not sure that he was so wrong. Are you?"

It was said in a casual tone, but Gamble caught the swift flick of Kyo's eye—the fisherman judging his cast. And the strike came quickly.

"What do you mean?" said Lamb, his voice emerging abruptly, not amiably. "You're not that stupid."

Kyo smiled; he was not reeling in yet. He was playing his line and enjoying every maneuver. He leaned casually against the table and curled the fingers of his left hand around a cigarette. They would have been delicate-looking and girlish if it had not been for his exceptionally pale nails, which were sharply trimmed like little knife blades at the tips. He spoke lazily. He smiled straight at Lamb.

"Why," he said, "victory and defeat are relative things, you know, and not the affair of a moment. Or—they're simply attitudes or ideas and who is a loser who doesn't know it? Who won at Thermopylae?"

Lamb seemed to feel the firm but subtle tug of the line. He was getting angry and he actually took a half step forward. Along with the anger, Gamble sensed his puzzlement which delayed him and disturbed his timing. Gamble himself felt as if he were watching a newsreel that had nothing at all to do with his own experience.

"Look here," Lamb said, "I don't know a thing about these ancient Jap battles, but who won at Saipan? Who won in the Philippines?"

Kyo took a drink with a kind of relishing sip as if it were a single bubble of the finest brandy that he would roll around on his tongue. Then he put his glass down and suddenly seemed to be weary of the whole business. "There is a folk-saying for the occasion," he said. "In American books we are always quoting proverbs, you know. This one goes, *Makeru ga kachi!* That means: the defeated is the real victor." Slowly he stood erect in his theatrical way. "Or is that too much oriental sophistry for you, Captain?" He walked off.

The captain was quiet with a kind of paralyzed violence. Then he made a stabbing gesture at Kyo's back. His face had turned a dirty reddish color like a badly tinted photograph portrait and it was full of fine branching lines as if it had been struck and all the glass had cracked in the frame. All the boyish quality had gone out of his features and in the fluctuating light from the fire he looked like an old man, a dangerous old man.

He turned to Kidder and said in a low vicious voice, "I'd like to kill that son-of-a-bitch . . ." And Kidder took his arm and said something mollifying.

Gamble had forgotten him; then he realized that Kyo was not the real connoisseur of the scene—just as the audience is not aware of the director. Kidder was the person he should have been watching—which brought him back to the question he could neither form nor answer. He wondered if Kidder were improvising, working along toward some calculated denouement. Or did he hope that it, whatever it might be, would create itself?

Gamble danced with Fumi. "Mac, do you know those men well?" she asked. She was frowning across the room at the major who was managing all things at once—to talk, to smile, to stay in the center of the floor and to foxtrot competently in time with one of the old songs with one of the Naguchi sisters who was at least a foot shorter than he. He was a phenomenon of social grace and Fumi stopped what she was saying to watch him. "You'd think he would smash her," she said with awe, "but he never does."

"No," said Gamble. "Why do you ask?"

He had known Fumi long enough to perceive that she often got at things naively while he fumbled for them with a laborious and muddled process of thought.

"I don't think the major is bad," she said. "He had an argument with Kay in the kitchen and he tried to kiss her, but I feel sorry for him. I don't know why. There's something weary about him. It's the other one who seems sinister. I'm afraid of him. Or is that being silly?"

"What about him?"

"Oh, don't try to make me be logical, Mac," she said. She had the habit, at times like this, of looking off, as if she were gazing across immense spaces or into the sky. "Let's say he has a secret. I'm like a girl in a play who keeps thinking, 'There's something mysterious about that man.' Now go ahead and laugh at me." Then suddenly she said, "Oh look at Kidder!"

With his face screwed and his arms pumping up and down, he was illustrating some anecdote to a group by the fireplace. "Doesn't he look like a witch?" Fumi asked. "Imagine him in a black cloak and a broomstick."

"I think you're mistaken about the captain, though," Gamble said doubtfully. He didn't want her to know that he shared her feeling. "You people are supposed to be the ones who are inscrutable. Americans aren't. Or at least Kyo is always telling me that we are perfect illustrations of the physical law that every action creates an equal and opposite reaction."

"Oh, wise old Kyo," she said. "He thinks he can be clever by being just a little wrong."

The tunes they danced to were all old ones, remembered from some vast distance of before-the-war. To Gamble they suddenly brought back all the flavor of long-past college proms, parties at cottages, all the half-forgotten faces of girls, the sound of laughing in the summer darkness, the soft words and the ill-kept promises. The long dry-nausea of the war years disappeared under their touch of sound, as if it had been a story read in yesterday's newspaper and he felt that none of them here was, in reality, with any of the others. Each face or voice was simply a clue to all that they remembered and all that they seemed to have lost so quickly.

Except for Kyo. And the captain. They remembered something else.

A little later Gamble was standing alone by the record player when he looked across the room and saw the major's big sad-amiable face in the firelight. There was an instant of revolution in his mind and he realized his absurd mistake. There were still two or three people in the kitchen, rattling things and getting out more beer, but the rest of them had settled in a group around the fireplace and had begun to talk. The lamps had been put out and only the jumping brightness of the flames shook on the ceiling and illuminated their faces. In each one it seemed to bring out a peculiar truth. With his ponderous charm the major was talking to Fumi and Carpenter, his big hands making slow undescriptive circles in the air as he tried to explain how this and that had happened. It wasn't he that Kidder had meant at all.

Gamble was hearing the mixed sound of their voices and catching scraps of sentences borne along on the general flood: Kidder's voice, like somebody practicing scales on an out-of-tune piano in a distant building; the major's droning up and down the hills of his story; Fumi's laugh like the jangling of thin teacups; an occasional sentence from Kyo pitched in like a stone from a slingshot; Carpenter's rhetorical undertone; Miyako Naguchi's sharp one like persistent footsteps over broken glass. Gamble realized that Kay and the captain were not there.

He watched the doorway until they came in—separately —a few minutes later and quietly took places by the fire. He wondered if the captain had been apologizing, but he could tell nothing from the expression of either. Kay sat down by the major and quickly got interested in his story; the captain stood back by the end of the mantelpiece with his face lost in the shadow and only now and then showing by the glint of a button or the impatient movement of a sleeve that he was still there.

Gamble took a chair and sat at the outer edge of the half circle. Up until now he had not had time to try to place things—the evening had been so filled with unconsecutive incident and conversation. He returned to his original feeling that Kidder's story about—he was sure it was the captain, now—had been some kind of contrivance, leading or misleading toward some eventual consummation. Perhaps only Kidder would be able to see it and relish it when it came. The idea of Kidder as a kind of connoisseur with a taste for evil more rare and more acute than any normal one was beginning to obsess him. An air-drawn fancy, he could tell himself, but he could not shake it off. It may have been the very incantation of the word Nagasaki. No one in Japan mentioned Hiroshima or Nagasaki unless it was impossible to avoid. It was a horrible public secret, a familiar and always present Medusa-head just behind your back.

A hand releases a lever and a city is destroyed, perhaps much more than just a city. But afterwards is there a difference in the hand? Can you identify it by slight nervous movements under the skin, some oddity in the muscles, some disturbance of conscience in the blood that runs through the veins?

Factually, of course, Kidder's story was perfectly possible. Air corps officers from all over the Pacific took leave in

Japan or came there on trips and it might easily be true that this man had been bombardier on that inconceivable flight. At any other place Gamble might simply have walked up and asked him; not here.

This young captain with the college-boy face had suffered some strange mutation of feeling so deep and so destructive that Gamble felt like a man on some uninhabited coast who tries to imagine a submarine earthquake by the bodies of dead fish left on the shore. All this was beyond any act or word; but Gamble had seen it and known it in his face.

And so Kidder's story was perfect, a work of art. But Kidder's art was to deceive and Gamble began to be frightened. What if he were applying a hideous generality to a particular occasion? What if Kidder were only using this man as a kind of appropriate example for an inclusive metaphor? Gamble began almost to hope that the story was literally true. He intended to ask as soon as possible.

Then when Gamble heard them singing around the fire, he was suddenly ashamed of his enormous fable and he abandoned it. There was an old accusation against him: he saw the world as a kind of demonology and he drew plots where there were no plots and tried to see designs in what was actually the wilderness of daily life. He did not recall who had first made it; anyway it was true.

A surly young officer with a gift for being tactless. An old newspaperman who lied by habit to try to make him sound interesting. A rather ordinary air corps major who was trying pathetically to stave off middle age. It amounted to that.

Having abolished his scenario, Gamble spent the rest of the evening in the middle of a kind of aimless movie full of stray talk and chance movements across the screen. On a bench in the garden he was smoking a cigarette with the prettier of the Naguchi sisters who told him a long story of a lost love, or of a love that was not lost but that she wished would be, or something of the kind. A little poodle came into the story (sniffing his shoes, Gamble thought, and likely to surprise him with his teeth on his hand), but whether it was a present from her to him or from him to her, he did not understand. It was cold out there and at last they went in. "Now aren't I right?" asked the girl. "Oh yes, perfectly, of course," he said.

While they were dancing (by the firelight only) a frightened bird got into the house and sailed and swooped under the beams. They all stopped to watch and though Fumi opened the windows, the bird couldn't seem to find them. With a grin on his face the major picked up a glass and drew back while everybody said, "Look out! No, don't!" and threw it with all his strength at the pulsing shadow.

But miraculously the glass sailed out of a window without spilling a drop and the bird followed it.

The shadows were huge black flames on the wall—echoes of the red ones in the grate. Fumi had an odd perfume with an odor like sage. Hiro, very tipsy, contradicted Kyo, very sober. Gamble had promised to get somebody a fresh drink, then forgot who had asked for it and drank it himself. The beer ran out and somebody brought out a bottle of Santori whiskey. They played the songs from the very bottom of the record cabinet—"Red Sails in the Sunset" and "My Blue Heaven." Gamble ate something and was surprised to discover he couldn't taste it. Somebody hiccoughed violently in the kitchen, laughed, then hiccoughed again.

It was over suddenly as if the film had broken. The lights

went on and there they were, foggy-eyed in the brightness, the room a litter of piled ash trays, papers, sticky glasses. They were saying good night. *O-yasumi nasai.* Good night. Good night.

They went out to the lane and climbed into the jeeps. Gamble taking Kidder and the major in his. Kidder slumped in the seat, his head rolling forward on his neck as he dozed. In the back seat the major hummed to himself something like a dirge. Gamble followed the fleeing red eye of the other jeep down the bushy lanes and narrow streets laddered with heavy shadows. The cool breeze stung pleasantly on his cheeks.

Darkness sinks into Karuizawa like ink into a blotter. If you go high enough above it you can see all the rising land around glazed with a kind of aluminum frost of moonlight, but the valley itself where the town is, you will see as a great irregular black shroud across the ribs of the land. Down in its winding lanes it is an underworld of odd shadow-caverns into which all the appointments of the daytime town —fences, houses, gravel walks, gardens, steps—seem to have withdrawn. Even the Machi seems like a path between two low silent cliffs on either side. Only here and there on the roads, like an abandoned fancy, there is a lamp post to startle the darkness. There is one on the Mampei road, a desolate spot that Gamble always passed with a superstitious feeling. It had been pointed out to him as a curiosity soon after he arrived and he had heard the story. One night a German businessman who lived down the road had been returned home after having been "questioned" by the Japanese police. One of his friends, another German, sat by his bed until late at night, but finally he fell asleep. When he woke up, near dawn, his friend was gone from the bed and after a little while he found him hanging from the post, the light he had required still shining on his dead eyes.

In a few moments they drew up alongside the other jeep in front of the Mampei. Except for a light here and there from a hallway window it was dark. The pitch of the roof caught a little moonlight though, and Gamble could see its whole long outline as he stood for a moment before going up.

It was a work of pure *heimweh,* pure nostalgia, built in the style of a small Alpine inn. Gamble imagined a lonely German hotelkeeper with a memory of *das Vaterland* growing dearer and bigger in his mind through the years finally building this huge, exaggerated, many windowed version of his dream. It was half timbered and between the two great gables on either side a small watchtower stood up. A comfortable porch stretched all along the front.

But behind this orderly facade, as if the dream had gone a little confused and ambiguous in all the years of its dreaming, the building rambled away with many chance wings and unsuspected corridors, now vacant and echoing. Most of the rooms, except for the ones in the front reserved for American use and certain apartments in the rear occupied by refugee German families, were empty. Going down a corridor once, Gamble had stopped to look in one, smelt the dead air and saw a kind of graveyard full of strange white monuments: the shrouded furniture.

They lingered for a moment in the cool air and smoked a final cigarette. When the rest went in, the captain and the major stayed behind and Gamble, looking back, could see their two shadows conferring on the ground in a patch of moonlight, one straight and thin, the other bulky and a little bent. Gamble was sick of them and beginning to be sick of his own head, which had started to rock with a slow ache. But before he got into bed he did look out of his window again into the yard and saw them in the same place, still facing each other like a big numeral *1* and an *8* cut out of black cast iron on a signpost. A few moments later he thought he heard footsteps on the gravel.

His dreams were all about some kind of hunt or chase dashing through briery underbrush. At times he was the hunter with a knife and net and at others he was the prey. He could feel a slow engine moving in his head.

And when he finally awoke he was still running. His forehead was wet and the muscles of his legs were stiff. He opened his eyes and saw an oblong of warm sunlight across the carpet and saw that the color of the sky beyond the windows was dazzling blue with only a few minute chalk marks of clouds in the distance. In the garden there were birds and somebody was whistling down the hall.

Painfully he lifted his legs out of bed and rubbed his eyes; then for some reason he had a notion to go to the window and see if the captain and the major were out there.

Surprisingly they were—on the same spot, still conferring. For a moment he blinked sleepily at the magic, unable to understand it. Then he realized that they were wearing coats, gloves and helmet liners and that their gear was loaded on one of the jeeps. Then they walked over and got in.

"Hey!" He leaned out of the window and yelled as they started up.

The captain yelled back something about having to leave and about parking the jeep at the railway station for them to pick up. They skidded around the corner into the driveway and were gone. Neither of them waved.

He wanted no thanks or good-byes from them but when the jeep had pulled down the lane and out of sight he was left with the sense of his unanswered question. He would never, now, know who they were. But the question had become something more than one of simple identity.

He stayed a minute and stared at the Old Man. He was resting quietly in the sunlight with his knees drawn up. Gamble remembered hearing that he had been quiet that way for a long time. Only once, in local memory, had he ever got angry. They had built one of those stick-and-straw villages on his side and shortly after he had erupted a great shower of hot stones and molten lava—just enough to clear away the obstruction. After that he had been at peace and nobody had dared build anything on him again. Later in the day he would begin to smoke, but it would be the reasonable, meditative smoke of an old man.

He went back to bed again and woke up an hour or so later with the sun hot on his eyelids. Somebody was shaking the door, he realized, and hammering at it with sharp staccato raps.

"Mac! Mac!" It was Fumi.

He put on some clothes and let her in. She was panting, her fingers trembled and her face was flurried. It was bare without its make-up, full of consternation. She came over and took his hand.

"Oh," she said, "where is Kay?"

He caught her eyes touring the corner of the room and he felt a little angry. "Did you expect to find her here?"

"Oh, no, no, no. Please, Mac, I don't know what to think. She hasn't been home all night." She clawed one cheek with her fingernails.

"Maybe she had her own arrangements. Fumi, don't be so upset. Everybody's not like you."

She sat down on the bed and began to cry. "It isn't true," she said. "Listen to me. Last night after the party I went to bed and Kay was straightening things up a little. Then a jeep came and I heard her talking with someone—now I think it was that major. Somebody said your name. Then after a long time the jeep went away and I must have fallen asleep. She wasn't in her room this morning. The bed was still made."

She stopped crying and dug at her eyes with her fingertips. She said that she had tried to call. Usual success with the Karuizawa telephone. Then she had bicycled over.

"I think she's here in the hotel . . ." she began. "Oh, God." She started to cry again.

Gamble told her about the officers' early start. He decided that Terry would be of most help and he went down to find him in his usual place on the porch, reading a detective story.

"You look through the north corridor," Gamble told him. "If you find her, just tell me. We don't know what's happened."

Terry told him where the captain and the major had been staying and he and Fumi went directly there. The door stood open and in the room they found only a few odd souvenirs of the two men: a splash on the wall, an abandoned necktie, a razor blade on the bathroom shelf. Gamble began to doubt that Kay was in the hotel, but Fumi was already hurrying out into the corridor that seemed to stretch away endlessly.

Each door opened onto undisturbed silence and darkness. The dust, like sudden clouds of insects, would spring up and whirl in the slivers of sunlight that came through the blinds.

Gamble would push the light switch and each room would be
a copy of the last. A mirror furry with dust in which they
looked like peering dolls, humped sofas like sheeted camels,
an old radio set like an upended coffin in the corner, a forgotten pair of sunglasses on a table, giving them a green
stare, pages from an old *Nippon Times* pinned around a
lampshade, a broken golf stick. The remnants of interrupted
life.

Fumi's impatience turned to despairing haste as she flung
doors open, snatched at curtains, shined Gamble's flashlight
into closets, ran panting from room to room. At last they came
to the end of the long gallery of spectral rooms and impersonal echoes. Another hallway joined it at right angles
and there was a small window with a windowseat in the
corner. Fumi sank down heartbroken, her hand spread on the
pane and her face warped with torment.

Gamble found himself caught in one of those queer moments of indifference or impersonality that sometimes came to
him in moments of crisis. Afterwards he would feel guilty
about it, but now, without knowing why, he felt a kind
of analytical curiosity. In a cold, disinterested way he was
noting the changes and distortions in Fumi's face. Last night
it had suggested a peculiar beauty, that perpetual youthful-
ness caught in an ancient mint. Now in the beam of sunlight
from the window it seemed to him that the silver portrait
on the imaginary coin incorporated all the history of grief,
poverty and pain from every transaction it had ever had part
in through all the years. He tried to leave it. He tried to say
something comforting.

Fumi had forgotten him, too, and she seemed to be talking
not to herself but not to anyone in particular. Outside the

window, Asama had begun to send up a little smoke into the empty sky.

She said, "Oh, it's no use. It's the same, same thing. Always asking it. The house in Tokyo burning up. When we heard from the Philippines. Hiroshima. The moment when it happens, you ask it. Why me, why us? Just before you bleed to death or the heat shrivels you up. It wasn't *I* you meant, I'm innocent. It was those others, but now you've missed them and you've hit me . . ." Gamble could see that she was nearly hysterical. He took her arm. "Fumi . . ."

They heard a sound from behind a door in the other corridor, a sobbing breath.

The door stuck and Gamble had to heave his shoulder against it to get it open. It gave after the second push. Kay was on the bed.

She was twisting on the mattress, crying with the harsh futile sound that you hear in the throat of an old pump that has long since gone dry. Her hands covered her face and Gamble could see her white teeth cutting into her fingers. He knew that she must realize they were there, that she had been dreading it and that now she didn't care. Fumi ran to her. There was just enough light through the shutters to show that she was bare and just enough to show the red lines drawn below her ribs like a musical stave without notation; there was blood on the pillow. The faint haze of sunlight showed that her clothes, scattered on the floor among the dust covers and pieces of a broken bottle, had been ripped to pieces.

"Oh, Keiko, Keiko, darling," Fumi moaned. "What is it? Who did it?" and she covered her body with one of the dust protectors, though it continued to writhe as if touched by fire.

Gamble did what he could. He brought water and they

bathed her face. Fumi made her drink some of it and gradually she quieted and except for a slow hoarse panting, lay
still.

Then she began to whisper compulsively; they couldn't
stop her. "Came in the jeep . . . he hurt my arm, Fumi . . .
pushed me into the room . . . oh, oh . . . and I struggled . . .
all night . . . choking . . . the room . . ." Her breathing lessened
and she collapsed.

Gamble was going for the French doctor, but Fumi
seized his arm *"Not here,"* she said. "She must go home."

So instead he found Terry, who brought the jeep around
to a back entrance and helped Gamble carry her down the
back stairs. Around the flimsy cotton sack, Gamble wrapped
one of his own blankets and they laid her in the back of the
jeep. Terry was gentle and efficient, better than either of
them. "You can't come," he said to Gamble. "No room. I'll
stop for the doctor on the way and come back for you later."

Gamble walked around the side of the hotel to see if anyone had noticed them, but the place seemed deserted.
Through the dining-room window he could see a woman on
her hands and knees scrubbing the floor, but she was intent
on her work. The porch was unoccupied. Somewhere somebody was practicing a waltz on an out-of-tune piano. Gamble
started. It reminded him of something. He ran up the stairs.

In the room again, he pulled open the blinds and let the
sun in. He felt sickened by what had happened to Kay; but
it was the fact of the room that was most obscure and appall-
ing. In the sunlight he could see its ruin.

All along one side, about knee-high, the plaster had been
kicked in and chunks of it lay trampled on the floor. The
drapes had been wrenched from their rings. The glass table
top had been battered with something heavy until scarcely

a square inch was left uncracked. An upholstered chair had been torn up and its cotton guts scattered around it. A straight chair lay like a broken-legged corpse in the corner. The table lamp had been battered against the mirror with particular fury, as if to obliterate a face.

Gamble sat down on the bed, where the blood had dried on the pillows in an irregular maplike design. He looked at the broken glass, the wrecked walls and torn cloth and he wondered if the senselessness made any kind of sense. He felt as if he had come on the scene of a re-enactment and a rehearsal and that he was sitting in the replica of a street, a city, a whole country, the world.

Then he heard a footstep in the hall; he saw Kidder's face in the doorway.

"The carrion bird!" he said bitterly. "Well, come in."

But Kidder wasn't as he had expected. He looked worried and even a little afraid. "I guess I know what happened. I saw you taking the body down. God, this is terrible, Mac."

Gamble didn't enlighten him. Kidder was trying to explain. "That guy—he must be crazy. Listen, Mac, I was wrong about him being what I said he was. I was misinformed by a certain . . ."

"All Cretans are liars, said the man from Crete."

"What do you mean by that, Mac?"

"I mean get out. Right now."

He went. He was of no more importance than his explanation. Gamble had worried about identities, but now he knew that identities didn't matter, that, dreamlike, they were interchangeable and he felt that he himself, all soldiers, were a part of that terrible interchangeability.

THE END
OF PITY

IF YOU looked, you could probably find Gillespie in your family photograph album. He would be that Uncle Thomas or Uncle Edward from Milwaukee who stands shyly clutching the crook of his umbrella and stares with shocked eyes at the camera as if he had just witnessed something remarkably lewd. Perhaps the painted drop behind him will suggest some Venetian scene or the Swiss Alps, for this is the uncle who traveled. Dozens of summer trips took him all over the continent of Europe and frequently into the Holy Land. He was, most likely, an architect or an amateur of architecture with an extensive and loving knowledge of the cathedrals of seven countries and a great penchant for describing them—to the annoyance of the rest of the family. He is remembered as tender-hearted, generous, nervous in the presence of large animals and, of course, a bachelor.

Shave off the sideburns, take away the umbrella and the frock coat; put him in o.d.'s, a helmet, combat boots, and there is Gillespie.

There was something infinitely charitable about him although, with the rest of us, he belonged to a most uncharitable organization, the Counter-Intelligence Corps. On some dusty road in France he would suddenly stop his jeep, saying, "That child looks hungry." Then he would get out and, cajoling the dirty boy in a mellifluous French that would have charmed Racine, would hand him his dinner K-ration.

In the eyes of the Quartermaster Corps Gillespie was a bottomless well. No sooner was he issued clothes or supplies but they disappeared, a bounty shared by all the northern provinces of France and half of Belgium. Whenever Gillespie came back to a village he had visited before, the commotion was extraordinary. The kids came running; women leaned out of windows to yell and even the idle drinkers at the cafe raised two fingers in greeting.

There was a story about Gillespie that somebody told. One evening he stopped in a border village in Alsace because he had noticed a parked convoy of trucks that were bringing Polish d.p.'s, former slave laborers, out of Germany. Major Stoneman, a crusty and somewhat pedagogical G-2 officer from New England, was with him, fuming at the delay and telling Gillespie to be quick about it. In a few minutes Gillespie had got rid of his monthly cigarette and candy ration among the clutching hands and, smiling, had come back to the jeep.

"What're you, a one-man relief organization?" the major had asked.

On the road again, the major had grown philosophical in his own way. "The quickest way to crack up is to admit everybody's plea," he said. "There is such a thing as too much compassion."

Gillespie only laughed as if it were a joke he had not quite understood. "Some day it will hurt you," the major had said abruptly.

It seemed at the time that Gillespie had been hurt as much as possible. When he stood in the rubbish in the interior of Cologne cathedral a look of pain came over his face and he had to sit down for a few moments. He kept his eyes shut when we drove through Aachen. When an old farmer who had been hit by a stray bullet in some village skirmish died while Gillespie was trying to give him first aid, he was depressed for days afterward. In his eyes there reappeared again and again a look of anguish and dismay that he could not hide. It was as if a gentle antiquarian had come home to discover that housebreakers had not only wrecked his collection but had murdered his family on the way out.

If Gillespie had not been so efficient at his job, he might have been ridiculed more often. Captain Hind, the detachment commander, would sometimes refer to him as "Florence Nightingale," but he respected Gillespie and depended on him. Gillespie had mysterious sources of information. Sometimes he heard something of value to us from old sacristans in village churches, refugees who had come through the German lines, or perhaps from a child who had watched the German troops from her bedroom window at night as they moved out.

He was chief of the detachment office and he kept the records, wrote most of the reports, knew all of the directives and was the only one who could handle our G-2 colonel when he called up in a fit of rage.

Only Gus Desroches seemed to despise him. Desroches called him "Lady Bountiful," gave imitations of his odd, gentle way of talking and saved his most grisly stories for moments when Gillespie was near.

Gus came into the dining room singing in his harsh whoop:

> *Goodbye Piccadilly,*
> *Farewell, Leicester Square,*
> *It's a long long way to Tipperary,*
> *But my heart's right there.*

Nobody paid any attention because in the past two weeks we had all become used to his joke. He liked to call the English "blighters," the Germans "Boches" and us "The Old Contemptibles." "If they got rid of Kitchener and Joffre," he'd say, "we might win this war."

He was a Cajun Frenchman of about thirty, lean, black-browed, sunburned and rough as a swamp fox. Without being educated, he had a great assortment of information, all things of odd shapes and sizes. He had been a G-2 sergeant in an infantry outfit until a month ago when one of our men had been taken to the hospital and he had been sent as replacement. He became known for his reckless driving, his ability—like a divining rod's—for finding cellars with wine and liquor, his tough way with German civilians.

The captain looked up from the paper he was reading. "Don't sing to me, sing to the Germans," he said. "You'd be worse than poison gas. By the way, Gus, I have something I want you to do."

With elaborate motions he came to attention—this was his good-soldier parody—and said in a monotone, "Yes, sir. What is it, sir? Ask me anything, sir."

"You may not know it," the captain said, "but we have a tent, a damn big pyramidal tent that was issued to us back in France. We've never used it and we've dragged it halfway across Europe with us so far. I'm tired of wasting the space in one whole jeep trailer and we can't abandon the thing because we're charged with it. So this afternoon I want you to take one of the jeeps and a trailer and haul that tent down to Divisional Quartermaster at Neuss and get rid of it. Make 'em give you a receipt. Don't bother to come back until you're shed of it. Understand?"

"Understood," said Desroches. It was plain that he didn't care for the job. It would mean several hours wasted in hunting up a reluctant supply officer and persuading him to accept a mass of canvas that he wanted no more than we did. The captain was never quite sure what was considered expendable and what wasn't.

"Now where's lunch?" the captain asked.

Desroches strode over to the dumbwaiter and yelled down the shaft to the kitchen. "Hey, Maria Louisa! *Essen! Kuchen! Raustoff!*" An answering wail came from below and in a few minutes the dumbwaiter appeared. "Professor Koch's house incorporates all the newest inventions of the nineteenth century," Gillespie said. The whole place depressed him.

Professor Koch had left Oberkassel in haste; we were his unforeseen heirs. His was a tall grim stone house on a street of similar houses. It was quite dark inside and though Professor Koch had gone away physically, his soul could never be evicted. His clothes and his old-fashioned frock coats still hung in the closets upstairs; his pipes still stood in their racks on the library shelves; his walking stick's ivory head still gleamed in a corner of the hall; his personal smell of tobacco, powder, boot polish and hair oil still drifted in the rooms. He himself, luckily framed and behind glass, watched us balefully from a table in the library. His autographed copy of *Mein Kampf,* his personally inscribed picture of Rosenberg and some other similar paraphernalia lay on the junk heap at the back of the garden.

The dining room was as dark as the rest of the house. There was a dingy Turkish carpet on the floor and a great deal of oak furniture that seemed to have been designed out of a love for mere obstinacy. In the corner was a Dresden stove, a smooth brown cliff of tile. The Koch family portraits burdened the walls like lessons against the sin of gluttony. Each of them seemed to have been painted after a particularly heavy meal while the artist suffered with indigestion and the sitters from torpor. Their cheeks seemed stuffed, their breathing difficult and even their eyes seemed to swim in a pale lustrous gravy. It was hard to enjoy food here.

Gillespie left as soon as he could and went along the hall to the small front sitting room that served as an office. He found that Desroches had left without his noticing it; he discovered him sitting in the front room with his feet crossed on top of the desk. He had been talking to an old woman who must have just come in. She was sitting in a chair in a dark corner of the room near the bookcases. Gillespie started to turn around.

"Don't go away, Gillespie," said Desroches. "Here's an interesting monument for you." He went over to the window and pulled the curtains wider apart to let in more of the reluctant gray light.

She was unusually tall even as she sat there and when she arose in alarm she gave the effect of a great flagstaff covered with ragged pennons. She wore an ancient lavender dress from which flew and fluttered a hundred filmy points of cloth. On her head was a round straw hat with a hard brim, a kind of huge saucer, and in her hand she carried a knitted bag.

Gillespie had to look upward to her face. It was a queer face, all creases and canals and it was covered with heavy powder of an orange tint; even at that there was something handsome about it in a Brobdingnagian way, something that suggested lost looks. Her lips were working and she started to speak, but Desroches held up his hand. She sat down. Then he stepped into the middle of the floor with his arms folded, giving her a critic's stare out of half-closed eyes.

He imitated Gillespie's deliberate way of talking. "Now isn't this splendid?" he said. "An excellent example of an early Gothic ruin. Notice the vaults, the spires, the flying buttresses, the wonderful gables on this old crock. Early thirteenth century, wouldn't you say, Gillespie?"

Gillespie, for once, was suddenly angry. He felt the skin of his face getting tight and cold. He suddenly stepped between Desroches and the old woman, only a few inches away from Desroches, breathing almost into his face. "Either tell me what she wants in a decent way or get out of here and let me talk to her myself." Gillespie realized that it wasn't his own voice—it was harsh and quick. There was a look of astonishment in Desroches's black spotlike eyes and he pulled away. Then Gillespie realized that a moment before he had thought of lashing Desroches across the face and had even seen the place on the bridge of his nose where his knuckles would land. He was amazed at himself and he too stepped back, his fingers trembling.

Desroches went over behind the desk and sat down again, lighting a cigarette. He looked suspiciously at Gillespie and then smiled. Possibly it was a contemptuous smile, but, Gillespie noticed, it was also a cautious smile.

"It's nothing," Desroches said. "She's just another one of those crazy characters that come in with some story or something they want us to do for them." Gillespie was going to do it, whatever it was.

"What does she want? Who is she?"

"She's French, she says—used to be married to some German. She's been head housekeeper or governess or something at the Portuguese legation for a long time. A big house down by the river, she says. The family moved out during the raids and she's lost track of 'em. The troops moved in and they won't let her into that area. She says there's some important property of the Portuguese government that she ought to get and she wants one of us to take her down there. I doubt it." He turned again to the old woman and said in French, "You're wasting our time. Get out." But he had already seen what was going to happen.

"I'll talk to her," Gillespie said.

"All right if you want to. She's your type." He walked to the door, then paused and said, "Wait'll you get a load of her. She's off her rocker. She don't know whether she's speaking French or German." He went out.

As if nothing had happened, the old woman leaned forward at Gillespie and smiled humorously. *"Monsieur, vous êtes très gentil,"* she said in a sweet miniature voice. *"Notre haus ist . . ."*

Their house was a considerable distance away. Gillespie and the old woman, a strange couple, walked down the

long street in the stony afternoon light. She had begun talking again almost from the moment they left the door, talking
amiably in her comic mixture of the two languages as if she
were a child who had never learned the difference between
a speech half forgotten and one partly learned.

Gillespie was inattentive, wondering at his own rage of a
few minutes before. He thought now that Desroches had not
backed down because he was afraid of Gillespie's somewhat
womanish anger, but because, in his tough practical way, he
had discovered a joke in the situation, a good example of the
absurd daydream in which he thought Gillespie existed.
With the closing of the door, the old woman would no longer
be a reality for him but, to Desroches and the others, Gillespie would always be an unbelievable continued story that
went on daily before their own eyes.

There were occasional holes in the street and more and
more often they had to avoid piles of dirt and broken stone
shoved up against the gutters. Oberkassel is like a dock stuck
out into the river Rhine and beyond that, on three sides, is
the great industrial sea of Düsseldorf. Over on that side the
German troops kept up a pretense of war like a natural
habit of life whose origin and purpose is no longer remembered. At night the artillery fired across the river with
varying sounds, depending on the kinds of guns and their
distance. In the minds of sleepers on this side the sounds had
become domesticated: the dull slamming of a door, an iron
pot dropped in the kitchen, the wind banging at a window
sash. Mortar shells had a hollow pop like the bursting of an
electric light bulb in the next room; but that was different.
They were fired mostly in the daytime and sometimes you
would round a corner and find a child or a stray dog dead in

the street and the austere gray fronts of the houses pocked and pitted for yards from the recent burst.

In her small tuneful voice Mme. Laurec was telling him all the unnecessary things that came into her head. *"Je suis sehr traurig,"* she said gaily, but that was an indefinable feeling, it seemed, coming partly from the loss of M. Laurec, a jewel of a man, who had passed away some seven years ago, partly from the little flat with the nasty kitchen where she now had to live, and partly from worry over "her darlings" of the da Camara family—the consul's—with whom God knew when she would ever be reunited again.

There was a trolley car like a great toy dragon with a smashed face, abandoned on its tracks in the middle of the square. A line of people formed in front of a butcher shop. An extremely bow-legged old man in a German army cap was sticking a military-government poster on a wall. In the little park there were signs of spring and in places cut branches and green leaves littered the pavement.

But as they went along the narrower streets toward the river, damage became more frequent and the town more empty. Jeeps passed them once or twice. Two soldiers leaned against the doorway of a shut-up church, smoking and arguing, their voices sounding like the quarreling noises of squirrels at a distance. A heavier shell had smashed the pavement in one place and they had to cross the edge of the crater on planks. At the bottom of the hole lay exposed a tangled crisscross of pipes and wires, the city's iron veins and tendons under its concrete flesh.

There was a barrier at the end of the street made of three lines of bright new barbed wire strung between a lamp post and an iron railing. A corporal with a fixed bayonet on his

rifle was meandering alongside it, ducking a cigarette behind one cupped hand. He looked at them speculatively out
of the corner of his eye and then decided not to throw it
away.

While Gillespie explained and showed his credentials,
Mme. Laurec supplemented with smiles, incomprehensible
sayings, and a fluttering of all her flags. The corporal stared,
then grinned. "All right," he said, "but don't get out on the
river bank." As Gillespie helped her through the barbed
wire he laughed and yelled after them, "And watch out for
the dame; she's got her eye on you."

She pointed to a gate further down the street. Evidently
in front of them were the back gardens and rear entrances
of a number of large houses that faced along the river, which
was invisible from here. An almost continuous stone wall ran
along the sidewalk and beyond it Gillespie could see trees
and the tops of voluminous bushes. The street was carpeted
with leaves and twigs clipped off by the mortar shells, wanton
gardeners that had left ugly gaps in the foliage.

At the gate she produced a large brass key, but it was not
needed and they passed through into the handsome dis-
ordered garden of the da Camara house. Following her along
the path, Gillespie began to realize that this was no ordinary
garden, but a prospect, a miniature country laid out in front
of him, an imitation Portugal perhaps. The gravel path wound
through a small forest of pines. Along a small knoll wooded
with dwarf trees ran a baby river with its own islands and
bridges, flowing away from them off through the model
forest. Beyond the grove was an open space like a small
meadow at the end of which was a little turreted summer-
house like a castle and back of that, in a surprising illusion, a

long dark mountain range stretched out of sight. It was a boxwood hedge, carefully clipped and carved to look like distant sierras.

But Mme. Laurec was clucking at the bushes she saw up-rooted and the branches of trees that had been broken off. Once she stopped to examine a flower bed and another time to set up a wooden bench that had been overturned. Her lips pursed and she looked around censoriously.

She had another key in her hand, but the back door was half open, hanging on loosened hinges with its bolt torn out of the wood. She touched it in surprise and wanted to ex-amine it closer, but Gillespie urged her on. They came into a hallway and she led him through a door that opened off into a large low kitchen with a white tile floor and a great black range that took up the whole of one end of the room. The tables and counters were full of empty wine bottles, opened cans, orange skins, waste and litter. Mme. Laurec shook her head in astonishment and stared at Gillespie for a moment with parted lips.

He was beginning to get impatient. He reminded her gently that they could not linger too long and reluctantly she went back into the hall. They followed it until they came to another door which, she explained, was the door to her own room. It was small and when the blackout shades had been pulled back, they saw it had not been disturbed. A low dresser, a bed with the mattress folded back, a mirror, a fat white jug on a washstand, were what it amounted to. She fumbled in the drawers among some clothes, put a few things in her bag, then led the way out.

The next trip was up a narrow flight of steps that led off the hallway. When they reached the top Gillespie was no

longer sure of his geographical position in the house. The
silence, the musty smells, the echoes made him feel uneasy.
Mme. Laurec no longer paid him any attention; he could
go or stay as he pleased. She went from room to room with
some idea behind her fixed frown that she would not express
and that seemed to have no connection with the "valuable
property of the Portuguese government." Gillespie, watching
her, began to feel that she was looking for something intently
but without any notion of what it might be.

She halted in an upstairs sitting room, her back to him.
Then dreamily she moved across the room to a chair with a
dust cover on it. She shoved it out in front of the fireplace,
then, leaning on the back, she stroked her fingers over the
cloth, smiling and murmuring. Then she crossed over to the
sofa and leaned down, stretching out her arms. After a while,
with a sadder expression, she went to the table and traced
her fingers over the polished surface, no longer seeming to
notice the layer of dust they disturbed.

She moved out to the center of the room again. She
paused, nodding at someone Gillespie could not see. She
gave a little suppressed laugh, made a kind of half curtsy and
reached out her hand to the empty air; then, turning, she
quickly walked out of the room.

He did not try to understand this except in a visual way.
For a few minutes he lingered in the room, getting out a
cigarette, staring at her fingermarks in the dust, noticing the
oblong lighter patches where the pictures had once hung on
the walls, holding off a few minutes before he should go to
her and warn her they must leave.

During the moments of pantomime, he had realized a
change in her, or in his view of her: it made all the difference.

While he had talked to her in Professor Koch's parlor and later when he walked down the street with her she had been a queer old thing, the coquettish *grande dame,* dainty giantess. He had just been crossing up Desroches. But he had been all overwhelmed in feeling sorry for her in those last few seconds, not for her queerness but for her sudden familiarity. She had abruptly moved into human scale, become real, personal, living, appealing to him.

Then he went into the hall and on to an open door beyond which he could hear her voice in muttered exclamation and conversation. He came on her silently and stood in the shadow. She had opened a little wardrobe dresser and had bent down to reach into one of the drawers. It was obviously a nursery. The walls were a bright blue and two small beds were shoved up against the further wall. Mme. Laurec at first had seemed to be merely straightening and examining some clothes. Now she took out a small sailor blouse and held it at arm's length in front of her. In the dim light her face looked scarred: tears had worked out two wavy runnels in the orange powder and one hung, delicately uncertain, on the end of her nose.

Gillespie stepped away from the door, further back into the hall. He waited, hearing a confusion of whispers, sighs, endearments, mumbled talk. Drawers opened and shut. There were long moments of silence. Finally he heard her coming out.

She smiled at him thankfully. *"Wir gehen,"* she said and led the way down the corridor which widened at last and drew light from some windows. Gillespie saw that they had come to its end and that here was the main staircase, an open one that made a broad gradual turn and descended to the entrance hallway of the first floor. At the end of this hall was the outer door, double-sized and of heavy oak. They went down. To the right of the stairway one of the inner doors was partly ajar and toward this she walked confidently.

Again they stepped into a half-dark room and Gillespie could not adjust his vision at once. He could see three extremely tall narrow windows almost entirely shrouded by blackout curtains at this end of the room. It seemed to him that directly in front of the middle window was a black dully gleaming piece of furniture, a grotesquely carved, elaborately ornamented object, flanked by piles of pillows on either side. He blinked and stared, trying to make it into some familiar shape—table, chair or flower stand. He touched the blackout curtain. A little light sprang in. It was a heavy thirty-caliber water-cooled machine gun standing there on its tripod.

"What's this?" Someone walked out of the darkness at the far end of the room. A light came on and Gillespie was facing a bulky surprised sergeant with a carbine in his hand. Another soldier came in from a doorway Gillespie had not seen in the darkness.

"God, I thought it was the captain at first," the sergeant said. "Whad'ye want?" Gillespie told him, indicating Mme. Laurec who was staring at the stripped room with all its furniture piled against the far wall.

"All right," said the sergeant. "Don't go near any of the front windows though, and when you leave, go back through the garden." He rested one hand on the pile of sandbags near the machine gun and squinted out through a peephole in the window shade. "We got a delicate mutual-assistance agreement with them Heinies across the river. They don't fire on us unless somebody makes an ass of himself and shows a light or sticks his head out the window, and us likewise.

"Some air corps guys come up here looking for souvenirs last week and they probably made too big a target or some officer was around, so the Heinies blasted 'em. So we shot up their o.p. in the factory over there. No trouble since."

"We'll be careful," said Gillespie, "Ah!" said Mme. Laurec. The sun had suddenly come out and the black shades were punctured and threaded with sparks of gold. She turned at once and went back through the door they had come in by.

"O.K., Sergeant," Gillespie said. "We're going now. Sorry we bothered you." He followed her out into the hall.

"Are you ready to go now, Mme. Laurec?" he asked in French.

She had moved across the hallway toward the front door. She turned around and faced him, her back against it. "Yes," she said with dignity. "I have found what I was looking for."

With all its mottled powder, dried tears, lines and wrinkles, her old face looked serene and young. It had the same distant innocence that had come over it during the minutes she had smiled and gestured and moved around in the room upstairs. She was smiling again and Gillespie felt stricken because, assenting with his heart, he was powerless to raise his hand. He let her go.

She was opening the door. She was standing on the terrace outside. She was raising her arms in the sunlight, the thin dress clinging to her tall body while the tag-ends of her clothing were ruffled and flipped by the breeze from the river. Automatically Gillespie recoiled into the shelter of the inner doorway, waiting.

Gillespie still felt dazed an hour later as he sat alone in the dingy, dark, red-and-brown room that had been Professor Koch's parlor. More than anything else he felt a dull disgust and hatred for himself. He felt self-betrayed by all the feelings that had been so natural to him and now it seemed that the old woman could not have been real at all but a delusion that he had made up against himself, a knife he had sharpened to cut his hand, a trap he had set for his own foot. As he remembered her smile in the doorway it returned to him not with warmth or meaning, but as a bony grin. The afternoon lengthened, the room grew even darker; he sat with his face in his hands.

He had not noticed the noises on the stairway, the distant slamming of doors in the house, the chiming of a clock. But suddenly there were voices in the corridor; the door opened and Captain Hind walked in, followed by Desroches.

Desroches laughed, exploded. "I got rid of the old bitch! What do you think of that?"

"How do you mean?"

"Enemy action, enemy action!" crowed Desroches. "The Boches shot her up themselves!"

"Here, what's this?" said the captain. "There's something the matter with Gillespie." The captain went over to him.

But Desroches didn't notice. He turned to another man who was just coming in the door. "You know what happened, Langer? I took that tent out in the trailer this afternoon— on my way to Neuss to try to turn it in—and I got down to the next street, just going around the corner, when what in the goddamn hell do you think happened? A mortar shell dropped right in the middle of the trailer! Didn't hurt me, didn't hurt the jeep, cut the trailer up just a little—but it blew that old mess of canvas into a million rags!"

THE THIN
VOICE

THEY had come down to Heiligenkreuz in Major Danney's civilian car and that was some comfort. But now they were standing in the dark on the schoolhouse steps, hunchbacked under the wind which was saw-edged with icy rain, waiting while Langer tried to get the key to work in the lock.

The major explained things over again to Welsh. He was standing with his feet apart and his head lowered as if to butt, hulking blackly between Welsh and the glassy yellow stream of the headlights. His face and head were lost in a cap of shadow as if covered by an executioner's hood; his ponderous voice seemed to contain the tone of an underlying question as though someone were still waking him and he was still asking why. It was about five-thirty in the morning.

"The general's orders," he was saying to Welsh, "are to screen this entire vicinity with a fine-toothed comb. Every male German between fifteen and sixty-five. Understand that, Welsh? No slackness, now; *thoroughness* is what we've got to have here."

Welsh tried to nod as curtly as he could with the rain

coming down his neck. This was what happened when you had to work for Danney; he took you in. There seemed to be only one permissible way of behaving with him and if you refused to play son to his father—but none of the junior officers ever did. They were sarcastic behind his back but he patronized them to their faces.

The major was a professional soldier. He was a big man with an enormous red-cheeked face; he looked like a cruel, clean-shaven Santa Claus. All the world around him was his garden and other men he dealt with were simply his disgraceful children. Behind his back in one hand he carried an invisible razor strap and in the other a bag of hard candy. So Welsh tried to be mildly insolent if he could manage it; but it never worked, it wasn't even recognized.

"Yes, sir. I've gone over all the directives several times. I think I know the procedure." Welsh's words seemed to blow away with the wind but Major Danney's dropped like separate rocks.

"Now, Lieutenant, the posters have been up for several days and the Burgomaster has been warned to get his people here. All you have to do is to see that they *are* here and that every one of them is properly examined."

"Yes, sir."

Langer had got the door open and they could step out of the blasts of rain into the entrance hallway, which was dark and cold. Langer and Bart went on into the further room, their footsteps on the boards retreating like the hollow ghost-raps heard at a seance. Unable to stare, unable to create an effect by twitching his ferocious paternal face, the major took hold of Welsh by his upper arm.

"Now this is an important Counter-Intelligence assignment. We want tabs on every ex-Nazi in Germany." His voice rumbled like stage thunder in the narrow hall. "And we want all of the big ones behind our stockades. Understand, Welsh? Now you know all of those identification papers they carry better than I do. You and your men." The voice slid downhill, becoming a little more affable; Welsh guessed what it was.

"And I don't think I'll really be needed here. Anyway, in the original plan I was only supposed to be a kind of supernumerary observer." The voice took a brisk upturn. "So I'll leave it to you."

It was too dark in the little entrance for the major to execute one of his dramatic departures, but he attempted to give the sense of one. As his hand felt for the doorknob he said, "I'll be back at 1700 pronto. Trucks for Nazi officials and German deserters at 1715." He jerked at the door and it came open. A slash of wind and rain like a flung hawser hit him in the face and he staggered and lost his breath. Then he had to go bent and coughing outside; Welsh could hear him shaking the iron railing as he went down the steps and slamming into his car while Welsh, behind the door, felt himself smiling like a villainous child.

Now Langer had turned on an electric light and Welsh could see the doorway into the schoolroom. When he went in he saw Bart standing directly under the bulb in the middle of the little regiment of wooden desks. With his fists on his hips he was staring around the room and it made Welsh think of his old nickname. Dressed in o.d.'s, with his brown wet hair sticking up like vestigial antlers and his heavy overbalanced face, all nose and nostrils, he did seem to be a sad and cantankerous moose.

But almost immediately Welsh saw his own self reflected in the rainswept window, approaching the teacher's desk like the ghost of a child in a misty antique mirror. He saw bitterly how well the image fitted Major Danney's conception. He noticed his own silly blond hair and his mouth clinging like a small white oyster to the lower part of his face. He looked like a choirboy.

He threw his briefcase on the desk with an angry slap and turned away from the window. "Bart," he said sharply, "is there another room we can use for an office? We'll use this for a waiting room."

Bart answered slowly. "Yes, Langer's in there now. He's making some coffee on the Coleman stove."

Welsh then noticed the door behind him and he went on into the other room, a smaller one, but Langer had already begun to set things up. He had placed three tables in a row along the wall under a red-and-green map of Europe. He had started the Coleman burner and put on the coffee. He had remembered cups, sugar, condensed milk. He had carefully put their papers, notebooks and pencils on each of the desks.

"Let's have a fire in here, Langer," Welsh said peevishly. "It's goddamn cold."

"Okay, Lieutenant," Langer said without turning to face him. "I built it in the stove there. All you have to do is touch a match to it."

"Well, light it then," said Welsh.

But a minute later he was sorry for that and he said mildly, "You've done a good job in here, Langer," but Langer didn't answer him.

When the coffee was ready he called for Bart and they sat

down at the tables. In his thin voice Lieutenant Welsh began to go over the details of procedure. Examine all identification papers and hold back all Nazi party officials and all para-military officials above a certain rank. All ex-soldiers not having a proper German army discharge. They knew this as well as he did and it was as if Welsh were trying to convince some invisible audience of his knowledge and authority to command.

"And especially," he went on, "we have to look out for ex-guards or officials from the concentration camp at Waldberg. Many of them live around here and we haven't picked up all of them by any means. Their names are on that list." Bart's smile might have been sarcastic and Langer might have been looking deliberately bored, he was not quite sure.

His voice, lighter than cigarette smoke, seemed to float up above him and disappear without being noticed. "Above all," he said with as much emphasis as he could find, "above all, what we must have is *thoroughness*." He waited a moment and while he waited the last words seemed to repeat them-selves in Major Danney's voice.

Abruptly he got up, avoiding their looks, and hurried into the next room. He walked up and down the aisle between the desks trying to work off his shame and rage with himself, crushing one hand in the other, and repeating silently, "Jesus! Idiot! Idiot!" He could hear Bart's half whisper from the other room, "What got into him?"

Finally Bart called to him, "Better come back and finish your coffee, Lieutenant. I think the first ones are coming." Then he heard the outside door opening and the voices and footsteps of people coming into the entryway.

He walked slowly back. Langer had already come out to

talk to the people who were now crowding into the school-room, telling them what was expected and getting them formed into a line. Bart didn't look up when he came and Welsh had time to finish his coffee before Langer got back.

The first three men came into the room and stood before the desks, holding out their papers. The one in front of Welsh was a humped thin farmer in a long dark overcoat that made him seem to be a badly wrapped package; he smelled of pig manure. Welsh noticed that on his face the beard stubble looked like iron filings collected on a magnet. He held out his papers in fingers like thick half-smoked cigars. Welsh took them and, opening the worn *Soldbuch*, discovered the man in front of him as a smooth-faced smiling boy in the identification picture. He checked the necessary entries. War service 1914–18. Wounded. Recalled to the *Landsturm* in 1938. Exempted from military service because of age and infirmity.

At his left he could hear Bart's thick uneven voice saying something, so Welsh spoke to the old man. He was pleased with the effect. Bart was from German parents in Iowa and Langer was from Chicago. Their German was fluent but in-correct, full of Americanisms. He knew that his own, though school-learned, was excellent and precise *Hochdeutsch*. A man just coming in the door stopped to stare at him. "You talk like our priest," the old farmer said.

And Welsh felt even better as time went on. He dealt con-fidently with each set of papers as it lay on the desk before him. The shuffling lines of men slowly passed by with their hard subdued faces and their work-deformed hands. Their breaths were strong and bitter and the ammonia-sweat-and-dung smell of cowshed and barnyard stuck to their clothes.

In time their looks had come to resemble those of their animals, their aged horses and cows. They seldom spoke.

Every now and then someone would be singled out and sent to the lean-to on the back of the school. Once it was a fat man in a velveteen coat who had been of some importance in the local SA organization. Usually it was a soldier who had simply come home after the surrender of the army without bothering to get a discharge slip. "It's a ridiculous piece of red tape," Welsh said to Langer.

One of these men was in front of him now, a tall boy with a white face and a mechanical leg that did not obey him. He explained in short jerky sentences that he had been wounded in Russia and, after the hospital, had been sent home to convalesce. Yes, he said he knew he would have to go to prison camp, but if the Herr Offizier would be so kind—he lived in a village about three miles away.

"What's his trouble?" Bart asked. "He's holding up the parade." Welsh ignored him; he told the German to go on.

At home, the cripple said, was his pack with everything he owned. Surely the officer agreed that a man would need dry socks, some soap and a razor at least in the prison camp. He hesitated. And—if the lieutenant would understand—he had an old mother. He wanted to say good-bye to his mother.

"*Nein*." Bart said. "*Das ist streng verboten.*" Welsh flared up.

"It's none of your business, Sergeant. I'm taking care of this man." Bart stared; two red marks like bee stings rose on his cheeks. "Yes sir," he finally said; "I didn't mean anything," and turned away.

"You may go home and get your pack," Welsh said in German. "You may say good-bye to your mother, but you must be back here in this room at two o'clock exactly." He repeated it, "*Zwei Uhr genau.*" The boy started to salute him, hesitated, then bowed instead.

As the morning advanced, the rain slowed and ceased but the wind still ripped at the window frames and it hadn't grown light enough to put out the electricity. Welsh wondered why they were not getting the work done as fast as he had expected. There were confusions, delays, long explanations, questions that had to be repeated to him. Some of the men had been party members and their explanations of how they had been forced to join were monotonously the same. Only three of them were found to have held rank of any importance at all.

When noon came there were still about a hundred men in the outer room. Bart told them to go home and come back in an hour. Langer made coffee to go with their cold K-rations and they ate without speaking, Welsh still sensing the antagonism of the other two.

He finished first and, putting on his trench coat, went through the schoolroom where several men had remained behind and now sat eating lunches, cramped in the small seats, staring dumbly out of the window. Welsh opened the outside door.

Glad to get away from Bart and Langer for a moment, he stood on the steps. He lighted a cigarette and looked up and down the blank little street that led to the town square. He noticed by the sign that it was called *Schillerstrasse,* and that in the center of the square was a stone cross like a queer huge bone. But these were vacant symbols and there was nothing either poetic or pious about Heiligenkreuz. The houses along the street, all blackish stone, reminded him of a row of pris-

oners he had once seen, all lifers, still, cold-faced, and growing older without hope.

As he was watching, a little girl came out of one of the
houses and started down the street. She was carrying a large
earthenware jug in her arms and it looked almost too heavy
for her. When she was a little past the door of the schoolhouse, she suddenly seemed to trip against an uneven stone
in the road and, falling forward, let go of the jug, which
bounced once in the air and then seemed to fly to pieces.
There was milk inside the jug because there was immediately
a white puddle in the roadway in the middle of which the
girl fell to her knees.

She didn't make a sound; she didn't cry. She stood up and
wiped her stockings and then, almost as if she had looked
forward to this castastrophe, she squatted down and began
to gather the pieces of the jug and put them in her skirt.
Welsh watched her pick up each one, shake it a little and
put it with the others. At last she had recovered the whole
jug, fragment by fragment. Then she turned around and
went back up the street the way she came.

It suddenly seemed to Welsh that he was doing the same
thing.

But first lieutenants were not supposed to generalize, he
thought. So when he had finished his cigarette he looked at
his watch and went inside. It was nearly one o'clock. As he
did so, he thought about Major Danney and he realized that,
in spite of everything, he was looking forward to seeing him
at five.

Bart and Langer were not alone when he came in. There
were two men with them, both trying to talk at the same
time. At first Welsh saw only their backs but they turned

immediately and, without pausing, directed their wordy duet toward him. *"Langsamer! Langsamer!"* Welsh yelled. *"Einer nach dem andern!"*

They stopped at once. The younger man wore a tight blue pullover that gave him the look of some kind of athlete, a fancy boxer or gymnast perhaps. His pale blue eyes were so deep-set that they looked like puddles of water at the bottom of twin craters; he had a long pump-handle nose.

The other man gave the impression of tough old age. He had a square-set face, marked at random with deep creases and crevices. His blond hair was white at the roots so that it seemed hard to tell whether it was becoming white with age or, having already become white, was gradually yellowing with still greater age. His left hand was only a purple stump, like a ham butt.

With his good hand he held out a brown booklet which Welsh then took and examined. His name, it said, was Heinrich Zorn and the book was a membership book in the Social-Democratic party, dating back to 1924. Neither of the men had spoken after Welsh, so Langer began to explain.

"This man says that he's just been released from the prison camp and before that he lived here in this town. He's here in the 'interest of the anti-fascist truth,' as he puts it, and he says he can help give us a line on everybody who comes in. What about it, Lieutenant? I think he might be useful."

"Who's the other one?" Welsh asked.

"He's a French slave laborer. He's been working on farms around here since 1942. He says he knows all the important Nazis in this place and he wants to help too."

As if performing in elocution class, the man with the yellow hair put his one hand on his heart and stepped forward a step. He talked for nearly five minutes. He gave his father's name, the exact day and place of his own birth, the date of his graduation from a technical high school, his address in the town and his wife's full name before she was married. He said that he had always been against the Nazis for many reasons. They had destroyed the freedom of the German people, they had plunged the world into an unjust war and furthermore, he had private information that the important leaders of the party were dishonest and immoral in their personal lives.

He said that he had suffered all that a man could suffer. They had confiscated his property and made him endure years of imprisonment because he had opposed these injustices. As soon as he mentioned the Konzentrationslager, he seemed to be unable to go on. He waved his blunt purplish stump in several futile circles and repeated, "*Ja . . . sehen Sie . . . sehen Sie.*"

Welsh explained what they were doing while Bart brought a couple of chairs. The old man stowed his book away and sat down solemnly, but the Frenchman remained restlessly standing, talking to Langer.

At first Welsh thought they were going to be a help. As the afternoon lines began to come through they had some information to offer about each man that stepped up to his desk. This man had been a Nazi, but of no importance. That one had three sons killed in the war and was known to say things against the government. These pieces of information were whispered hoarsely in Welsh's ear.

When the German with the mechanical leg came back, exactly at two o'clock, Welsh tried to catch Bart's eye. But Bart either deliberately ignored him or else was too busy.

Welsh began to have trouble with the two volunteers. The old German got into a long wrangle with one man over some obscure neighborhood swindle that happened in 1929. He was always jumping up to make accusations. The Frenchman now and then shoved a man out of line and made him go to the end or hauled someone in ahead of everybody for a special hearing. Welsh had to explain to them over again that this was not a court of justice, that it was simply a kind of registration.

Somehow they managed to get through the afternoon and to finish with most of the papers. At about four o'clock the electricity failed, leaving the room in a closet-like half light, but only a few men remained. Welsh tried to hurry things.

The Frenchman had disappeared soon after the lights went out and Welsh hoped that he was gone for good. For the first time all day long there was nobody standing before him and he looked around the office in the growing darkness. In the dimming light he could see Bart and Langer talking to two of the last-comers. He was tired of the endless series of faces and the interminable papers, and he was just ready to say something about closing up when he heard sounds of heavy walking outside, a tangle of voices, a yell. The door was kicked open and a knot of wrestling men were pushed through.

The Frenchman was one of them and he disentangled himself first, going over to stand by the wall. There were three others, and as they finally stopped shoving and jerking, Welsh saw two chunky round-faced men with blond hair heavy as wheat, holding between them another man. The two on either side looked like angry twins. They were of the same size and bulk, the only difference being that one had on a dark tunic and the other was dressed in gray. *"Ich bin Russisch Offizier,"* said the one in the tunic. *"Kriegsgefang'ner. Ich bin Hauptmann Krotolenko jetzt von Waldberg Lager."*

But Welsh was staring at the man in the middle. At first his face had dashed wildly from side to side, teeth showing and hair flying, as in a spasm. Gradually it had become rigid and now it was looking straight at Welsh, thrust out at him like a gargoyle.

There was something epigrammatic about the face as if a great number of hideous generalities about the human race had been neatly summarized in its features. Some animals are traditionally corrupt in the fables—they had all contributed to his looks: the vulture his nose, the jackal his eyes, the lynx his mouth, the fox his expression. But that is all euphemism, Welsh thought, and animals are only blamed as a kind of evasive figure of speech. Actually his face was intensely human. As Welsh stared he thought he could see something in it—at the same time—of the gravedigger with his spade, the officiating parson with his book, the hypocritical mourner, the corpse itself and, finally, of the man who drove him to suicide.

There was blood around the edge of the mouth and, as it opened slowly like the opening of a secret door, Welsh could see that a tooth had been knocked out. When the man tried to speak it did sound like some wild animal bark.

"Er ist Tartar," the Russian officer was saying and he went on in broken German to tell how he and Captain Mihailov had been prisoners at Waldberg for three years. This man, captured somewhere in Russia by the Germans, had become one of their guards. The worst, the Russian said. He had tortured the prisoners, he had beaten men to death. Captain Mihailov

had seen him pluck out a living eye. Now they had found him. He was hiding in a farmer's stable.

"I know that man," said Zorn.

"This is not a court of justice," Welsh said. "We'll send him to prison. Each man must be tried."

The Russians didn't seem to understand. Krotolenko said that they would be pleased, if such were permitted, to be present when the Americans shot the man. They had been looking forward to that.

Welsh repeated his sentence; the officer looked puzzled. He began to talk with the other man in Russian and Welsh was aware that both Bart and Langer had stood up. The old German had hitched his chair nearer and was tapping the stump of his wrist against his knee. The room was quiet until the Russian spoke again. He said that he had talked with his brother officer and that they understood what the American officer meant and that he and Andrei Petrovitch were willing. Could they borrow a pistol for a few minutes?

Shaking his head, Welsh looked at the face again. The mouth was still opening slowly and closing, the eyes were rigid. Bart said, "Oh, Christ. Let 'em have the bastard."

"No," said Welsh slowly. "No, they can't."

Suddenly there were footsteps in the outer room. The door opened and Major Danney, like a god from the machine, stood there smiling in his buttoned-up gray trench coat and his neat green hat. The three men stepped back a little. "What's this?" asked the major. "Who're these people?"

Welsh explained and Major Danney stepped up to inspect the prisoner's face as if it were a piece of ordnance. He stepped back quickly and then he turned to Welsh. "Goddamit," he said suddenly. "What are you waiting for, man?"

"You'd let a son-of-a-bitch like that get away?" he roared. "Welsh, lend that officer your .45. Tell them to take him out of town—make as little fuss about it as possible."

The light in the room had failed so far that he could barely see their faces. Bart was staring at him with accusation; Langer's look was grim and cold. He saw Zorn's eyes glaring out of his scarred-up face; in the half light the Frenchman looked murderous. "Welsh!" said Major Danney. Welsh lost his head.

He stood up and he seemed to be shouting in his bodiless voice, "Goddamit, what is this? Are you a judge? Is this a hanging-jury? Is this a bloody Jacobin club? Don't you realize that even the worst human being deserves . . . has a right . . ." His voice was rising to a scream. "You can't kill a man like that."

At this moment the prisoner wrenched his arms and just as quickly one of the Russians caught him by the throat. Agonized and crazy, Welsh lunged at them, but almost at the moment he started forward Major Danney swung his arm in an arc and the heavy gloved hand chopped Welsh so hard across the face that he was thrown back over his own table.

Welsh fell forward to his knees on the floor. Everyone could hear him crying and the tears were mingling with a stream of blood falling from his nose. Major Danney began to give orders.

They picked Welsh up and made him lie down flat across the tables. When he could see clearly again the room was empty except for Langer, Bart and Major Danney. Langer gave him a handkerchief and helped him wipe off the blood. Bart took off his combat jacket and put it under Welsh's head for a pillow. They were very kind to him. Major Danney sent for his driver and had him bring a bottle of cognac from the car.

Major Danney put his hand on Welsh's shoulder and said gently, "Are you feeling better? I'm sorry this had to happen, but you lost your head, son. Take a little drink of this and you'll feel all right in a minute. In a minute you'll feel better, son."

THE
WISHBONE

THERE was somebody running in the room below and from
the moment she aroused herself she knew Jimmy's muffled
yell. He must be racing out into the cold sun parlor leaving
the door open behind as he had been told time and time
again not to do.

Submerged again in the flow of sleep, she seemed to see a
minute Jimmy rushing away between her outstretched hands
and repeating in a cricket's voice obscene words from the
telegram that had come last night. She herself was searching
for him and trying to explain, "Don't you know you must
never say such things?" but in a moment she was lost forever.

Until her eyelids fluttered and she felt a breeze like a knife
on her forehead, she slept. But then, waking a little, she
brought her arms out from under the blanket and laid them
on the icy coverlet to help; a thin river of arctic air was
coming in under the four inches of open window. Not a
woman who ever let temptation in minor matters affect her,
Jesse Kimberley denied the deep warmth of the bed and the
fact that it was Saturday by projecting her lean body gently

from under the covers and lowering her feet to the floor that felt like a field of ice.

As she closed the window, she understood the shout and, although she could not help it, her heart jumped like a girl's. The streets of Jenison, Michigan, the broad lawn by the house and the two Canadian maples in the yard were overlaid with the thick gleam of the year's first snowfall. She lived so much through the feelings of Jimmy, Kate and Mark that ideas of Santa Claus, sleds going downhill, sleighbells and ice skates came to her at once.

And now as she dressed in the feeble circle of warmth made by the electric heater, she could hear the noises they made as they went through the chests under the window seats in the upstairs hall to pull out skis, heavy gloves, ski poles, the pair of real Canadian snowshoes nobody ever wore, wax for the skis, high-top boots, hockey sticks and puck, galoshes and ice skates. In two weeks they would be into the adjoining window seat to pull out the boxes of Christmas tree decorations and would carry them in procession down, leaving strewn behind a track of imitation silver snow, celluloid Santas and colored light bulbs on the stairs. But the excuse was winter, and winter, after all, is a wonderful event, she thought; always new, exciting and bleakly beautiful. Somehow she had an almost religious faith that it was good for the children and would make them grow up vigorous and self-reliant. Mrs. Kimberley had an uncertain distrust of people who came from softer climates where there was no ice and snow.

When she finished and went out into the hall, she could hear their voices in the kitchen and she noticed that the window-seat cover had been left open with one torn brown legging hanging over the edge. She went down the stairs wondering if Mark had had trouble starting the car this morning and feeling glad that she had not been there to hear his ill-temper as he went back and forth from the garage with steaming teakettles of water. As she went into the kitchen she heard Kate's voice.

"*Shouldn't* it be, Margaret Mary? Why *won't* the river be frozen over today? Do you think it will be thick enough to skate on by tonight? It's freezing outside, isn't it? Oh I'm so happy. And Daddy promised to get the bobsled out the first day it snowed."

Carrying their dishes of hot Wheatena, Margaret Mary moved in her stumping walk across the kitchen. Her wooden leg was always a source of suppressed wonder and sly looks in the morning at breakfast (strongly discouraged by Jesse) when they recalled it over again. But this morning there was something new.

Mark was just finishing his orange juice by lifting the glass high and letting the liquid slide down his open gullet.

"Mark, how many times have I told you that you'll choke to death some day if you keep on drinking your orange juice like that?"

"Oh, Mother," they all said, "it's snowing outside. It's snowing outside. It's winter!" "We're all going to Bunker Hill right after breakfast," said Jimmy. "I hope those guys from Christian School show up this year, because we'll be ready for 'em." He was paddling his spoon in his breakfast food with a scowl that made him look older than twelve. He was fair and somewhat chunky, with a smooth broad Scandinavian face and Mrs. Kimberley sometimes wondered how he belonged in a family of tall, bony, generally dark people. First he was going to be a football player, then a doctor, then a millionaire, he said, and somehow nobody ever seemed to doubt his word.

"Right after breakfast I want one of you to go up and shut the window seat and leave it as neat as you found it. I'm always picking up after you children and I'm tired of it," said Mrs. Kimberley as she sat down across from Kate and poured herself a cup of the coffee Margaret Mary had just put on the table. There was a special treat today, she noticed. The cream had frozen in the tops of the milk bottles and that, with a little sugar sprinkled over it, was as good as ice cream. Mark had a big spoonful halfway to his mouth when he stopped and said, "Mom, I heard somebody ring the doorbell last night about midnight and then I looked out the window and saw Pete Squires go away on his bicycle. What'd you get, a telegram?"

Then she remembered what she had forgotten. "Yes, it was a telegram." Kate and Jimmy said, "From who?" and Margaret Mary turned around from the stove to listen. "Oh, it was from your Aunt Carlotta. She's coming for Thanksgiving—it's nothing to get excited about."

"Aunt Carlotta?" said Mark. Jimmy, who was two years older, said, "Oh boy, will she bring me some postage stamps from Paris this time?" "Aunt Carlotta's the pretty lady in the photo album, dummy," said Kate to Mark. "She has oodles of money and she lives all over the world just like a princess and two years ago she sent me that real china doll for Christmas." "*You* can't remember her," said Jimmy scornfully, "but I do. The last time she was here she told us about when she went to a horse race in France and one of the horses knocked into the fence and all the others ran over the rider until he got killed. That's the same one, isn't it, Mom?"

"Yes," said Mrs. Kimberley, "I'm afraid so. But anyway,

Kate, she isn't as beautiful any more as she was in that picture, I expect. I think you'll find her quite an old lady—even older than I am and nowadays she doesn't have so much money as she used to, so don't get your hearts set on presents. She's coming all the way from New York to spend Thanksgiving with us. I want [how could she say this?] you children to be nice to her but don't pay too much attention to what she tells you. She's—a little queer at times and she may say a strange thing now and then."

"You mean she's crazy?" asked Jimmy.

"No, she's not *crazy*, Jimmy. She's just—just eccentric after living in all those foreign countries. She's nice and you'll like her, but just don't take what she says too seriously." "All right, Mom," they said. But she knew they didn't understand because she hadn't put it in the right words.

The talk turned to Bunker Hill and the possibilities of ice skating. Then the three of them ran to the closet where their overcoats were. She could hear Jimmy struggling in the hall with the laces of his high-top boots, somebody slammed the window-seat cover, and next she could hear their voices in the yard as they scrambled in the wonderful snow.

"So *she's* coming," said Margaret Mary, sitting down to drink a second cup of coffee. "You'll have to excuse me this time if I don't put a hot-water bottle in her bed every night—she'll have to do it herself."

Mrs. Kimberley stared at the snow-covered birdhouse in the elm tree just outside the window. "Yes, Margaret, I know you don't like her, but please try not to show it. She won't be here very long and Mark is fond of her, even though she's just a half sister to him."

"Isn't anybody in town who likes her," said Margaret Mary.

"Last time she was here she went to see Reverend and Mrs. Burkhard and what with all her foreign ideas and those stories she nearly scared the old lady to death. You know as well as I do that Mrs. Burkhard took to bed with a fever for a whole week after she left . . ." "Now, Margaret, don't exaggerate. You know Mrs. Burkhard is in bed half the year 'round with her 'fevers' and I don't think Carlotta told her anything particularly shocking."

But as she went into the living room to straighten up after Jimmy's stamp-pasting session of last night, she reflected that Margaret Mary was right. The whole town had disliked Carlotta Kimberley ever since—when? Since she was a child? Or since she had gone away long ago to marry a Frenchman and live in Paris?

The town remembered her most vividly from her recent rare visits after her husband (a man with an unpronounceable name—another mark against her) had died, and, according to general gossip, her income having shriveled, she moved to New York. Mrs. Dutcher staring out of the post-office window seven years ago had seen a spare somber woman with the eyes of a gypsy fortuneteller being driven up the street in the station taxi. She had turned around to tell somebody, "Carlotta Kimberley's in town again," and, without really knowing what she meant, almost instinctively, added, "That means trouble."

There was no trouble, of course, but there was talk when, on the next fine day after her arrival, Carlotta walked with Jesse Kimberley down the street to the Congregational churchyard at the far north end of town to put some flowers on the mound of frosty grass by the tombstone that read, "Dr. Lucius Kimberley 1873–1918," but none on the ground beneath the smooth marble of the identical, uncut stone that stood exactly alongside, as smooth and nameless as on the day Dr. Kimberley had stood scowling in the July heat and watched it put there.

And there was more talk as they came back along the sidewalk after the female part of the town had had a chance to muster at upstairs windows, gather on corners or concoct errands that compelled them to go the length of the town to Keeler's dry-goods store. Then it was that the general opinion was passed and the details were collected for the damaging critiques of teas and socials.

Mrs. Harry Lewis remarked particularly (although it was impossible to get Mr. Lewis to respond with more than a grunt) that the New York fashions *this* time had gone too far and the church people of America, if nobody else, would never allow such short, immodest skirts that barely came to the knee, such ugly, flimsy scraps of felt for hats, such awkward loose-hanging coats to pass for decent clothing. Mrs. Van Steenberg noticed the clothes and, what was more, took particular note of the amount or color Carlotta Kimberley wore on her face—like a Halloween mask with paint on the cheeks and lips and even shading on the lashes and eyebrows, she suspected. Mrs. Potter said that nothing would ever make her bob *her* hair and go around looking like a fast woman. It was the next day that Carlotta had called on Mr. and Mrs. Burkhard and was (or was not) the cause of the fever Margaret Mary had described.

She found the Crown Colonies collection scattered under the sofa and the United States commemoratives flown like frightened birds into the woodbasket, but finally each one had been painfully gathered and put back into the little transparent paper packets; and Jesse closed the *U.S. Special Giant Postal Stamp Guide and Universal Album*, putting it back on the bookshelf from whence it would undoubtedly be pulled in a week or two for another frenzy of pasting, swapping, rearranging and debating.

She finished putting away the paste and scissors and then she heard the postman's rap on the door. For a minute she looked out on the glaze of white lawn that sparkled in minute points from the sun like a field of diamond dust. Dr. Baer, going by in his puffing old Ford, waved to her and nearly skidded into the snow plow that was coming up the other way on Dickenson street. Chase Boyle, running along the sidewalk to make a slippery slide there, yelled and threw his snowball, purposely short, just to show he knew that she didn't mind and that she liked the winter too. Mr. Dutcher, in his fur cap and his overcoat like a badly refitted horseblanket, kept on shoveling the snow off the sidewalk by his house. She knew that he was swearing under his breath and that after a while he would swat Chase Boyle, partly because he was such a nuisance, but mostly because he was so happy on this day of all days.

She collected the mail and sat in the easy chair by the lamp sorting her own letters and the advertisements out of the thick bundle that would go on Mark's desk. Then suddenly something made her think of Carlotta again and her hands dropped to her lap while she stared into space, which was more and more her habit lately.

Carlotta had never been well received. In those younger days she would wander along the river bank by habit, Jesse thought, because up in the town sometimes they would speak to her and sometimes they wouldn't. No boy ever walked along with her. Jesse preserved the picture, a browning mental souvenir, notched at the edges. "Poor Carlotta," she used to say with pleasure and then she would run curiously up behind to go her way for a while on the leaf-spotted path. But Carlotta didn't know, or at least she seemed not to in spite of the open and immediate way small-town girls have of letting you know. She just walked there "for pleasure," she said, with her hair done in a black knot behind her head and the brown triangle of her face turned upward toward the tree branches.

One day when Jesse was coming home late from a visit she took the short cut by the river path. It was late fall and the wind whipped and worried the trees, now and then throwing a scatter of raindrops through the branches or into the roughened water. Jesse saw Carlotta there on the path, deeply wrapped in her coat and more alone than anybody else in the world, walking for pleasure. When they came close Carlotta's face looked green and deep-shadowed as if exposed by lightning, and to Jesse's quivering "hello" she made no answer. Going up the hill toward home, Jesse fully expected to find the news that Carlotta was dead awaiting her. But, of course, she didn't. Then, drying her wet face before the fire, she realized that Carlotta had told the truth.

Jesse's life belonged to hayrides and bazaars and girl's club meetings. It belonged, lightly, to a boy now and then, to Sunday school, and later to dances and parties and trips to Detroit, new dresses, talk, gossip, friendships. Carlotta was excluded from all this; she belonged to nothing. And then Carlotta went away to boarding school in New York. Once or twice a year Jesse thought of her, but she never wrote.

Once or twice a year she came to brief life on the lips of

other people and then for an instant the gloomy story hung wordlessly about Carlotta's name like smoke in the air, although no one meant to recall it and no one troubled to tell it any more. It was a bad dream of Jesse's childhood that refused to dissolve; it had always been with her. Jesse never remembered when she had heard it first and never remembered belonging to it but the pressure of the name "Carlotta" in her mind was that of a hand against a door that opened and let her into a frightening half-forgotten room.

The young doctor Lucius Kimberley, who had just relieved old Dr. MacIntosh of his practice and had settled in the Baker house next to the Baptist church with his wife and child, came home late one evening from a call at a farmhouse out in the direction of Grand Rapids. Driving his slow and tired horse down the street toward home, he had seen Jesse Blaisdell who was still out on the lawn looking for four-leaf clovers in the dying light because somebody had told her if she found one four-leaf clover she would find another and another and as long as she kept finding them she would be rich and lucky the rest of her life. "Have you seen Carlotta this afternoon? Has she gone home?" Dr. Kimberley asked the little girl; but Jesse shook her head because she didn't know. And Dr. Kimberley had gone home to unhitch his horse, to put it in the stable, to walk up his front steps whistling, to light the gas in the living room, to call for his wife and to get no answer. And he had gone through the red plush drapes that hung across the arch to the dining room and had found there pretty Julia Kimberley lying on the floor with a grotesque wide red mouth where her white throat should have been and a little girl smiling and splashing in the puddle that spread over the rug.

Jesse did remember her mother scrubbing to get the red-black prints of a child's hand off the plaster of the dining-room wall.

But now she shook her shoulders as if to cast off the thought and bent her head again to search through the mail for odd household bills and foolish advertisements that would only annoy Mark if he came across them.

The rest of the morning was taken up with odds and ends of duties, things that must be done before the week-end was over. She phoned to send a telegram to Carlotta; she decided on menus with Margaret Mary; she burned a great pile of wastepaper in the fireplace; she straightened up Mark's "den" and dusted the books on the shelves. Just before dinner she went across the street to see if Mrs. Packard could get her some chestnuts for the Thursday dinner. The morning passed quickly and the children were home before she knew it.

They were fighting a retreating action down the street and across their own yard against some of the boys from the Christian School. A shower of snowballs came looping across the street just as they reached the shelter of the porch. Some of them thumped against the roof, one flew to pieces against the door, another hit the mailbox with a clang. But they all got inside without damage and Jimmy leaned back out the door to yell, "Yah! You haven't got a Chinaman's chance!" And there were more thumps on the porch just after he ducked inside.

Around the sofa where she was sorting the clean socks with holes from those without, they gathered, their coats spilling gobs of melting snow on the carpet here and there. Jimmy said, "We sure as heck showed those guys from Christian where to get off! There wasn't one of 'em dared come up the hill all morning." Mark said, "Mom, d'ja hear about Chase Boyle? Old man Dutcher pushed him into a snowdrift and so Chase hit him behind the ear with a snowball—hard-packed, too—and Mr. Dutcher's over at Boyle's right now, swearing mad, and he says he's going to get the cops on Chase. Can they put you in jail for hitting a guy with a snowball?" Kate said, "Mama, the river *is* frozen over hard. Betty McAllister told me so and she was down this morning and she even walked out on it for about twenty feet and it was as hard as the sidewalk and she didn't even see a crack. We *can* go skating tomorrow, can't we, Mom?"

Mrs. Kimberley answered, "Oh? No, I don't think they can. That's nice, but you'd better wait until your father finds out for sure. It may still be dangerous and I know it won't be smooth enough until they pour some water over the top." Then—"Jimmy, pick up that snow you're spilling all over the rug and take your hightops off in the vestibule before you come into the living room again. Aren't you children hungry? Margaret Mary's got some hot vegetable soup for lunch."

They went to take off their wet coats and shoes, to put on slippers and to wash up before lunchtime. Mrs. Kimberley rolled up the socks that had no holes in them and put the others in her workbasket in preparation for the afternoon. She went upstairs to leave them and, before she came down, she stood for a few moments in front of the mirror staring at her own long collie-like face, at the straight brown hair traced with gray drawn around her skull like a smooth headpiece and ending in a bun behind. She wondered if Carlotta had really grown any older in looks. Although no picture ever showed it, she remembered Carlotta as handsome. But her beauty belonged more to the tones of her voice, her manners and the secrecy of her temperament than to face and body. People used to say in an oddly excited tone of voice, "That Kimberley girl is strange. But there's something about her . . ." They meant that there was something about her that they did not quite dare call beauty. But although Jesse envied her too, she was more candid with herself and she would try to define why the things that were beautiful about Carlotta should be foreign or those that were foreign about her should be so beautiful.

She sighed at last and turned away to go downstairs where Margaret Mary had four steaming bowls of soup ready and was putting the rest of the lunch on the table. Mark would not be home until one o'clock, when he would sit here with her, his finger clutched in the handle of the coffee mug that had his name painted on its side in gold gothic letters, his eyes staring at the columns of the Grand Rapids paper while he ate. Kate had come in already and a moment later Mark and Jimmy arrived, shaking hands over some secret deal.

Mrs. Kimberley was quiet as she bent her head over the plate. The mingled after-image of a girl's face, the whipping trees in a stormy wind, stains on a wall, a voice she had heard from the far past, wordless but low and disturbing, flickered in her mind. At a distance she heard the children's talk, jumping from one subject to another. Almost by hearsay she knew that the winter sun outside the window was bright as an egg yolk and even somewhat warm. She knew vaguely that it came though the bare rose-bush latticework outside the window and cast a great bar of light across the table. A hundred miles away, Margaret Mary was humming over the steaming pots on the stove and the children were discussing all the possible aspects of the coming of winter. In her trance she realized these things.

Chase Boyle, though none of the three liked him much, became a sympathetic figure and Mr. Dutcher (even if he had been nice to them last Fourth of July) turned into a bad-tempered villain who shouldn't be allowed to have a sidewalk if he wouldn't let kids slide on it. The McAllister twins, it was decided, were the most interesting people in town, with their new ten-foot toboggan painted dark red on top which had arrived as a special surprise from Marshall Field's in Chicago in time for their birthday last month. Pete Squires was going fishing through the ice again this winter and already had his shack out down by the shore. All of the kids at school were selling tickets for the turkey raffle and the one who sold the most would get the pair of real tubular-blade ice skates like the one in the window down at Webster's. Greg Lewis said he had sold a hundred and fifty tickets, but it couldn't be true because everybody knew what a liar he was.

Jesse looked at the folded newspaper under her elbow but the words said, "Carlotta, Carlotta, Carlotta." The voices went on in the background of her hearing.

"Where you going 'safter, Jim?"

"None of your beeswax."

"Aw, c'mon. Didn't I give you that box of b-b's for your gun?"

"Okay. If you hafta know. Pete Squires said I could ride to Irving with him on the truck."

"Ask him if I can go too?"

"I want to go too," said Kate.

"You keep out of this," said Mark. "How about it, Jim?"

"No sir. This is private business."

"I'll tell Mama about the fight you got in at school and she won't let either of you go."

"You shut up!" they both said to Kate.

Kate began to cry a little. "I want to go too, Mama. Make Jimmy and Mark take me with them!"

Jesse awoke, suddenly aware that they were quarreling and remembering the tomato-soup fight Jimmy and Mark had had a few weeks ago. "Now what's the trouble?" Jimmy told her.

She said, "If Jimmy wants to go for a ride with Pete I don't see why he can't go alone. Why don't you two go down and see if the ice is thick enough to skate on? Anyway, you just had a trip to Grand Rapids last week and Jimmy couldn't go." Accepting the settlement, they began to talk about something else.

Rescued by the distraction, Jesse now began mentally to count the places at the Thanksgiving dinner table, deciding between fruit cocktail and shrimp, planning the stuffing that would go into the turkey and wondering if the oven could be relied upon to keep the same roasting temperature long enough. The lunch was nearly over when she raised her eyes at last. Mark and Kate had taken up her idea and were planning a walk along the river bank to prove how thick the ice was and Jimmy had already left for his rendezvous. "Now don't go out on the ice," she said. "It may still be thin and I don't want you falling through"

Margaret Mary contributed, with her back turned, a long monologue on the danger of frostbite and chilblains to children who were allowed to run around in the cold all day, but Jesse barely listened as she finished her second cup of coffee.

Stamping the snow off his shoes, Mark came in the side door and gave her a frosty kiss. The cold had changed his brown hardy face to a bright rust color and snowy crystals glittered in his eyebrows. "I've been out to look at John Patmos's dairy," he said (why she was the only one in the family who didn't shout she wondered). "I walked. Don't dare trust a car on those country roads." He threw his overcoat on a kitchen chair and sat down. Margaret Mary put a bowl of hot soup in front of him.

"I sent a telegram to Carlotta this morning, Mark," Jesse said. "I told her we'd be delighted." In spite of the boiling heat of the soup, he was pouring spoonful after spoonful into his mouth. He answered, "Mmmph?" Margaret Mary went into the dining room and then they could hear her feet on the stairs. She's gone to read the paper, thought Jesse.

"Mark, listen. I've been having some ridiculous ideas this morning, but I thought I ought to tell you." He looked up from the plate. "Of course. Go ahead. You always say that just before you tell me something quite sensible."

"No. It isn't sensible. It isn't really anything I can put my finger on either. But—I don't know—it's just that I'm *afraid* to have Carlotta Kimberley come to our house. There's no real reason; I don't want to be superstitious just because— because she's had an unfortunate life. But Mark, somehow, it's the children. Do you understand? Can't we send her another telegram and ask her not to come?" Mark had stopped eating and, pinching a soda cracker to powder between thumb and forefinger, looked seriously at her.

"I don't understand what the children have to do with it, Jess. I know that there's something about Carlotta that people in this town don't like. Some kind of an instinct, I guess. I've heard people say they didn't 'like' her or didn't 'trust' her or that they felt something was 'wrong' about her. Now that's just silly, Jess. I can't understand it. I was brought up with her and I guess I know her pretty well. It's really all small-town nonsense. Remember the fights I used to get in when other kids called her names?"

Then it went on as this same conversation always went on when they talked about Carlotta. Mark just sat stoutly and told the obvious truth, as he always would do to anybody on any subject. He would patiently search over the whole history of Carlotta. No, these feelings were all quite foolish. And who can trust "feelings" anyway? They are just as likely wrong as right. Facts are facts. You have to trust what you know—and had Carlotta ever done anything wrong? She was a good girl, smarter than most in school. Nobody could accuse her of anything out of the way. She went away to boarding school simply because the other girls wouldn't get along with her. Then she fell in love in a perfectly ordinary way. Guy was a good man, an honest respectable man who just happened to be a Frenchman (people in this town still think of all Frenchmen as natural sinners). He'd known Guy and Guy was all right. Never seen a more decent man in his life. A good businessman, too. Jesse would always try to interrupt, but he would not let her. Now he waved his soup spoon in the air.

Then he would go on to describe Aunt Willa's visits to Paris (and if there ever was an old holy terror it was Aunt Willa). How pleased she was with Guy, how clean and sunny their house was and how happy Carlotta seemed all the time. Then, beginning to wind up, he would always talk about Facts. These were the real facts. You had to trust to facts. If you ran every which way according to small-town gossip and superstition, you'd just end up by making yourself miserable. And Jesse would bow her head to the logic and say, "You're right, Mark." He always had words handy, like small change in his pocket.

The meal went on; he mentioned a few incidents at the bank, said John Patmos had two of the finest Guernseys he'd ever seen, and then they talked over Christmas presents for the children. Mark promised a shopping trip to Grand Rapids if the roads were clear after Thanksgiving.

He finished in a great hurry, pulling out his watch and then stabbing it back into his vest pocket; he wrapped his blue scarf twice around his neck, threw on his overcoat and stopped for his galoshes. "No, Jess," he answered her. "I won't have time to read them now. Nothing important today, was there? I'm expecting a letter from the insurance people in Grand Rapids." Then he slammed the door after himself and was ploughing through the snow in the side yard. "Jimmy must clean the walks when he comes home," she called to Margaret Mary who was just clumping down the stairs with her wooden-legged tread.

Mrs. Kimberley went to her room where the darning lay in a snarl of red, blue, green and gray in her workbasket on the bed. She dipped her fingers into it and began to sort the socks. The black one belonged to Mark senior and this mateless red one brought a picture of Jimmy, shoeless, dancing a kind of lonely improvised hornpipe on the polished walnut of the dining-room table. Then he had cried when she slapped him —public tears meant to announce that he had sinned and had properly suffered. But they dried soon. Five minutes later she heard him with Mark and Kate at the radio putting on a cheerful show. It was the Frontiersman program and Jimmy was directing everything that went on. "All right, boys, now lower her into the water." (Grunts from the radio. "Steady there"—the voice of the Frontiersman.) "I know she'll float, she's a good canoe"—Jimmy's voice. "She floats all right"— the Frontiersman. Mark and Kate were shaking with laughter. Jesse moving about in the dining room wondered how he always did the same trick so well. He must have listened to that program a thousand times, she thought, to learn just what the Frontiersman and Chief Torn Blanket were likely to say. It was only later when she was writing a letter in her own room that it struck her to wonder why Jimmy had been dancing on the dining-room table. If she asked him he would give a reason. But what would the real reason have been? She never would know. He had been all by himself.

So she knew her oldest boy by what he told her and he never told her lies, exactly, but he never told her the secret truth hidden behind the actor's smile and the quick, disarming, entirely reasonable reason he always had for grownups. When Jimmy went away from the house she tried to follow him on a path through her mind, but it always ended quickly when he slid under a hedge or dropped into an alley out of sight and she could never imagine what had happened to him.

She sat down in the chair facing the window over the lawn and took up her darning. She worked slowly, stretching the heels or toes over the darning form that looked like a hard brown toadstool. Which one did she love the most? The question echoed in some faraway corridor in her head like a familiar, long-unheard voice. It recalled some distant sensation of being kissed—by? It must have been her mother. Yes, "God bless Mama and Daddy. Amen." Then in the cottony warmth of the bed she would ask herself the question and give her answer.

As she finished one sock and turned to another, she fol-

lowed Kate and Mark. They never disappeared. Or seldom,
Mark with his leather cap, dark blue coat, solid legs, walking
along with a serious face at what he saw, like his father calling Kate's attention to "points of interest." "Look, Kate,
there's a barrel frozen in the ice." "It looks like 'n old bear."
"Don't be silly. It's just a big barrel. Probably floated down
from the mill. There aren't any bears around here any more."
He never told lies, came straight home from school every
night, did his arithmetic lesson in an old ledger that Mark
had given him or read a book that he had borrowed from his
father's bookcase. His greatest thrill was to be allowed to go
with his father to the bank on Saturday morning to fill the
inkwells.

Kate shadowed Mark as he shadowed his father, but she
never succeeded. She was a thin little girl with knobs at her
shoulders and knees, yellowish-brown hair and wide-apart
teeth. Mark could make her cry by calling her "funny-face."
Sometimes she would come to her mother's room sobbing
with shame, saying, "I hate to be a girl. I *hate* to be a girl."
Then after the tears would come the confession that Mark,
who was drawing a cowboy-and-Indian fight on brown wrapping paper had said that girls couldn't draw pictures of
horses. Only boys could. Then for a long time—two or three
days—Kate would love her mother more than ever and would
sit there while she darned, defiantly drawing picture after
picture of horses (that all somehow looked like pigs) in a
drawing pad and saying, "Mama, you're so nice. Can I go to
the grocery store this afternoon with you to help?" And she
would say, "That old Mark can go duck his head in the wash-
tub. I won't help him finish his old picture"—something she
never dared say to Mark himself. And a few days later she

would be patiently covering the sky of Mark's picture with blue crayon, although it was a weary job and he would not even trust her to draw in the yellow sun on the upper right-hand corner.

But it was Jimmy who escaped her. She remembered, three or four years ago, the day she had been hanging up washing in the back yard when the shiny car stopped by the front porch. Then Jimmy had come around the house with a tall fat man in a blue suit who talked in a high studied tone of voice, "Madam, I represent the Imperial Typewriter Company and we've had a request for a demonstration from Mr. James Kimberley at this address." (Between the flapping sheets she could see the small figure in overalls hiding itself around the corner of the house.) The man had puffed up his cheeks and looked ruffled when she explained that it was a mistake, that Jimmy must have filled out some coupon without knowing what it was and he slammed the door of his car sharply when he went away. Jimmy had run down to the river a few minutes afterward and never—even to his father—would tell just why he mailed in that coupon.

Dropping one faded gray sock, she looked out of the window and caught sight of Kate and Mark, home from their walk, now laboring to build a snowman in the yard. A long gray ribbon trailed across the ground to where Mark bent and strained over the big snowball, trying to roll it onto his sled. The afternoon was dulled to an ashy gray and soon it would be dark. She wanted to help them finish it before they had to come in from playing. There was an old straw hat in the garage, coal lumps in the basement, a broomstick under the stairs. She wanted to be out there in the new winter with them; instead, these torn socks . . . She heard Jimmy's voice in the hallway, impersonal and questioning, "Mother?"

He came into the room, "I cleaned the walks." "Wonderful! Jimmy, you're so good. Come and tell me about this afternoon." "I have to wash up for supper now, Mom." "Oh, please," she said and her voice sounded younger than his. "Well, I sold some tickets for the raffle and helped Joe Van Steenberg with his paper route. Then I came home and shoveled the walk. That what you asked about?" Then he was gone.

After supper Mark did his geography lesson and Kate played four games of parcheesi with Jimmy. The games ended in bitter disagreement and later on Jesse heard Kate sobbing to herself in bed. She went in to comfort her, but Kate only rolled to the other side of the bed and pushed her face further into the pillow. When Jimmy came in to say good night to his mother, he announced, "I'm teaching Kate not to cheat," and turned away as if there were no answer to that.

After Jesse had gone to bed (Mark still worked over some letters in his study) she could not doze off for quite a while, but when she finally did her last thought was, "Tomorrow is Sunday and Carlotta will be here on Tuesday."

Monday noon when the children came home from school, Mrs. Kimberley first heard a great bang at the door and then bursts of voices going off all at once. Mark charged into the room like a runner who has not been able to stop at the tape, his schoolbooks falling on the floor behind him. "Mom!" he said in a deadly serious voice. *"Jimmy has won the pair of real tubular ice skates from the raffle."* Then all three of them were in the room, dancing and pulling at her skirts. Jimmy could barely talk. He held up a certificate that was good for one pair of ice skates of the kind described below at Webster's hardware store, Jenison, Michigan. "How grand!" she said. "I'm proud of you, Jimmy! But let's sit down to lunch before Margaret Mary gets angry and you'll tell us all about it."

"First take off them wet overshoes," said Margaret Mary. A little calmer after they had changed to their slippers, they sat around the table, leaning toward Jimmy who was so proud he hardly knew where to begin.

"Well, it was this way," he said, folding the certificate and putting it in the leather billfold Jesse had given him for his birthday. "I got a few ideas last week after that big fibber Greg Lewis was saying he'd sold a hundred and fifty tickets for the raffle. One of them I got when I went down to the bank and heard that Dad was sending out some kind of an ad or statement to everybody who does business there. So I borrowed a rubber-stamp outfit from Harry and printed a whole lot of little cards that said, 'Buy your ticket for the wonderful turkey raffle from Jimmy Kimberley. Our representative will call.' So then I put a card in each envelope and two days later I went around to see everybody who got one and tried to sell a ticket. Most of 'em bought one, too. I even found out that they didn't have a raffle over at Irving, so I hitched a ride there and sold some. Then there was a salesman in at Keeler's the other day and he said he liked me because I was a go-getter and he liked to see go-getters and right there in front of Mr. Keeler he bought five tickets." He gasped for breath.

"I sure got ahead of Greg Lewis all right, but now I feel sorry for him because he worked awful hard to sell those seventy-five tickets, so I'm going over after lunch and ask him if he wants to come down with me and pick out the skates. And don't tell him, but I'm going to let him try 'em out first." Kate and Mark were overcome as much by Jimmy's generosity as by his salesmanship. Kate said, "Oh that nasty old Greg. He really only sold *seventy* tickets because his grandfather bought five and what does an old man like *that* want with a turkey anyway?" Mark said, "Let me be next on 'em, hey Jim?"

The excitement gradually lowered as they ate lunch, but the talk was all about skates, skating and ice rinks. "I may get up a hockey team of my own," said Jimmy. "I know we could beat those guys from Christian if they had a hockey team." Margaret Mary gave Jimmy an extra-big slice of chocolate cake for dessert and nobody made the slightest protest. Mrs. Kimberley decided to ask Mark what it was that hockey players used besides a stick and puck. There might be gloves or helmets or something of the kind in the Grand Rapids stores. She wondered if it wasn't a dangerous game and she thought Mark might try to divert Jimmy's interest into figure skating or something less rough.

When Mark came home he was pleased to hear about the prize. He slapped Jimmy on the back and shook his hand and promised that he'd be present at the tryout of the new skates. The three children went off to the Lewis house to find Greg before the schoolbell rang. Mr. Kimberley sat down at the table and began to devour the pork chops and mashed potatoes that Margaret Mary set before him.

"How are the Thanksgiving plans coming?" he asked. "Oh, everything's well in hand," Jesse answered. "I'll get the turkey on Wednesday afternoon and there are just a few other groceries we'll have to buy then."

"You remember that Carlotta will be here tomorrow," he said. "Her train comes in at 2:30 and I'll go down to the station to meet her. I guess she won't get a royal welcome in Jenison, but I don't think anybody's really mad at her either. People can't hold a grudge for seven years."

After Mark had gone and she was in Kate's room wiping the dirty fingermarks off the white woodwork, she repeated to herself his words, "After all, people can't hold a grudge for seven years."

The next morning she was surprised to find herself looking at the clock every now and then with a feeling of anticipation almost. The last time, Carlotta had brought her a fine silk parasol from Paris, such a pretty knickknack that she had never been able to use it, though many times she had admired the azure brightness, spreading it out in the sun parlor and watching the light gleam through. For Mark she had brought no gift at all, which, though it did not seem an unfriendly action, signified a difference in her feelings towards the two of them. Sitting back on the sofa before the fire late one evening after Carlotta had left, Mark explained the whole thing in his usual way. He always cut through the doubtful cloud of Jesse's feelings with words as crisp as figures and arguments as straight as ruled blue lines on a ledger page.

"Of course she brought you a present and none to me," he said. "Remember the stories my great-grandfather Kimberley used to tell about this part of the country when it was Indian territory? The fur traders used to come up here and they'd bring gifts for the Indians but they never brought presents for the settlers and missionaries. It's the same way with women. They think of all other women they have to deal with as savages. Enemies possibly. Men are just like the friendly settlers—they don't get anything while you women are pacified with presents." Jesse had been amused at the time and she laughed; but it also explained everything wonderfully.

At noon the children harried her, asking to be allowed to stay home that afternoon and the next day. She finally gave in by compromise. She wrote a note asking for them to be excused from school on Wednesday. Jimmy, dominating the lunch table, said that Webster's had no skates that fitted him and that a pair had to be sent for especially. They would be here from Grand Rapids on Wednesday and the grand tryout would take place Thanksgiving afternoon. There were still no reliable reports about the safety of the ice, but Kate said that Pete Squires had told a girl in the seventh grade that he planned to go fishing "this week or next" and that the ice was thick enough to hold up an elephant.

Mark came home late for lunch and at about a quarter after two started out for the railway station. Jesse had just time to finish a note to her sister in Minneapolis when Mark was back; they were opening the front door and she could hear the bumps of luggage being set down in the vestibule. She ran out. She kissed Carlotta and helped her off with her coat while Mark carried the bags upstairs to the guest room. Carlotta's brown skin glowed from the outside air. She sat down in the big wing-back chair and began to tell Jesse about the trip while Jesse all at once felt a flow of feelings that combined what she liked and disliked, admired, envied and hated about Carlotta Kimberley. Carlotta's low voice, so even and supple—no longer a memory but sounding here in the room. Carlotta's confident, restrained manners, her assured smile, and (again as always) the sense of cruelty and superior humor hidden beneath the outward grace. In ways Carlotta surely was beautiful (how had Jesse ever doubted it?). It was in her voice, in the exceptional eyes, in the grave ellipse of her face, which was as neat and handsome as a drawing.

"Tedious," she was saying, "nothing more tedious than being juggled around all day in a hard seat in the company of the most tiresome travelers you have ever seen. First there was an old man who looked like Briand. He talked for a hundred miles about the new breed of chicken he is developing on his farm in Ohio. Then an old woman, the usual hypochondriac with a whole valise full of pink and green medicines. Oh yes, and I forgot the ex-police chief who was so gallant. After he had learned that I lived in Paris he considered me very naughty and he leaned forward in his seat to tell me all sorts of confidences. Oh, Jesse, he was funny, but it bored me all the same." Then she asked about the children and Jesse described them a bit, comparing her own rather thin voice with Carlotta's easy low tones and envying the fashion of her dark blue dress of the softest wool.

Mark came in and the conversation went pleasantly if haphazardly over all the events of the past seven years. Carlotta said that New York, at last, was getting on her nerves and that she needed this little rest in Michigan. Mark talked about the bank, the new schoolhouse, the surprise everybody had had when their old classmate, Will Hollister, who had seemed so worthless to everybody in town, had made a fortune in real estate in Detroit. Carlotta told about Guy's elder sister in Lyons who wrote her often and, believing that it was impossible to exist on American food, sent her packets containing pâté de fois gras, petits beurres and confiture. Jesse made tea and they talked about their scattered relatives, about New York, about Jenison, about the investments Carlotta was worried over. At exactly three-thirty the children burst in.

After she had greeted each one with the gravity she might

have shown a senator, Carlotta said, "I'm a little tired now, Catherine, Mark and James. I'm going to rest until dinner, but after dinner we shall have a good talk together—and— I have a surprise for you then." She went to her room and Jesse went to the kitchen where she looked over Margaret Mary's shoulder at the food on the stove until they both became nervous. Then she and Kate set the table in the dining room, bringing out the cut-glass goblets and the good silver that was used only three or four times a year.

Margaret Mary's roast was splendid and Carlotta talked well during dinner, paying a great deal of grave attention to the children and exclaiming over Jimmy's prize. She told him a story about a famous Norwegian figure skater she had known in Paris, making him sound very funny and real. Jesse saw the awe and admiration in their eyes.

After dinner all of them but Jesse, who had decided to help Margaret Mary with the extra dishes, went into the living room where Mark had built a log fire in the fireplace. In the kitchen they could hear the laughter and the running conversation from the other room. Jesse heard Mark excuse himself and go upstairs after a while. He had work to do on an important transaction that would come off at the bank next day, she knew.

When the last saucepan was dried and Margaret Mary's tread sounded on the stairs, Mrs. Kimberley finally went into the living room. "Mother! Look at the keen presents Aunt Carlotta gave us!" Kate held in her arms an enormous book of colored pictures. Jimmy's model-airplane building set was spread out on the sofa. Mark was taking lead soldiers out of a flat wooden box where they had been carefully packed in straw. She admired each present in turn. "And here's something for you, Jesse." Carlotta handed her a box with a ribbon around it. "Something for the Indian," Jesse thought as she tore off the wrapping. It was a heavy silver bracelet, much too fine and showy for her ever to wear. "Oh, it's lovely, Carlotta! Thank you ever so much," she said. A little unsettled and somehow irritated by the children's joy and the presents, she went to her room to get her knitting. She felt that she must have something to occupy her hands while she sat there.

When she got back all four were gathered on their knees about the bright lead army on the floor. Carlotta was saying, "*Le soldat est blessé*. Repeat it, Jimmy." He answered very slowly, watching her face. "Ler—zoldah—ay—blessay." "Very good," said Carlotta and, pointing to another one that had fallen over, "*Le poilu est mort*. The doughboy is dead." This time Kate answered, "Lew—pwahlou—ay—morr." "Fine!" said Carlotta, turning him upright. "They call them poilus because they don't shave much. *Poilu* really means hairy—like a bear—but now it is the nickname for the French ordinary soldier."

Jesse scanned the array and noticed what fine toys they were. There was a group of cuirassiers with flowing plumes and silver breastplates, mounted on running horses. The foot soldiers were little statuettes exact in every detail from the ridged helmets, the horizon-blue uniforms, to the overcoats turned up at the back. There were generals and messengers, nurses and even wounded men lying on cloth stretchers that others carried. "*Le général*," said Carlotta, pointing him out. "*La cavalerie. Le drapeau. Le canon. Le canonnier.*" Then, smiling and pointing to all the soldiers in general, "*Le chair a canon*. The cannon fodder." Jesse broke in. "It's time for you children to be in bed. I think you'd better go now." Carlotta looked up, still smiling a little. "Aw, Mom, tomorrow's a holiday," they said.

"I know, but your Aunt Carlotta is tired after her train trip and you'll have all day tomorrow to talk to her. So let's pick up the toys now." "I want to kiss Aunt Carlotta good night," said Kate.

After the children had gone, Carlotta said good night almost at once and, though she tried to continue with her knitting, Jesse found that she had made so many mistakes that she would have to unravel all that she had done. In a few minutes she too went to bed, to sleep uneasily and for the first time in years to be troubled with dreams.

The next day was sunny and temperate. Carlotta slept late and she was still in her bedroom when Jesse went to the grocery store with Mark. They did the final shopping for Thanksgiving and bought a bagful of hard candy for the children. As she stood by the canned-goods counter, Mrs. Lewis came up to her. "I'm glad Jimmy won the raffle prize," she said, "and I want to say how nice it is of him to try to make Greg feel better about it. He was very disappointed at first. But we're going to try to get him a pair of skates for Christmas —the same kind if they're not too expensive." The Lewis's little restaurant did not make money, Jesse knew. It would surely be quite a sacrifice. She wondered if it would be too obvious to have Jimmy give Greg a pair of skates for Christmas. She smiled and said, "Well, we'll talk about it soon. It's too bad Greg didn't win them."

They loaded the back seat with groceries and Mark drove slowly home, skidding here and there on icy spots in the street and trying not to slide into the curb.

When Jesse took off her coat in the vestibule, she could hear Carlotta's voice among the voices of the children in the living room. She stopped to listen and heard Carlotta saying, " . . . then we saw the man high up there on his tight wire and we saw the balance pole break. He was teetering back and forth and then he couldn't stand any longer. We saw him way up there like a bird with a broken wing twist over and drop, drop . . ." Jesse was balancing on the dizzy height while she saw the body turn over once and then far away below her spread out and hit the ground and break into red pieces. "Mark! Jimmy! Kate!" her voice shot out like a shrill whistle. "Come here at once!" They appeared. Nervously struggling with her coat, she said sharply, "Go out and help your father with the groceries. There are too many for him to bring in by himself. You ought to be ashamed." Only Jimmy looked back curiously at her over his shoulder.

As soon as they had gone, she walked into the living room, moving with tensity and stiffness. She felt her legs quivering as she cleared a shoebox off the easy chair and sat down. Her voice seemed queerly to vibrate as she glared into Carlotta's eyes and said, "I won't have you telling my children any horror stories. It's cruel and perverse to fill their minds with ideas of bloodshed. You're—you're changing them. I won't stand for it, Carlotta."

Carlotta's face was smooth and undisturbed (condescending, Jesse thought). "But, Jesse, my dear, I don't understand. Bloodshed? I was simply telling them about a circus performer I saw fall from a tightrope once in Paris. But you didn't let me finish, Jesse. He saved himself by diving—ever so cleverly—into an incredibly small net. He wasn't hurt at all."

Jesse felt herself recoil, herself the accused now instead of Carlotta, the face she looked at was so gently natural, the hands, the eyes, belonged so to themselves. Barely noticing what it contained, Jesse had cleared her chair of a shoebox. Now, being so rashly wrong, she leaned forward in confusion and pretended to examine the skates.

"I'm afraid you mistake me, Jesse."

She had to answer. But luckily in a moment her quivering had stopped and the vibrations of her heart had left her voice, at least.

She said, "I'm sorry, Carlotta. I *did* mistake you. I was frightened for a moment. But don't you see why? They're so young; they're still such *children* that I'll do anything to keep them from discovering the ugly things until they must."

Carlotta's face wore that most quiet, most tempered, most unsmiling of smiles. "Jesse," she said, "is there anything actually so ugly about that one fact you fear so much? Mustn't we all find it out quite early? It seems to me that Jimmy and Mark and Kate soon won't be children any more. They're growing up, Jesse. . . . but I promise not to scare them with stories."

Jesse stood up to go and suddenly, without a word, everything was wrong again. As she went out the doorway she could feel Carlotta's cold, secret smile against her back.

Thanksgiving dinner came and went. The turkey appeared on the table, enormous and brown-glazed, an Everest around which lay the foothills of creamy yellow squash, mashed potatoes, unstable knolls of cranberry jelly, piles of biscuits, peas, lakes of gravy. In two more hours Margaret Mary would carry away nothing but a skeleton and some exhausted dishes.

All morning there had been an undercover argument

among the children—an argument carried on in corners and beyond doors that Jesse sensed more than heard as she worked on the pumpkin pies. In the end it was never brought to her for a decision but when dinnertime came, as if by a treaty, Jimmy took his place on Carlotta's left and Kate sat on her right while Mark sat across from her.

After grace the turkey was carved; dinner began. Mark told some of his Indian and early-settler stories; the whole of Jimmy's magnificent strategy in winning the skates had to be re-analyzed. Then Carlotta told some stories about France. Her temper completely restored, Jesse laughed with them all. She even found herself admiring the beauty of Carlotta's narrow brown hands (interrupted twice by silver rings) against the white damask. She saw the admiration in the children's eyes as Carlotta talked.

At last they arrived at the custom of the day. She had almost forgotten but Jimmy reminded them all. He had pushed back his chair and he was standing up with the wishbone in his hand.

"Who's going to pull it this year?" He looked around.

Kate said, "Let Mama and Aunt Carlotta," and there was a moment of silence when their glances touched across the plates—until Jesse looked down. "No," she said. "Somebody else."

"Are you afraid you'll lose, Jesse?" asked the low voice.

So they decided on Jimmy and Carlotta and Jimmy said, "Make your wish now," as their fingers strained in the air. It snapped. They were laughing with relief and Jesse lifted her eyes to see Jimmy with the lesser white fragment in his fingers. She flinched. He was saying, "Well I don't care anyway, because now Aunt Carlotta gets her wish."

But in the end the dinner slowed all of their feelings to

drowsiness and there was little talking when Margaret Mary finally brought in the red moons of pumpkin pies and the steaming coffee pot.

Eventually the children were excused and they returned to their presents in the living room. Carlotta herself had nothing to say and after the coffee she went to lie down on the sofa and listen to the radio. Mark reminded himself of an unavoidable errand, but he promised Jesse he wouldn't be away long. With slow fingers Jesse and Margaret Mary washed the dishes. Then Jesse went to her bedroom.

She intended to rest for just a moment, but the ceiling grew indistinct and the walls around her evaporated into fog. The grandfather clock in the hallway persisted a moment longer but then he died in the interval between a tick and a tock.

Hours had gone when Jesse finally stirred. The light through the windows had gone winter-gray and her hands were cold. Then she noticed how soundless the house was. She sat up and, as she disencumbered herself from sleep, uneasiness grew instead.

She walked to her door and opened it; but there was no radio-voice, no footsteps, no squabbling, no sound at all. Her fear, like a sharp fingernail, pressed deeper.

"Jimmy!" she called, took a step on the stairway. Waited. "Jimmy!"

She was halfway down the stairs when she heard Margaret Mary's sleepy voice from above.

"They took the skates, Mrs. Kimberley, and went down to the river. Some time ago."

"Did Mark go with them? Did he get back?"

"Not that I know of—just the lady, Jimmy, Kate and Mark, junior." Her voice sagged. Jesse heard the door close.

Then she ran. She ran down the steps and through the hall

to the kitchen and through the kitchen out the back door. It flew open behind her but she had no time to go back.

She got out into the wide field behind the house and she was running over the uneven ground toward the river. As she ran her heart pumped fear through her body, making her feel a strange mingling of weakness and forced strength. Her breath, sucked from the cold atmosphere, dragged against her throat like windy sandpaper.

As she ran the icy crust of the snow bit against her ankles. The dry stalks that stuck up above the snow broke against her skirt and the cold air flowed through the pores of her light dress and froze her skin. Her anxiety made the field look still immensely wide. She could see nothing but the flat desolate crust of the snow, the trees far ahead of her at the edge of the river, which looked like a border of thorns, and the sky. The sky was a sick gray and long ugly clouds gave it the appearance of roiled and filthy water.

Her hair flew raggedly in the wind and her hands became cold underneath the nails, then up to the wrists. It was a hopeless race against nothing. The far edge of the field seemed no nearer.

Once Jesse told herself that she was being completely absurd, exposing herself for no reason at all. But her heart was beyond convincing; she kept on running.

At last the field began to slope and the slope led to a rounding edge and it was here at this edge that she stumbled and fell on one knee because the scene below her was so horrible and expected that it might all have been foretold.

Against the dull white of the snow on the hill were the black figures of about twenty people, all of them crowding, staring, pointing out to the place in the ice. Mark and Kate were there; she recognized them as they stood a little to one side, hand in hand. But not Jimmy. She looked everywhere for him.

Pete Squires was on his belly on the ice, painfully crawling out on a ladder to where the horrible black gap in the ice showed. That gap in which Jesse now felt herself freezing, drowning.

Her eyes excluded all the rest. She could see only that deadly parallelogram of pitchy water. She might have screamed; but her throat had been sewn up.

Gradually she recovered and she saw the people, the shore, the trees again. Finally she became aware that Carlotta was standing halfway down the slope with her back towards her. Jesse stared at her. She imagined the cold half smile now decorating the lips as Carlotta watched the show.

Then Jesse was suddenly running down the hill, lightly, gently. There was something black on the ground behind Carlotta and Jesse picked it up, swung it in the air, crushed it down on Carlotta's head with all her strength.

Time vanished for a moment; then Jesse's eyes cleared as it from a flood of black tears and she looked again. The scene was the same except that Carlotta now lay flat with her face in the snow. A little curlicue, a splash of dark blood sank into the snow like red ink on a blotter. No one had noticed. Slowly Jesse looked down at the object in her hand and slowly it took its place in her mind as one of the real tubular-blade steel ice skates.

Then, as inevitably must happen, she heard Jimmy's voice calling to her as he ran down the hill and she knew the enormous hopelessness of having lost her cause.

THE ACADEMIC STYLE

THREE figures were walking in the green-gray and burnt-umber late-afternoon landscape: Doctor Cashel, head of the college art department, and two artistic persons from New York. Cashel was tall, lank and heavy-faced, like an incidental thought of Daumier's. Margaret Elgin was one of Degas' pretty girls—twenty years later; she was cat-faced, stocky, springy, low-slung, and she wore her gray bangs like a badge. Roy Tendon was out of the school of Velasquez with his little trimmed beard and narrow temples, his shiny and vacuous eyes. The campus was a plane of dark green and the buildings rising on either side were ambitious collegiate Gothic by an unknown master, circa 1911.

"I have a subject I want to consult with you about," Cashel was saying. "It's of considerable importance to us and not entirely without interest to you, I'd imagine. No, this way. I live over behind Science." They rounded a corner and followed a neat line of hedge. Two students, a boy and a girl, were lying stomach down at full length on the grass facing each other and staring into each other's eyes without moving.

122

The three stepped carefully over them and continued along the way.

"But that can wait. Right now I wanted to tell you both how much everyone appreciated your critiques of the student competition this afternoon. You gave a—what can one say? —new *perspective* on the paintings. Very interesting indeed. You know, we don't go in much for the more modern lingo of art criticism here and I'm sure we all learned something."

"I'm sure," said Miss Elgin. She was the editor of *Art-View Review* and she had taken the job seriously and had done most of the talking. She had adopted the manner of a well-known criminal lawyer taking the unpopular side of a local case. Tendon had irritated her by standing around, running his fingernails through his beard and interrupting occasionally with a few pessimistic *non sequiturs*.

"I hope the students got the message about relaxing and going over to total freedom," said Miss Elgin. "Do you think so?" She squinted at Dr. Cashel's face and saw no traces of the message there. "They seem to be so bound up with their tight, constipated little forms, one's rather at a loss to *see* them."

"Maggoty academic," said Tendon suddenly. "A plate of still life putrefying in the sun. See what I mean?"

"I think everything you said was very striking," said Dr. Cashel firmly, gesturing them toward a gravel path which led between rows of spirea bushes. "Especially, Miss Elgin, your statement that 'in creating a work of art we pass life through the sieve of our own insanity.' Very striking." He winced as he said it. "We, of course, take a rather more traditional approach."

"Oh, I think it's impossible really to spoil a good painter," said Miss Elgin. "They shed the excess baggage. Oh, here's where you live, eh?"

Dr. Cashel was opening the big oak door of a fairly new Tudor cottage, which was set among some pines at a little distance from the college buildings. He stepped aside for Miss Elgin, but Tendon entered first and immediately walked into the living room. It was a big room with embrasured windows, bright print drapes, some Muirhead Bone drypoints on the walls, a large gray limestone fireplace, and a white kitten. Mrs. Cashel was standing by the sofa waiting for them.

"Miss Elgin, Mr. Tendon, so glad to see you again," she said in a happy, lathery voice. "You must be worn out after your lectures and the critique. You surely deserve some good hot tea! We rather pride ourselves on the variety we can offer. Come, what is your favorite? Oolong? Souchong? Ming? Young Hyson?"

"Bourbon straight," said Tendon, looking around for the most comfortable chair and finding it. "On the rocks. No soda or water, please." He showed his teeth at her. "Very good, though, that line about the tea. I'll have to remember it."

"I'll take Scotch," said Miss Elgin.

"Of course, of *course*," said Dr. Cashel. "Talking's dry work, Amy, my dear. A drink is surely called for." He went out into the dining room and began banging cabinet doors. Mrs. Cashel hovered a few moments with a disappointed smile. Then she went to the kitchen and came back with a small tray of cakes and cookies and a steaming teapot, from which she poured a single cup.

"Magwich, honey," said Tendon in a high, quarrelsome voice, "you went on too much about Gorky and de Kooning in your talk. These kids never heard of them."

"They have now," said Miss Elgin.

"Sure, it's okay to tell them," Tendon answered, "but when you say something like 'the new age replaces plastic form with spastic form,' you catch them with their pants down. Mind you, I'm not criticizing the statement—it's nice. Very nice. But they didn't get it! I noticed some of the people even giggled. You have to begin way down on a level . . ."

"Oh, Christ, Roy, why didn't you say something halfway intelligent over there when you had a chance?"

Tendon said grumpily, "You should've just said the pictures all stink."

Miss Elgin glared at him. "You may be a good painter, Roy, but you don't know didildy-squat about teaching or criticism."

"Well, well, what's this?" said Dr. Cashel coming into the room with a tray of drinks and a slight flush on his face. His sober cheerfulness had been restored. "Here you are, Miss Elgin. Here you are, Mr. Tendon."

Roy sulked and looked at the tray. "I asked for a highball with plenty of soda," he said.

"I thought I heard—" said Dr. Cashel.

"You got it wrong," said Tendon, looking out of the window.

Dr. Cashel strode to the kitchen, where they heard a tap being turned on. He came back an instant later with the glass filled to the brim and put it down with a decisive rap on the table next to Tendon's elbow. Then, as if waiting for a class to settle down, he sauntered over to the fireplace and stood before it with his hands together behind his back. He looked out from under heavy brows with his student-quelling stare, but Elgin and Tendon were still busy glowering at each other.

"Oh, let's not be unpleasant," she said. "It does irritate me to do all the work and see you sit around and do nothing but declare your genius."

"Who told the silly damn Art Club all about Abstract Neo-impressionism?" he asked.

"Well," she said, sending a shower of sparks from her cigarette all over the carpet, "who gave the main lecture on Trends After Pollock? Who spent literally hours with that stupid girl with the sunflower painting? Who—?"

Dr. Cashel had to be admired. A slight tendency to rise on his toes was his only visible reaction to the dialogue. When he broke in, it was with his usual steady, deliberate voice. "Please, Miss Elgin and Mr. Tendon, there is no need to differ! In our eyes you share the credit equally. We are very grateful for what might be called your 'introduction to modern art,' and I thank you again.

"Now it's on a related subject that I hope to get your advice. First I should give you a little background—it all began, as we say, with Dean Champion and his relatively recent taste for modern art." He was well launched and there was nothing for Miss Elgin to do but cast her eyes up and lie back in her chair and for Mr. Tendon but to sit there and suck at his glass.

"Dean Champion," said Dr. Cashel in a voice paced for easy note-taking, "is a man of wide cultural interests. He knows traditional art to his own satisfaction. In recent years his summer visits to Provincetown and Mrs. Champion's keen interest in the modern have given him an enthusiasm for that world of experimentation which you yourselves so well represent." He gave a downcast smile, as if imagining a picture of the Dean in a Palm Beach suit, his big pompous face sunburnt bright, pottering around the strange canvases in some seaside studio.

"Also," said Mrs. Cashel from her seat at the writing desk, "didn't you say she sunk a good bit of money into that orange and green thing over their mantelpiece?"

"These good people might consider that description a bit deprecating, my dear. They tell me it's a very fine example of the work of a man named Kandinsky. It's called Number Ninety-five, I believe. But back to the point—

"The Dean has frequently expressed some dissatisfaction with our conservative outlook in the Art Department. He has said a dozen times if he's said it once, 'Oh, Rembrandt and all that is all right, but what about Picasso? What are you doing about Picasso, Cashel?'

"Naturally," said Cashel with the faint print of a smile on his face, "I told him we were doing nothing."

"Oh, quite right," said Tendon absently; "he's pretty well past and done with."

"The main question," Dr. Cashel continued, "eventually became one of means—just exactly how we were to fit modern art into our program here. Last spring, you see, Dean Champion persuaded the Tarleton Foundation to give a rather generous sum to establish an 'artist in residence' on the campus. That brought the whole matter to a head. You can imagine that the teaching staff had some trepidations about this—"

"Yes?" Miss Elgin asked, sitting up straight; Roy Tendon was nodding with interest.

"Well, it suffices to say that the Dean's enthusiasm prevailed in the end," said Dr. Cashel, spanning an ocean of indignation and embittered debate with this one small sentence. "It was finally decided to make a beginning this semester by inviting two prominent spokesmen for modern art to judge the annual competition and to give the two spring lectures in the Fine Arts Series." The head of the Art Department gave a slight, perhaps involuntary, bow toward his two listeners. Each gave a little hunch of the neck in return.

Dr. Cashel rubbed his shoulders gently against the edge of the mantel as if affected by an itch of anticipation. "As the selection of this 'artist in residence' falls mostly on my shoulders, I decided to use this very excellent opportunity to solicit your advice.

"The resident artist, preferably a painter, will be someone capable of teaching a class in modern theory and technique. He will not, according to the stipulations of the grant, be overburdened with classwork and he will be allowed considerable time and freedom for his own creation. It won't be an onerous job, I assure you." Tendon and Miss Elgin were both leaning forward, elbows on knees. Cashel paused for a moment to look bleakly magnanimous.

"The resident artist will receive a house rent-free during his year of tenure. The Crispin house has been mentioned—a rather nice place of about twelve rooms, with a good view overlooking the river."

Tendon shivered and quietly kicked over his empty glass. Miss Elgin ran her tongue around her lips.

"The resident artist will have a studio built for him wherever he chooses, but preferably fairly convenient to his house. I have seen the plans approved by the college and the Tarleton people and I must say the place will be nice—the north wall and half the roof will be glass. Complete stocks of everything necessary for painting or sculpting. A lavatory. A very pleasant adjoining room with a fireplace and modern furniture, meant for relaxation or entertaining. A high-fidelity sound system will be built into one of the walls for music. The whole place will be air-conditioned—at any rate, I believe you can see it will be quite pleasant. . . ."

Miss Elgin's jaw muscles moved spasmodically, but she said nothing. The painter's dark face had turned burnt sienna, with patches of white on his forehead and cheekbones. His breathing was audible.

"Of course Dean Champion and the donors realized that a practicing artist cannot simply be shut off and cloistered here on the campus." Cashel shook his head once or twice. The other two shook theirs slightly in return. "No. The Dean wisely pointed out that he must be *au courant*, in touch, aware of the changing currents, so to speak. Therefore, provisions have been made for travel without expense to the artist." Cashel smiled broadly and looked out the window into the far distance. "Personally—if I were he—I should prefer a couple of trips to Paris during the course of the year. But I suppose some would prefer a number of shorter trips. Perhaps to Arizona, Mexico City, New York, and so on."

Roy Tendon's shuddering returned, as if he were gripped by a malarial chill. Margaret Elgin's fingernails punished her wrists.

"I might add that several of the Dean's friends are wealthy collectors. There is a reasonably good chance of purchases or commissions."

Miss Elgin and Tendon both began to speak at once.

Dr. Cashel held up his hand, "Oh, I think I know what is on your minds and I don't blame you. You've been thinking to yourselves that the conditions sound fairly suitable, but an artist at work can't simply be uprooted and brought here without attractive compensation. And you are quite right. After much consideration, the Foundation officers decided not to exceed the salary of a full professor. It will be a modest but sufficient $8,000 a year. But, Miss Elgin and Mr. Tendon, you don't seem ready to comment? Have we neglected anything?"

Tendon had mastered his seizure. He began hastily, "No, no. Why, it's excellent, sir. I'm just thinking—I'd say immediately that your man ought to be young, but not too young. Ought to have had some recognition, but no silly overpublicized reputation. Ought to come from New York, of course. And, Dr. Cashel, having been a student of François Kohn, I'd say you'd find your very best men in that group. Undoubtedly. Also, I'd think your wisest move would be to get somebody using the Abstract Neoimpressionist style."

"I've heard some praise of the Neo-Cubist group," said Dr. Cashel slowly.

"No, sir. Emphatically no! Not at all," said Tendon.

"Well, why is that?" asked Cashel.

"Oh, mmmh, it's—they have filthy habits," Tendon answered. "No, definitely an Abstract Neoimpressionist if you want to be in the running at all. Speaking personally, sir, I want to say that I myself might . . ."

"Why does it have to be a man?" Miss Elgin asked sharply. "Roy's just assuming it has to be a man, whereas it seems far more logical to me that you need a woman for the job. The majority of your art students are girls, aren't they, Dr. Cashel? A woman could probably see their viewpoint much better in working with them."

"That's true," said Cashel meditatively, "I hadn't thought

of it. No, no reason why the Tarleton lecturer can't be a woman." He turned to her. "A woman who not only paints, but who has a good background in modern aesthetic theory— someone who can lecture and write as well. Someone who not only knows the world of vision created by Pollock and de Kooning, but who knows the developments that have followed after them.

"As a matter of fact, I think that I can say without exaggeration . . ."

"Just a moment," said Dr. Cashel.

Tendon and Elgin stood up and were advancing on him from left and right. Elgin's eyes glittered at Tendon and his beard stuck out in spearlike defiance at her.

"Maggie's out of her head. It ought to be—"

"Roy hasn't the faintest notion of—"

"Please! Please!" said Dr. Cashel loudly. "I know that you are both anxious to be helpful and I'm deeply grateful for any suggestions that you may offer." He waved them to their seats again. "Your enthusiasm, in fact, is quite gratifying. I must say this, Miss Elgin and Mr. Tendon. I want you to think the matter over. Please consider it carefully overnight. Talk about it between yourselves if you want to. In short, give yourselves every opportunity for grave, deliberate, discriminating, far-sighted and wise recommendations." His voice had risen in volume and it rolled deeply around the room. He suddenly dropped it to a gentle, confidential tone. "I may be wrong in telling you this, but—in strictest secrecy—I have such a feeling of reliance in you I feel nearly certain that I shall accept one of your recommendations."

Silenced, the two listeners could only nod dumbly, like two shy, polite children.

Cashel shook hands with both of them. "So glad you came to tea. We'll plan to have lunch together tomorrow before your train leaves and I can get the names you recommend." Just as they stepped outside, Dr. Cashel said, "Oh, one oversight. I forgot to tell you that by the rules of the Foundation grant no judges of the annual competition are eligible for the artist-in-residence post. Unfortunately that eliminates both of you."

Roy Tendon in red stocking-feet, in a paint-stiff brown bathrobe, with a bottle of bourbon under one arm, stood knocking persistently on the white door. He looked jumpily up and down the dim Alumni House hallway and then knocked again. "Oh, for Christsake, Magwich, open up," he said in a hoarse, muffled voice. "There's no use blaming *me*."

"Go away," answered another hoarse voice just beyond the door.

"We've *got* to talk it over," he said.

They had taken separate paths from Dr. Cashel's house, each trying to remember what the other had said to make things go so wrong. The cold war had remained during dinner with Miss Elgin at one end of the Village Inn dining room eating shad roe and Tendon at the other end eating pork chops. Each then went back to his own room in the Alumni House and had maintained silence until nine o'clock.

He rapped again. "Goddamit, Mag, there's a maid coming down the hall. She'll see me here trying to get into your room."

"Then go away."

"Too late. Hurry up. Open up!" The lock clicked loudly

and the door swung open. The astonished maid was just in time to get a ragged back view of Mr. Tendon and the whiskey bottle sliding through.

The two of them sat facing each other across the reconciling bottle. "All right, I admit then it wasn't entirely your fault, Roy, but what happened? What in God's name did we say?"

"All I know," he said, pounding his forehead, "is that the goddam gates of Paradise opened up for a minute. I saw 'Roy Tendon' up there in big letters. Then that sonofabitching professor . . ."

After a few moments he said in a loud, sad voice, "Know what my income was last year, Mag? I don't know either, but I think it was around $1,800. I went to a doctor and he told me to cut out drinking dago red for breakfast, but I told him I was too poor to drink anything else."

"Oh, stop getting sentimental," she said. "What the hell are we going to do about this? Let me remind you that Cashel gave us our travel money, but he hasn't paid our fees yet. And let me remind you that we promised him we'd recommend somebody for that job."

"He knows I've got talent," Roy said. "I'd ruin him just by being here, that's what he thinks. I should help him. I should recommend." Tendon was almost shouting, waving a hand in the air, and all the holes in his bathrobe were showing. "Why should I?"

"Calm down, Roy," said Miss Elgin in a pinched voice. "You still don't know what happened." She looked at him balefully.

"Look, Cashel invited us here for the lecture thing and promised us $150 apiece. When he got confidential this afternoon, he asked our advice. Then, on the way out, he says we aren't eligible for this job. What does that add up to?"

"It adds up to Cashel is a pig," said Roy sullenly.

"Oh," she said. "Try to think a minute. What does it mean?"

"Cashel doesn't like you," he said.

"Stupid!" she said patiently. "The old faker gets by as an art teacher, but he's never heard of anybody since Millet. He's shrewd in his way—he realizes there probably aren't two people in the country who know as many artists and as much about contemporary art as we do." She had a look of small triumph.

"Oh," said Tendon, pouring two more drinks. "You think he just wants to pick our brains."

"Right," she said.

"Well, in that case, we'll just refuse."

"We could, but he'd eventually get it from somebody else. Don't you see, Roy, we have quite an opportunity here."

"See what?" asked Roy, looking into his glass.

"*We have the chance to make the choice.* He doesn't know anything about live artists. He practically told us he'd take our advice." A happy smile appeared on her face, and slowly an answering smile appeared on his lips above the nervous beard. They looked at each other with the pleased expression of two researchers who have just discovered the death ray.

"Clyde Spitzel?"

He laughed gleefully. "Carlo Bonfanelli!"

"Greasy Franklin!" They were both helpless for a moment. Roy beat the chair arm aimlessly with one hand. Margaret doubled up and clutched her knees in both arms.

This went on for several minutes, and when they finally

recovered she said, "Now let's be serious. Who was that one-armed guy you used to share the cold-water flat on Spring Street with?"

"I know," he said. "Isaac something. Isaac Hooker it must be."

"Didn't he have some theories?" she asked.

"Of course, of course," he said. "You remember he always said the trouble with art was that it got polluted by the use of human hands? He thought the only real art was caused by bad accidents. He thought machines caused the worst accidents."

"He told me that once," she said, "and insisted on showing me the stump of his arm."

"That sure was a bad accident—about all you can say for it. Old Isaac," he said nostalgically, "never took a bath all the time we lived there. Even if we'd had a bathtub he wouldn't have."

"What was his painting like?" she said.

"Oh, he had a machine—very noisy old business with an electric motor and an old restaurant fan. He blew paint up in the air with some kind of a spray thing and the fan made it hit the canvas. Very messy on the room, of course. He tried squirt guns and pumps during one period, but they didn't work very well."

"I think we should consider him seriously."

"He had epileptic fits, too. Very frightening in their way."

"Good," she said. She wrote down Isaac Hooker.

"Did you know Ella Mongol? Had quite a vogue in the thirties." Tendon was working hard and his forehead was wrinkled.

"Everybody did. The one who was always organizing agitprop committees and going off to Moscow?"

"She just *said* she went to Moscow. She was such a trouble-maker I doubt if they'd let her in."

"I believe she painted *The Death of Sacco,* and *Lenin Watching the Execution of the Czar and his Family.* I think there was supposed to be something wrong about that last one."

"Lenin and executions were her two favorite subjects, anyway. She hardly cared about other subjects. She must still be around."

Miss Elgin wrote again on the piece of paper.

"You mentioned Clyde Spitzel," he said. "What ever happened to him?"

"He's out of prison now," she said. "I saw him not long ago in a bar. He said it was a trumped-up charge by some critics who were out to get him, but you can never trust what Clyde says."

"Was it assault with intent to kill?"

"I don't remember," she said vaguely as she wrote. "There was quite a fire afterward, I think."

And so they continued, recalling old times and half-forgotten faces. Merlin Palmer, the Surrealist about whom Dali was supposed to have said, "The man is mad"; Olga Ferenzi, whose studies of entrails were so much admired for a time; Maebashi, the sculptor who created a composition called *War* out of sticks of dynamite wired together; Don Pin, whose *Cannibalism in the Parlor* caused so much talk. As the list grew, it became something of a sentimental memoir and they recalled old times fondly. The past came back to them in a blur of warm colors, a collage of curiously kept details. Something went wrong with Margaret's hard eyes and she wiped them with a paper napkin; Roy remembered old friends with kindness and spoke gently of their talents. They spoke of Village basement parties at which people sat on orange crates or the kitchen table and debated Braque versus Picasso, declared for or against Dada, said how it was impossible to do anything—to *really* create any work of art —in a capitalist society. They recalled picnics at Woodstock with thin beer, and innocent nude bathing parties at Province-town with juniper-flavored homemade gin. From the mixture of memories, they recalled a dozen or more names, put them down, then had to scratch many of them out again. "I just remembered—he's a dipso. Hasn't been heard of for years." Or, "She married a rich Mexican and gave up painting." Or simply, "He's dead."

The whiskey sank in the bottle. "What a wonderful vital generation we are," said Miss Elgin enthusiastically. "The dim-witted colleges are just getting around to appreciate what we've done in art. Old Whozis and his job. They need us, Roy!" she said in a thick voice. "They finally got around to see how they need us."

"But we don't need them," he said belligerently. "I won't take the job—that's final. They can stick it—" but he fell asleep in the chair before he finished the sentence.

The sunlight, very sharp outside, was mild in Dr. Cashel's office. He sat with his chair turned so that it could warm his face and this made it seem less parsonlike and censorious. He seemed to be daydreaming if, by some exaggeration, a textbook or a slate blackboard can be said to dream. He sat there for quite a long time, with only his knuckles moving a little as his right hand rested on the desk blotter. Finally the door opened and Miss Burns, an Art History instructor, came in.

"I'm sorry to disturb you," she said as the best way of disturbing him. "Dean Champion wanted me to give you a message. He says he wants to know when you will be ready to make the recommendations for that resident-artist thing. He's very anxious to let the Tarleton people know, he says." Miss Burns was a very tall, thin woman with white hair above black eyebrows. She loved to transmit messages, especially those sure to cause trouble.

"What did you think of them, Jane?" asked Cashel gently. "Elgin and Tendon and their critique?"

"Hogwash," she said firmly. "Surely, Dr. Cashel, you haven't any intention—you aren't going to let those people make any suggestions about the resident artist."

"Yes," he said slowly. "I am. I've asked them for their suggestions. They're acquainted with far more of the modern artists than any of us here. I'll call Champion this afternoon and let him know."

"I see," said Miss Burns, drawing herself up like the Light Brigade. "Well, I must prepare for my nine o'clock." She turned abruptly and went out the door again. Dr. Cashel reached slowly for his telephone.

"I want to call long distance," he said, "Payford, Maryland. Mr. Amos Kensington Connaught, person-to-person. The number is 5128." He waited patiently for the call to go through, staring out the window at the sunlight on the clipped bushes beside the campus walk.

"Amos!" he said finally. "This is Charles. Yes, Charles. How is Marie? Fine. Fine. Is your arthritis any better? I hope you've been able to work lately? Yes, I know things have been hard for you, but I have some good news. I say I have some good news for you that should make everything better." He had a kindly, faraway smile on his face, which made him look more ugly and yet benign.

He listened for a while and then said, "Well, I think we can solve all those things. Listen, Amos, you remember the job I told you about? The resident-artist business here? I think I can pretty safely say they'll offer it to you next year. Yes, it means a wait of about a year, but it looks certain after that."

"No. No," he said. "It's going to be taken at first by somebody who won't work out very well. Then I think I can guarantee it will go to you." He laughed and bobbed his head. "No, Amos, no finagling involved at all, it's just that my plans are working out." He listened again for quite a while. "Yes," he said, "I'm anxious to see it. *Polynices Departing from Thebes*, eh? It sounds like a good subject. No—you're absolutely right, there's certainly going to be a revival of the academic style before long.

"What do you mean, radical experimentation?" he asked after a pause. "Have you lost your senses? Oh, along the lines of Correggio? I misunderstood you for a minute, old boy.

"Won't it be grand to be together again? Brings back old times, doesn't it? Remember all our arguments about Sargent and Whistler? And those swimming parties at Honfleur? Remember the scandal about Tidwell's *The Sabine Women*? And the parties in your studio when we all sat around on wooden boxes . . ."

THE
INVADERS

LIKE bright figures on a poster they suddenly appeared at the top of the stairway, outlined against the sky.

He was dark and she was blonde as the summer morning around her, a tall girl, trim and deer-faced as a printed model on a fashion page. She wore a fire-colored playsuit belted with white, blue sandals, and she carried a basket on her arm. She could not resist raising the other arm just as they reached the dune edge as if she were pausing to be photographed by some ready camera, constantly in wait for her newest step or gesture.

"Oh, how glorious!" she said.

He laid down the things he had been carrying and together they stood and looked.

That early June had been racked with storms and filled with an overplenty of rain. The doors and windows of the cottages to the right and left of them on the dune and further back in the woods were still blind with nailed-up boards or shutters and, driving along the road to the shore, they had met no one, because it was nearly the first day of real summer weather that year.

The dune was tall and it was as if they looked from a high theater balcony down onto a tremendous vacant stage. Over the slightly curved shoreline the small waves died, while the whole expanse of Lake Michigan out to the far horizon glistened like a sheet of stretched blue silk.

"We have it all to ourselves," he said. "That's fine."

She made a half-circle sweep with her arm. "Is that all it means to you? Look, Gib, doesn't it suggest something? I mean, doesn't it suggest something more than just that to you?"

He had decided to pick up their things again and had managed to get most of them into his arms. "Yes, it's a nice view," he said, "but I've seen it lots of times before."

"Not *that*. Don't you see what I mean? I mean it's like our life together after we get married—no one has been there before; it's all ours to do with what we please."

"I suppose so," he said, starting down the stairs. "But I hope it won't be as empty as all that."

"Now you're being nasty, Gib."

"No I wasn't. Now look out for these stairs. They're rotten and one good shake would knock them down."

"I wish you wouldn't snub me like that. Sometimes I think you don't appreciate things the way I do."

"I'm just busy with all this gear," he said.

She followed him down the steep stairs and when they got to the level of the beach they went directly down to within five yards of the water. As he laid their blanket out on the sand and put their surfboard, picnic basket and towels to one side, she stripped off the red garments; underneath it she had a bathing suit that shone green like the water in a quiet shoal. They lay down flat in the sun for a while and watched two clouds that swam like lonely white fish in the sky.

He watched them for a long time as they glided through the airy blue pool and out of sight. He closed his eyes, but after a few minutes he awoke with the feeling of lying in a bath of warm honey. The sun had risen higher and it seemed to be nearly noon.

She lay on her back and he could see that she was now asleep. To his eyes she was like the landscape of some familiar province as she lay there barely breathing. Sitting, he looked down on her as an aviator might look down on his own country and recognize the gentle heights, the rolling plains and the symmetrically built town of her face. He closed his eyes and lay back again. A familiar country? Yes, something like that. When he had asked her to marry him he was not quite so aware of the strictness of the borders and confines, he thought drowsily. Past the country club on one side, the suburban home on another, the good schools, the parties, the familiar names, was an unexplored wilderness, a wild Ireland beyond the pale. There was a certain dark frontier further than which one could not go. As he fell asleep again he dreamed about riding a bicycle around an enclosed track, with no exit.

In time she awoke and she awakened him by tickling his ribs and kissing him on the forehead.

"Shall we go swimming now?"

While they were dozing a brisker wind had come up, stirring the surface of the water into rough whitecaps that broke on the shallows about a hundred feet out. He picked up the surfboard and she followed him to the edge of the beach. Janet was somewhat afraid of the water. She had explained it by saying that someone had pushed her into a deep place once when she was a child and she had nearly drowned. She always asked a hundred questions to reassure herself before she finally put her foot in. Is it cold? It looks terribly cold, doesn't it? Do you think there's any undertow today? Now let's not go too far out, shall we? It *is* freezing, isn't it?

She followed by inches; he was already pushing the white board through the waves toward the spot where the breakers curled over. If you took the right moment and jumped on the board just ahead of a breaking wave it would carry you on the crest nearly to shore. He showed her how.

A wave rolled toward them, bigger than any of the others. "Now!" he said and boosted her onto the board. She slithered her body until she had got firmly settled and grasped the handholds at the side. He swung the front end around a little so that the wave would catch her evenly. It was almost on them. "Hold tight!" he yelled and dove beneath the water.

As long as his breath held out he swam beneath the surface. The ridged sand of the bottom slid under his hands and a colder current knifed along his backbone. It was quiet here; the water scarcely seemed to move. He opened his eyes and thought that a fish swimming in this green silence would never realize the dash and fury of the surface. But he preferred the waves. He put his hands flat on the sand and gave himself a push that plunged him up and into the air again. He looked for her.

But he had got turned around in swimming underwater and he was facing down the beach. He was suddenly aware that the beach was no longer empty. He tossed his head to throw the water out of his eyes and began a slow side-stroke.

There were two figures on the beach, two men walking along the edge of the sand about a quarter of a mile away.

They were not wearing swimming suits, they were fully dressed, and, though close to the shoreline, they were not wading. They walked along slowly side by side as if going down a city street. He caught the glint of the sun on skin and then he realized that one of them was black.

He had only a minute to wonder about them because in the next he heard Janet calling to him, "Hi! It got away from me, Gib."

She was floundering in the shallows where the wave had carried her and trying to stand up in the undertow. She got up and waved to him. In the tossing water he could see the white back of the surfboard being carried down shore. It was about halfway between himself and the two men walking along the beach.

Then she saw them. She slowly lowered her arm and even at this distance he could feel her astonishment. Not that there was anything odd about other people on the beach—it was usually crowded this time of year—or that there was anything particularly strange about those two, but they had become so accustomed in the last few hours to thinking of themselves as the only two people in the world, had so accepted and enjoyed their isolation, that anybody's coming would be a shock. He planned to remark something about Crusoe and Friday when he came up with her. But now he had to swim for the board and it was getting farther and farther away.

He went as fast as he could, but before he had gone very far, he hoped that the two men had sighted it. He hadn't noticed before how strong the down-shore current was. It seemed to push him along, but the board was traveling faster.

They stopped and one of them stooped and rolled up his

trousers legs. He was coming out into the water now and
Gib could see him lifting the board. Then they came on
down the beach at the same pace towards the spot on shore
where Janet was standing. Both of them had their arms
hooked over the board.

He reached the shallow water and stood up; when he got
to the shore they were just handing the surfboard to Janet.
"Thanks," she said with a smile. "It knocked me over and ran
away." They didn't smile in return. "O.K., lady," the white
one said, "It's O.K."

They were not men, but boys. They both seemed to be
about sixteen or seventeen, though they were short, shorter
than Janet. He took Janet's arm and they went up and sat on
the blanket and lighted cigarettes.

The boys stood and stared at the surfboard which lay
near the water where she had dropped it. They turned it over
and looked at the other side. Evidently it was sandy because
they scooped up water in their hands and tried to wash it
off. "That's O.K.," Gib said. "It'll be all right." The boys came
up and sat down carefully, about four yards away from them.

The white one had skin the color of skim milk. He was
either completely and prematurely bald or else his head had
been closely shaven recently. He had a small bunched face
with sharp features that reminded Gib of some kind of tool,
a monkey wrench, perhaps. The other one had close-cut hair,
too, and a flat face like an imprint in some thick warm tar.
They sat close together, arms folded over their knees and
occasionally seemed to give each other a slight push or nudge,
like a signal.

They were wearing high bootlike shoes, which they had
put aside on the sand but that was the only way they had

prepared for the beach. Their shirts and trousers were made of similar gray stuff and the pants legs of the one who had gone after the surfboard were black from being wet. Except for the slight movements of shoulders or elbows, they sat very quietly, gazing at Janet and Gib.

Gib felt that he had to say something. "Where you fellows from?" he asked.

"Flint," said the colored boy.

The other one said something to Gib. It was a strange accent, Polish, he thought, and the words were run together. "We come up to the beach, we hitched up for the day," was what it sounded like. It might be a speech impediment, Gib wasn't sure.

"Aren't you going in swimming?"

"No we ain't going in swimming." This was the colored boy and, though the words sounded unfriendly, the tone was soft and meaningless.

"We ain't got no suits," he finally said.

They asked about the surfboard. It was a neat board, they said. They had never heard of anything like that. Carried the lady right into shore.

After that no one said anything for a while. Janet had been rubbing sun-tan lotion on her shoulders, but when he started to light a cigarette, she took him quickly by the arm. "Let's go back in the water," she said and ran into the waves, still pulling her rubber cap over her ears.

She was ahead of him all the way out to the sand bar where the waves broke. They dove through one together and when they came up she said, "Listen, I wanted to talk to you. What do those two want?"

In the trough of the wave before the next one came, they

stood and looked back to the shore. The two figures had moved; they were a few feet out in the water pushing the surfboard around between them. They were being careful not to let it get away.

The next wave slapped the swimmers before they knew it; it seemed to break just behind their ears, rush over them and pull them violently towards shore. When they emerged, she took his arm with both hands.

"They're up to something, I know it. Did you notice their clothes? They look as if they'd run away from a reformatory." Her fingers gripped harder against his skin and her voice was drawn and uneasy.

He was a little dismayed by her show of nerves. "Well," he said, "I think it's obvious that they think we're in *their* way. They came up here to go swimming. They haven't any suits and they can't swim naked until we go away."

"Maybe you're right," she said doubtfully, "but they give me the shivers anyway. They don't seem like *boys,* do they? There's something awfully grim about them."

"Forget it," he said, pretending to duck her. "We'll move our things up the beach and eat lunch. They probably won't stick around long if we ignore them." He dove over the next wave and they started for shore.

A little compunction, a little guilt troubled him over his compromise with her fears. The boys had seemed only somewhat lost and lonely to him. If they lived in a crowded tenement, as he supposed, this stretch of empty sand and empty water must bewilder them more than he could understand. But he forgot about that as he raced her to the beach.

They did as he had said. The boys, now sitting close together in the same spot, watched their movements of gathering their things and going off without any question. They were still sitting there when Janet and Gib got out of sight around a place where the beach narrowed and the dune came close to the water.

"We might have offered them a sandwich," he said as they were eating. She shook her head.

"It was better not to. We'd have them around like flies all afternoon."

After they had finished eating they lay still on the blanket again, letting the sun cook them. He drifted again into that dozing state, dangling between real sleep and real wakefulness. Suddenly he was disturbed. It was nothing more than a momentary change in the light or the air, as if a shadow had passed across the sun. He felt that he must open his eyes, wake up. Slowly he did. They were sitting there less than ten feet away, staring silently at his face.

"What do you want?" he asked and sat up. They sat together just as before, one head dazzlingly black in the sun, close to the naked blue-white one. He felt that she was stirring on the blanket and in a minute she would see them too. It seemed impossible to explain their strange insistence, this speechless patience, in his own terms. She would be frightened when she saw them here again and a little of her panic would take hold of him, he knew—not entirely, but just a little more, and he was afraid of it.

He spoke slowly, "You fellows must be hungry." He waited for an answer but all he saw was a minute movement as if they had both at the same time shifted a little nearer the blanket. "Would you like a couple of sandwiches? We have some left over." They were silent.

He went to the picnic basket on hands and knees, taking

care not to disturb her. He reached in and took out the left-over sandwiches, still wrapped in wax paper. The white boy extended his hand and took them. Gib was aware that she was awake now and listening.

"Why don't you go away somewhere and eat them?" For a minute he was not sure that they would pay any attention. Finally they rose slowly and went about twenty yards away; then they sat down again. They began to unwrap the sandwiches.

"Get rid of them," she whispered. "They're planning something, Gib, I know it. They're after us." Her whisper was hysterical; he could see a white bloodless band running across her cheeks beneath the tanned surface. "I can tell."

"Nonsense," he whispered back, but the very violence of her exaggeration shook him.

"They have criminal faces," she said.

"Now don't be silly, Janet. They haven't done a thing. They're pests, sure, but that doesn't mean they're up to anything." But the confidence had gone out of his words and he was aware of an angry pulsing under his ribs. "By God, if I thought so . . ." he said. "Look!" she whispered sharply.

They had stood up, dropping their sandwiches in the sand, and were looking at some spot down the beach, near the edge of the water. "What is it?" she asked. They could not tell. Gib got up on his knees to see. The two boys were going forward in an awkward stalk. They both stopped to gather something and then broke into a trot.

Gib saw what it was. There were a dozen or more sandpipers scurrying in their delicate spinsterish fashion along the edge of the shore.

The boys were running very close to them now and the

birds took alarm. The boys stopped and began to throw the stones they had picked up as the frightened birds scattered on the beach or began to fly out over the water. One of the attackers gave a quick cut-off laugh and then they were running down to the edge of the water.

"They're coming back!" she said.

They stood looking down at Gib and Janet. The colored one laid the sandpiper on the ground as if it were an offering or a prophecy. Neither of them said anything yet; the colored boy smoothed the dead feathers with his hand and he smiled as he did so. When he smiled, Janet screamed.

"Get out of here!" The words shot out of her mouth. "Get out of here and leave us alone. You've bothered us enough today. We don't want you, understand? We don't want you; you can go wherever you're going and take your bird with you. *Go away!*" Gib realized that he had taken hold of her hand and that his other hand was clenched in a fist. His breath was pumping; he knew he was hers.

They were undecided and they both kept glancing down at the bird as if they expected it to tell them something. The colored boy made some kind of gesture with his open hand in front of him, the palm showing pink in the center. At last he said, "We . . . I don't know. We ain't botherin' you."

"Get out of here," Gib said. Now he was sure of himself. "We don't want you." The white boy sat down.

Janet's face was white now; it didn't seem pretty any longer. She was gathering her things and with no more words Gib helped her. They put everything together and started down the beach, walking close to the water so that they could move faster on the hard sand.

"Are they?" she asked after a while. He had kept glancing back. "Yes," he said.

The stairway was nearer; they had only about fifty yards to go. He looked back again.

"They're about a hundred feet behind us," he said. They hurried.

They got to the bottom of the stairs and she started to climb, panting from the exertion. He went a little more slowly, shifting the things in his arms so that he might drop them easily. He looked back and saw that the two were close behind them. They were standing at the foot of the stairs now. Their faces were raised towards him and it seemed to him for a moment that they looked only puzzled and curious.

The colored boy stood a few paces in front of the other with his hands dropped by his sides. Suddenly he made that odd empty gesture with the palm of his hand and Gib paused near the top of the stairway.

But it was the white boy who spoke in his queer accent. His voice was windy and panting, for he must have walked fast, too.

"Mister," he said, "give us a lift out to the highway?"

"No!" she said from behind him. "Hurry, Gib, hurry and for God's sake, watch out." Her voice had risen to the pitch of a bird's shrill dying scream. "Watch out!"

Gib ran up the last few steps. He could see the boys stand there for a moment and then they came forward and began to climb the stairs. He saw the black hand and the white hand clenched on the railing. "Gib!" he heard her say.

He threw the blanket and the surfboard on the ground and faced around. He watched them climb until they were less than ten feet below him. "Gib!" she whispered again.

They were close. He knew what he had to do from the tone of her biting whisper. He wrenched at one of the 2x4 railings and the rotted thing came away with the pull. He saw the two faces, one black, one white, tottering in front of him. He swung the club with all his force and he saw the whole rickety structure give way. At the moment the blood splashed on his hand, the stairway fell. It seemed to burst into chunks and fragments of wood and avalanche down the steep dune. In the tangle of wood and sand and bodies he could see a raised black hand, open in the air with a pink spot showing in the center of the palm.

A GUIDE TO THE MUNIMENT ROOM

"IT MAY never set on the British Empire," said Mrs. Turnbull, "but, my God, it never rises on the British Isles."

"*Please,* darling," whispered her husband, "those English people at the table behind you—"

"All *they* ever talk about is the weather," she said with lower volume but equal emphasis. "What I just said is probably an old Wessex proverb or something."

"Why are you being so difficult?" He raised his eyes to the ceiling, as if to discern a clearing sky. "It's bound to get better."

"But we're too old to wait," she said. "Listen, Jim. It's time to go back to civilization—and I mean Cleveland, Ohio. This is *monsoon* country."

Turnbull looked from his inconvertible wife to his undrinkable cup of coffee. "There is something I especially want to see in Bristol," he said with the mild obstinacy learned from years of outsitting, outwaiting, and outlasting her. All forces of nature eventually take a turn for the better was his motto.

"There is something *I* especially want to see. That's the way to the railroad station. Why can't we spend the last few days in London?"

Just then the waiter came and took away their breakfast plates. "A bit damp outside," he said cheerily.

"A few inches more of damp and your whole island's going to be under the North Sea—where it belongs," Vicky said to him.

"Hear! Hear!" said the waiter, moving away with the tray of dishes.

"You can't faze them," Vicky said, "*they* think it's fascinating."

"You've got to see England in bad weather to understand it," Turnbull said doggedly. "When you have good weather year 'round, you get a civilization of bikinis and outdoor movies. The Englishman values his roof and his fireplace— thus property, privacy, and respectability."

"And wet wool and a high suicide rate," she said.

"Darling—those people behind you! They've been staring this way," he said and turned his face toward the window where the water still busily rivered down the panes.

The man at the table behind Vicky called out, "Say there, are you people Americans by any chance?"

Turnbull mumbled "Australian," but Vicky turned and said, "Why yes, are you?"

"Natural born," said the man. "By George, Leila. I told you so." He looked like a jolly burglar with his smile, his pink benevolent face, his broken nose, and sharp safe-cracker eyes. A few strands of black hair were stretched carefully across his scalp like telephone wires from ear to ear. "We thought you were English people at first. Ha! Ha!" he shouted.

"That's just because we were caught in the rain this morning," Vicky said.

The couple came over and shook hands warmly.

"Jim Turnbull from Western Reserve, well I'll be damned! Listen to that, Leila." He seemed to feel Leila needed special guidance. "I'm Dunc Emerson from Ohio State. Practically neighbors! This *is* a pleasure. Meet my wife, Leila."

The handshaking was prolonged; Emerson wouldn't let them stop smiling. Around him in the air waved invisible red-white-and-blue bunting and Buckeye leaves. A genuine English couple in the far corner complained of the noise to the waiter and left. It called for a drink, he said, and Emerson ordered tea. They all sat down at the Turnbulls' table.

"What are you doing in this Godforsaken town, anyway?" Emerson asked. "I've just been to a meeting of economists in London—my field. Leila got it into her head to look up some distant relatives down here. Turns out they're all dead or moved away and I don't blame them, so here we are."

"Well," said Turnbull hesitantly. "We've been in England about a month now. This is a sort of—you might call it a literary pilgrimage. My field's English Lit. I always wanted to get over here and visit all the places connected with famous authors." He paused. "You know—it makes a lot of difference in teaching if you can visualize some of the scenes you're lecturing about."

"Say, that's a grand idea," said Emerson, gleaming. "How'd you like them?"

"I thought Stratford was a frost and I wouldn't live in Dr. Johnson's house for a million dollars," Mrs. Turnbull said sourly.

"But you liked the Lake District and Abbotsford," said her

husband. "We've had a lot of rain and Vicky doesn't like rain. This is our last stop," he added.

"What's here?" asked Mrs. Emerson in her girlish voice. "I didn't know anybody was born here."

Turnbull relaxed in his chair and stroked his lapels. A chalky professional note came into his voice. "Bristol is the birthplace of Thomas Chatterton, the poet, 1752–1770. 'The marvellous Boy, the sleepless Soul that perished in his pride.'"

"Never heard of him," said Emerson. "Why couldn't he sleep?"

"Oh, I've heard of him," said Mrs. Emerson, with a light in her gray tabby face. "Wasn't he the poet who killed himself? One of those unrecognized geniuses? But I didn't remember he was born here. How *very* interesting."

"Exactly," said Turnbull. "But it's been such an awful downpour the last two days that we haven't felt like venturing out. Of course it isn't the Pile Street birthplace site I want to see—nothing of interest's left there—the place to see is St. Mary Redcliffe church, with which Thomas Chatterton was so closely connected."

"The same one!" Emerson said. "The one we saw on our way from the station. Isn't that a coincidence? We thought it might be Lutheran. We're Lutherans. But the waiter over there says it's an Anglican church and he ought to know because he says he's gone there all his life." He reared around in his chair. "Hey, George, come here a second!"

The waiter came, with inquiring eyebrows. He was a white-headed man with a blunt patient face and an air of being employed against his will.

"This gentleman here wants to know about St. Mary's church—the one you were telling us about."

"Well, I really—" began Turnbull painfully.

"—was there some poet who used to work there, fellow named Chadderton or something?"

"Thomas Chatterton is well known in Bristol," said the waiter with false submissiveness. Emerson looked at Turnbull as if expecting him to be surprised by the news. Turnbull gave an insulted smile and tried to nod pleasantly.

"He is buried in the yard at St. Mary Redcliffe and there is a monument to him there," the man said quietly.

"What!" said Turnbull, sitting up as if he had got a bowl of soup in his lap. "Buried here? You're *very* mistaken. He committed suicide in London and was buried in the potter's field there. His grave is not known." Emerson looked delightedly back and forth between the two. It was plain his money was on the waiter.

"That's the legend, sir," the waiter said.

"If that's a legend, then what do you think is true?" Turnbull asked, growing exasperated in spite of himself and clunking his knife up and down on the table.

"Everyone in Bristol knows that a relative of Mrs. Chatterton's living in London sent the poor boy's body home in a box. Some even saw it here. Then his uncle, the sexton, took him out and buried him at night by the lime tree in the church yard." American notions must be dealt with firmly. The old man looked Turnbull straight in the eye.

Emerson's laugh sounded like something boiling over on a stove. Turnbull shook his head irritably in the midst of the bubbling. "They don't put everything in the Lit. books, eh Turnbull? You fellows can still learn a couple've things."

"Well," he said consolingly, "we've got some of the same problems. Economic theory doesn't always work out the way it's supposed to in the marketplace."

Turnbull moved his head as if to shake him off. "I suppose there's a ghost, too?" he asked the waiter sharply.

"A ghost, yes," the old man said in his mild way and waited to be taken up.

"A ghost!" said Mrs. Emerson. "What's it like? I never heard of a ghost in a church."

"It's the boy—and he walks," was all the waiter would say.

"Is he dangerous?" said Mrs. Turnbull.

"A suicide buried in consecrated ground? And a ghost in the church?" Turnbull said.

"I say!" said a newcomer at a table across the room. "If you aren't *too* busy." The waiter started, looked around, and said, "Coming, sir." Then he said, "Excuse me," and with a look of calm satisfaction he hurried off.

Turnbull appealed around the table. Emerson looked at him with a sharp smile; Mrs. Emerson looked interested in her bewildered way; his wife was not paying attention. "What garbage!" Turnbull said. "Ignorant people believe anything."

"I don't know anything about poets but it sounds on the level to me," Emerson said in a judicial tone. "This country's supposed to have plenty of ghosts, isn't it?"

Turnbull pushed his chair back suddenly and got up. "*I'm* going to St. Mary's," he said. "Not that I believe what that fool waiter was saying, but . . ."

"Oh Jim," Vicky said. "Sit down and finish your coffee. *I'm* not going out in any deluge just to see where some writer was buried and I don't think you should. You'll catch a bad cold and have a stopped-up head all the way home."

"Sorry, old man," Emerson said and yawned. "I guess I

was just trying to get a rise out of you with that waiter's story. Couldn't care less, if you'll excuse it. What the hell, Adam Smith's probably buried some place in this country and I never went to his grave."

"I'll go," said Mrs. Emerson with unexpected enthusiasm.

While Turnbull was getting his raincoat and umbrella from the room, he had feelings both of impatience and misgiving. Chatterton, a dim figure and the center of a forgotten hullabaloo, had never really made much of an impression on him. He was chiefly interesting, Turnbull thought, because of the way Wordsworth and Coleridge had been affected by the story of his life. He hadn't imagined that anyone cared enough to keep up an old wives' tale of secret burials and ghosts. It was like some tiresome movie mystery, a simpleminded—That was it, he thought, as he walked down the corridor. The old waiter was simple-minded. There had probably been some superstitious stories about Chatterton current when he was a boy and he remembered them. Turnbull felt a little better, yet he still could not get rid of a certain anxious feeling about the church. He had to see it. Perhaps, he coached himself, it would give him material for a lecture at any rate. Start off with the ghost story—arouse the students' curiosity. Then he could deal with Chatterton as a literary figure briefly and finally lead into the subject of the Romantics' conception of the Poet. He clattered flat-footed down the stairs and found Mrs. Emerson, wrapped to the chin in a tartan raincoat, waiting for him by the door.

In the taxi, they talked about nothing special. Mrs. Emerson said Dunc wasn't the least bit interested in sightseeing, hadn't even wanted to see Westminster Abbey when they were in London. She was interested in churches, she said, and sang in the choir at home. Turnbull advised her to see the cathedrals at Wells and Salisbury before they left England. He shivered and felt cold for no real reason.

The taxi crossed a bridge and drove down a street of crowded shop fronts; then it stopped. Turnbull looked through the blur of the windows and seemed to be looking from under water at the church, whose chiseled peaks rose in obscurity into the rain. It was on a low hill—the "cliff" no doubt—and it seemed detached from the wet gray city, like a ship floating above it. Turnbull paid the driver and awkwardly opened the umbrella outside the car door; then, under its cover, they trotted up the steps into the shelter of the church porch.

He opened the heavy door and they entered. Inside, they felt suddenly on their faces the cold air and entered into the everlasting winter of the Gothic stone forest.

They stood silently for a few moments looking down the long nave toward the chancel. The church seemed narrow and immensely tall. They stood in a kind of dusty half light; above them the windows looked like faded, intricate embroidery in color and above that the piers rose into a stratosphere of darkness. At the far end, beyond the choir, an arched window glowed with what seemed to be self-contained fire.

"Well, *I* don't see any ghost," said Mrs. Emerson.

"What?" said Turnbull. "Oh, no, of course not. I wonder if there's anybody we can get information from."

They looked around and realized that there were actually several people in the church. A man and a woman were standing under one of the bays near the choir; someone was walking around near the altar; and two workmen with a man in a dark suit were examining some of the stonework underneath a gallery just to their right. The man in the dark suit seemed to be detached from the workmen, watching them, but not actually supervising and so Turnbull went over to him and asked if there were a sexton or someone who could show the church. Without turning fully around, the man said, "I can."

Turnbull came back with him to where Mrs. Emerson was waiting. The man said, "And what do you care to see in this church?" He had a strange soft voice and Turnbull felt taken aback a little at the question and at the way the man preferred to stand a little distant from them in the shadow. It occurred to Turnbull then that he had probably made a mistake and got some kind of clergyman, maybe the rector himself.

"Oh, I'm sorry," he said. "I was just looking for someone to give us some information. I thought there might be a sexton around who wouldn't mind . . ."

"I don't mind," said the man curtly. "I do it often."

They were uncomfortably silent for a few minutes. Turnbull began to wonder if it was his day for running into all the local eccentrics.

"I was waiting to hear what you are looking for," the man said finally. "Architecture? These bays along the nave are Perpendicular in style with certain traits of the Decorated. I can show you some traces of Early English remaining from the older church. In the north transept—but I see you don't go in for all that."

"Well, not exactly," Turnbull said. "We were wondering—"

"Historical interest?" the man asked. "Look behind you to your left on the wall. You'll see the arms and armor of Sir

William Penn, Commander of the Fleet in the Dutch War. Pepys speaks of him, rather nastily I'm afraid, and he's better known because of his son, who founded Pennsylvania."

"Of course we're interested in everything," said Turnbull, "but I wonder if you'd tell us about Chatterton's connection with—"

The man seemed not to have heard and was slowly proceeding ahead of them down the nave. Turnbull was now sure he had caught the rector, but he wondered why the man behaved so oddly. Offended dignity? Anti-Americanism? Dislike of sightseers? Mrs. Emerson trotted along at Turnbull's side and whispered, "Ask him about the ghost."

"Shh!" said Turnbull, forgetting it wasn't Vicky with him. Then he added, "A little later." He felt confused and overexcited, hardly himself at all. He realized that, ever since he had stood up at the breakfast table and announced so loudly that he was coming, a queer infection had set in, an infection of the nerves. It had even increased during the taxi ride and when they entered the church. In the lofty remote dark of the place he had been startled to realize that he was looking around expectantly to see something he didn't wish for. When he thought about it, he was horrified and tried to study the architecture. "We all have an idiot within us," a colleague had portentously remarked to him once. I don't, Turnbull had thought calmly, but now here he was in a fever, looking for something he didn't believe.

It was really, he told himself, just curiosity about the scenes, the medieval atmosphere that had inspired the strange boy—but it wasn't any use. He was jumpy and sensitive to every whisper in the place.

He had plodded conscientiously through all the birthplaces, town houses, parsonages, cottages; he had stood among the books in famous studies; had stared at commemorated views; had walked around for the first time in long-familiar settings—and found them all deserted. The desks were forever neat now and the scenes had become the printed word. With a sinking heart, he began to feel that now they were meaningless.

As he focused his camera on the Avon swans or late at night in his hotel room tried to jot down a few impressions of their visit to the Old Curiosity Shop, he felt a total blankness. Once he had written down in depression, "The countryside is doubtless the same, but there is no longer any eye to see it," and in the morning had scratched it out in embarrassment. He couldn't let Vicky—or anybody—know.

He began to perspire as they walked through the cold church. He had a sensation of half seeing out of the corner of his eye something or someone walking along with them. He found himself listening to the footsteps on the stone to hear if there were more than three pairs. When he glanced around quickly, of course there was nothing in view and when he concentrated, the number of footfalls was perfectly natural. He hated the rumoring old man. He was discovering a dumb and gullible self within himself and this alarmed him. He was alarmed to feel himself shiver. He wanted to finish up, get the visit over with, go away, but the very scare he felt propelled him on towards an anxious appointment.

They had come to the crossing of the church and their guide paused a few paces ahead of them. "I should tell you," he said in his soft depressed voice, "that Queen Elizabeth when she visited St. Mary's called it 'the goodliest, fairest parish church in England.'"

"Oh," said Mrs. Emerson, "I do admire her so much. I'm sorry we missed her visit. Was it lately?"

"Around 1588, I believe," said the guide.

"This is the north transept," he continued after a moment. "Here at the end we can see a very good thirteenth-century effigy." He led them down to a spot beneath the window. A knight in chain mail lay stiffly on his tomb. He had a tough violent look on the face under the mail headpiece, even through the stone copy and all the years. It struck Turnbull that there must have been those around him who heaved a good sigh of relief when it was evident he was no longer breathing and thought, Well, the wild beast is dead. He had something like a stone blanket partly covering his legs.

"Was he somebody famous?" asked Mrs. Emerson. "Was he killed in some historical battle?"

"He's nameless," said the man, running his fingers gently across the cold forehead. "I really don't know who he was, though I think he died as great as any knight who ever fought for England."

"But isn't it gruesome to stick them right on top of the grave like that? It makes me shudder."

"It was a mighty race," said the guide to the statue, ignoring Mrs. Emerson. "I sometimes think they have only gone back to their native rock again." Turnbull thought it a senseless remark.

He wondered what kind of clergyman this was, if indeed he was a clergyman, taking people on tours of the church only to deliver a lot of cryptic remarks. But then, he thought, the man seemed fascinated with what he was showing them —the preoccupied attitude (chiefly back view) as he bent over the effigy and put his hand against it and the evident feeling with which he spoke. It was very queer. Turnbull had now had a lot of experience with guides, the surly ignorant kind and the erudite voluble ones. This man seemed different from any. Turnbull finally decided that they had picked up an amateur antiquarian, the kind who would prove to have all sorts of uninteresting church lore and who bicycled to remote villages to make rubbings of church brasses.

They moved on to the south transept, the choir aisles, the altar, and the Lady Chapel. Their guide led them to the tombs of the Canynges—first the mayor in his robes, with his wife, and then to the figure of William Canynges, *ye Richest marchant of ye towne of Bristow afterwards chosen 5 times mayor of ye said towne for ye common good of ye fame.* The tomb-figure's priestly face and dress did not seem to go with his Rotarian epitaph and Turnbull wanted to ask some questions, but the guide stood staring at the recumbent figure and did not offer a word.

When they came to a great yellow whalebone, he did open his mouth to remark that it was sometimes said to be the rib of the Great Dun Cow supposed to have been killed by the legendary Guy of Warwick. He took them quickly through the chapel and, keeping always ahead, came back finally to the nave.

With some effort Turnbull caught up and said, "Excuse me, but you haven't said anything about Thomas Chatterton. We're very much interested in seeing the room where he discovered his old manuscripts—that is, if it's open."

Hurrying on, over his shoulder, the man said, "There's nothing to see."

"But it's what we came for," Turnbull said stubbornly.

"That is, the church's interesting, of course, but we did want to see the Chatterton room." He felt that they were being directed toward the door, deliberately put off for some reason. It seemed to him that the man had taken them on a lengthy tour of the church more to avoid than to answer questions. Well, Turnbull refused to be rushed off like this. He began to feel suspicious. "That's what we came for," he repeated.

"You mean the Muniment Room," said the guide. "There's nothing of interest remaining." He increased his pace along the nave and their footsteps echoed in the emptiness.

"Whatever it's called," Turnbull said. The man seemed to slow down and hesitate.

"We were told there's a ghost around here," said Mrs. Emerson. "Of the poet."

The guide did stop. He seemed startled. "Nonsense. Nonsense," he said hastily. "Of course there isn't." He ducked as if he were about to put his head down and run, but he said reluctantly, "I shall show you the Muniment Room, then." He set off quickly toward the door by which they had entered the church.

"Monument Room? What's that?" asked Mrs. Emerson, but their guide ignored her. He entered the doorway; they could hear his feet on some steps, going upward. They both paused for a minute and looked at each other. Turnbull felt cold sweat like knives under each arm. "Come on," he whispered fiercely to the undecided Mrs. Emerson.

It was a spiral stairway and Turnbull began by taking Mrs. Emerson's elbow with the intention of helping her, but actually pushing her along faster than she wanted to go.

"It means 'Document room,'" he told her in a whisper.

"Records, papers, valuables of the church were kept there."

"It's dark in here," said Mrs. Emerson. "I have an eerie feeling. Do you think we can trust that man? I don't want to get out on any towers or anything. I have a *very* poor head for heights."

"Don't worry," said Turnbull, thrusting her on by the elbow, "everything's under control." It wasn't.

James Turnbull was aware of being a moderate man with a good sense of where the exact middle of anything lay. He was well known in the Department for the measured view, the golden mean, the common denominator. Blatant enthusiasm about your field was definitely not good. Turnbull had impressed a number of his colleagues with his simile of the pipe rack. He had a fine pipe rack in his study—this English Lit. business is a bit like it, he had said, smiling urbanely. The books to be taught, he explained, ought to be well broken in, used reflectively for a while, and rotated so they wouldn't get stale. He couldn't understand how in God's name one of them had brought him into this fix, climbing a flight of stone steps in the dark somewhere, so shaky he was beginning to feel sick, his heart chopping like an axe on a block.

Even though he kept sternly thinking, absurd, absurd, his legs at least and his nerve-ends were convinced that he was getting into danger. He was confused and horrified. There was going to be something or somebody in the room when he got there. Absurd, absurd. There was going to be something horrible. Calm down, shut up. There was going to be something he could not foretell, but would recognize at once.

Almost in a panic, he stumbled up the last few steps and

reached the top. He leaned through the doorway, steadying himself and biting his lips, and saw nothing.

It was an empty room. Turnbull caved against the wall and almost groaned at his own idiocy. What he saw before him was a low-ceilinged, dusty, hexagonal chamber with close-set narrow windows all around the walls. There was certainly nothing in it except dust and a few heavy chests on the floor beneath the windows. Their guide stood in the middle of the room and looked questioningly at him, apparently surprised at Turnbull's struggles with his breathing.

As he began to recover, he panted, "Steps gave me a bad time. Short-winded."

"I'm sorry," said the guide. Turnbull realized that this was the first time they had actually seen his face in any sort of light; the man really looked outlandish. His dark suit was quite worn, a double-breasted pin-striped model with the coat rather tight over a slight paunch. Though he had seemed to be rather tall and light-footed down there in the shadows, he now looked short and a little bit clumsy.

He stood looking abstractly in their direction for a minute or two and Turnbull, as he returned to a normal state, was surprised to notice that he had remarkable eyes. They were gray, too large for the face and too bright. Something shone in them like deceptive lights beneath the surface of water and one of them was larger and more staring than the other.

He had darkish yellow hair, somewhat long and combed back, a round forehead and a heavy mouth. It was the plump disappointed face of a child who had aged without really changing; minute broken veins mottled the boyish cheeks in one or two places and the juvenile mouth looked old.

He said reluctantly at last, "This is the room in which Thomas Chatterton found the fourteenth- and fifteenth-century manuscripts he used for his forgeries. You can see for yourselves there's nothing here."

"You'd think there'd be some kind of tablet or marker, at least," said Mrs. Emerson, who had been peering around the walls.

"Marker?" said the guide with a peevish look at her. "This parish owes nothing to Thomas or any of the other Chattertons." Now that he was offended, his eyes seemed to distend. "His father stole invaluable parchments from these chests—a great part of the history and literature of the old town of Bristol! And do you realize what he did with them? He took them home to use for cleaning papers and patterns. They cut *dolls* out of them for the children.

"His father was Master at the charity school in Pile Street. He had no more understanding than to take these invaluable manuscripts out of the chests and use them to cover the boys' copybooks. Did you know that? No, we haven't any reason to love the Chattertons here." His voice spiraled up indignantly.

"I suppose they didn't know about such things in those days," said Mrs. Emerson, unimpressed and still peering. "Couldn't help what his father did, could he?"

The guide took a sudden step toward the chests as if he were going to open one. "Thomas was the *worst*," he said. "Thomas took the old parchments of medieval poems and histories and rubbed out the lettering. Then he printed his own poetry on them. He learned to write his verses from the old models, in fact—he took names, dates, everything from them for his own work."

"That surprises *me*," said Turnbull, revived by the argument and now in home waters. "I'm sure you must be mistaken. I believe the Chatterton scholars say there was nothing in the chests but old deeds and legal records—no real histories and certainly no poems. All that are extant support that theory, I'm sure.

"And about the erasures," he continued, looking straight at the guide, "—well, I never heard that theory either. I think Chatterton was supposed to have made some attempt to make the ordinary paper he used look old, but—" he said in a jocular way, "if you've got other evidence, the scholars would be delighted to hear about it."

The man looked at Turnbull as if he had been kicked and his mouth trembled a little. He kept shaking his head. "No, no," he said excitedly. "There were poems—beautiful ones. The boy sat there on that very chest"—he pointed—"and with his knife scraped off the old lettering." Mrs. Emerson and Turnbull slowly revolved in that direction. But the dust on the coffer was untouched and the room as empty as ever.

"That was a funny way to act," Mrs. Emerson said. "Why couldn't he just write them on plain paper and send them in to a magazine?"

The guide rubbed his forehead and looked tired. He said dejectedly, "One can write them very well, you know, and nobody cares. Nobody reads poor Tom's poems, but Rowley is a different matter, he's historical . . ." He fumbled for something to go on with and his voice trailed off.

Turnbull, now fully himself, had been growing more and more irritated. A part of the trip he had anticipated with pleasure—and now he had been plagued by the town idiots all day. There was certainly something strange and retarded about this fellow. He could be some simpleton who hung around the church, learned a little guide's patter from the sexton or somebody, and got sixpences from unwary tourists now and then. The church authorities ought to put a stop to it, if that were the case.

Turnbull spoke severely, "I think you're wasting your efforts and our time with ridiculous stories. See here, I don't know what kind of a guide you pretend to be, but I just want to give you a little warning. Now and then you'll run into somebody who knows something about these matters." The man turned his face away. "I happen to be a college professor—of English literature—and I *do* know something about Thomas Chatterton, you see? You fellows think you can get away with murder, repeating any old nonsense for the tourists. I advise you either to get the true facts or else find some other line of work."

Turnbull stopped and suddenly felt embarrassed. The man had put his head down like a punished child and there actually seemed to be tears in his eyes. All his awkward self-assurance had disappeared. Turnbull said, "Well, I'm sorry. I shouldn't have said that, I guess. We ought to be going. Thank you very much, we . . ." He saw that Mrs. Emerson had taken a half-crown piece out of her pocketbook and he caught her arm quickly. No need to encourage him, anyway. "We do appreciate the tour." He turned and got Mrs. Emerson started on the stairs. When they were a few steps down, he heard the guide slowly begin to follow them.

At the church door, they paused again and saw the guide emerge from the stairway. He made an apologetic attempt to open the door for them and all three went outside beneath the north porch. The man waited submissively, with bent head, for them to go.

The rain had stopped and the sun showed behind a ripped flying curtain of clouds. Puddles of water gleamed here and there on the stone pavement. Turnbull felt fully on balance again and wondered why he had let the dark silence of the church play on his nerves so. It seemed untrue and unreal, as, when he was a boy, the dark cellar of the house had never seemed real when he was not in it. At any rate, the superstitions were all gone now and he would be glad to see the last of Bristol. He'd tell Vicky they could take the train to London this afternoon.

Their guide hadn't moved and it occurred to Turnbull that he was probably waiting for a final word of reassurance. "Well," he said in a friendly tone to the man, "it isn't too important after all, is it? The whole thing's only a matter of curiosity now. It might have been a different story if poor Chatterton had amounted to anything as a poet."

The man seemed shocked and he raised his head, glaring at Turnbull with vicious brilliance in his eyes—only his eyes because there was no changing the plump incongruous face.

"He was a great poet!" he said wildly. "He was a great poet and they killed him in London. They killed him!"

He lashed at Turnbull with his open hand, but it was a poor aimless try and Turnbull easily stepped back and wasn't touched. Then the door was shut and the man was gone.

"Well," said Mrs. Emerson. "It's a good thing you didn't let me give him the tip." She stared at the closed door. "What was the matter with him, anyway?"

Going back in the taxi, they agreed not to mention the guide's odd behavior. Turnbull explained that it was quite clear he was some half-witted fellow who hung around the church—but of course they couldn't have known. "I don't think we should do anything about it," Turnbull said, "we don't really want to get the poor fellow in any trouble, do we?"

WINDFALL

TAGGERT stopped on his way out to say good-bye to Vanderbilt. All the press had gone out of him; the points of his collar curled like wet leaves; his clothes drooped; his face looked bruised around the eyes—angry and purplish. "Well?" asked Vanderbilt, unable to think of anything else. "Well?"

"Remember the Commandos during the war?" Taggert asked. "They had a trick of sneaking up behind a German sentry—they caught him around the neck and used one of those razor-sharp trench knives. Fellow I knew said that some of the sentries were surprised when they looked down and saw intestines on the ground. They wondered for a minute where they came from."

"My God, Frank," Vanderbilt said, "it couldn't have been that bad. In spite of everything he still respects you —he really does." This was not what Vanderbilt had meant to say and the lie came stickily off his tongue, but Taggert wasn't really listening.

"The next time he shows respect for *you,* look on the

174

ground before you move," Taggert said rancorously. "The modern executive. The Commando of daily life. I took two steps before I knew I'd been fired."

"Was it mostly the Sherman business?" Vanderbilt asked uncomfortably.

"Partly, I guess—delicately alluded to. Crisscross. Then a short snotty oration on the mistakes of trying to sell property that hasn't been fully inspected and renovated. Costly loss to the firm—all that. I sat there wishing his ulcers long life and good hunting." The conversation was too visceral for Vanderbilt. He wished Taggert would stop talking and stop standing there holding his hand to his stomach.

"What'll you do now, Frank?" said Vanderbilt in a low voice, conscious that people were walking and conversing just beyond the office partition.

"Oh, bid good-bye to my wife in a civilized way, I suppose," he said, dropping his cigarette before he could light it. He kicked the cigarette under the desk and took out a fresh one. "She is prejudiced against the poor."

"Oh come," said Vanderbilt.

"It's true," Taggert said. "She's been on the verge for months and this will do it fine, just fine. No goddam belt-tightening and taking in washing for dear Betsy. She'd rather hang herself. I get the cat and she gets the convertible. Do the French have any way of making cat tasty? Some special kind of sauce?"

"Listen Frank, don't talk like that," he said with manufactured optimism. "You have a fine background. There're lots of real-estate firms in the city, lots of jobs. You'll be better off some place else in no time." He was not frosting the rock very successfully. He didn't really care much for Taggert, liked him a little, but saw Boyle's side of things, too. Boaster, blow-hard, full of wrong information, Taggert caused bad weather in the office. It was not that Vanderbilt had ever had any direct trouble with him, but his follies and his tongue made Boyle and Waley, the office manager, harder to get along with. After an interview with Taggert, they hated everybody. Alice, Vanderbilt's secretary, a plump, fatuous girl of twenty, had been crying at her desk last week after a word with Boyle and had spoiled two important letters by dripping on them.

He did feel sorry for Taggert, still. The thin tent of his self-regard came down so easily. Vanderbilt automatically reached for the next thought, hesitated. Taggert would probably resent being offered a loan. Vanderbilt had thought of fifty dollars, which was probably enough to be insulting and too little to do much good. Taggert might think it a handout, offered to get rid of him.

"Another thing, old man," he said, "can you lend me fifty? Just to tide me over for the next week or two while I'm looking?" He made an antagonistic little smile. "The whole world knows you've got millions."

After Taggert had taken the money, said thanks abruptly, and had gone, Vanderbilt knew Taggert had asked for some ulterior reason. After thinking about it, he decided it was the final touch to his anger and humiliation, the last well poisoned before he left the camp. It served to kill their short quasi-friendship, the only good relations Taggert had enjoyed in the office.

Money causes small deaths. Taggert, he knew, would never try to repay him, and thus would be satisfied that the break was complete. Vanderbilt had a sensation of sourness, like the recollection of sour wine. Taggert had not even forgotten to make a reference to Vanderbilt's name, like all the boring references made by everybody over the years. He sat there and moved two pencils around on his desk blotter.

He sat there for quite a long time, not wanting to go back to work, waiting for something to happen, at least for lunchtime when he could get Taggert out of his mind. Finally there was a stir outside, an attempt on the doorknob. The door opened and Alice came into the room, or parts of her.

Just her face and her sweater-covered breasts—three fat dumplings she habitually intruded into the scene. Alice always seemed to be projecting from behind doors, desks, water coolers, file cabinets, listening to private conversations with an innocent interested expression. His loan to Taggert was probably an office bulletin by this time.

"Doesn't the buzzer work?" he asked sharply. She looked hurt. He knew that the buzzer worked and he shouldn't ask that way. She intended the human touch and she could never learn to use the thing. She hoped, instinctively, for a smile or some unimaginable word that would enrich her morning, and thus she projected through doorways, smiling.

"It isn't a call," she said. "I just wanted to speak to you, Mr. Vanderbilt, if you aren't busy." All of her had got into the room now. "Are you happy with my work, Mr. Vanderbilt?" she said in a voice like gravy.

"What?" he said. "Sit down, Miss Ferris." Happy with her work, good God. Any sensible girl would have said, "Are you satisfied with my work?" but Alice had to make it "happy." She wanted to know if she were still welcome in the world this morning.

"I guess so. I think you do quite well," he said unhappily.

"Then I was thinking, I sure could use a raise," she said. "I've got a lot of new expenses. My girl-friend and I got this new apartment and it's in a more expensive neighborhood, see. Oh, Mr. Vanderbilt, we'd be honored if you'd drop in sometime. It's as cute as it can be and . . ."

"Well," said Vanderbilt, disliking himself, but disliking Alice even more, "merit raises come up for consideration in September. I don't know that Mr. Boyle would consider one for you this early. You've only been here five months, you know."

"But I thought if you went to him," Alice said, arching her back in the chair, "he'd make an exception. I have to have some new spring clothes and I owe some money on the radio and . . ."

He began to remember all his unhappiness with Alice. Number one—the perfume. It was acid-sweet, a peculiar scent that penetrated even the heaviest cigar smoke. It hung in the air of his office like the sign of some dangerous fermentation and even after she had gone out and he had opened the windows it came thickly to his nostrils. Visitors made rude remarks. A man in the bus stared at him and edged away. The stuff was very clinging.

" . . . and I want my mother to come and visit me. All that mounts up," she was saying.

Another thing about Alice he was formulating consciously for the first time—her unaccountable absence on any important occasion. A special-delivery airmail letter had to be taken to the airport, but where was Alice? No one had seen her for an hour. A contract had to be found, a long-distance call put through, some first-priority papers typed. She was at coffee; she had left for the afternoon; she was shopping.

She was telling about her dancing lessons and my goodness, Mr. Vanderbilt, how they cost.

In addition, her shorthand wasn't very good. She left out whole paragraphs in typing, and as for her spelling—none of these things had ever presented themselves to Vanderbilt as a body of evidence. In an indefinite way he had always thought of her as "trying hard" and "doing her best," but now he realized, because of the focus she herself had put on the question, that actually she deserved to be fired.

She ought to be got rid of as quickly as possible. He ought to get some nice innocuous girl with plain brown hair, reasonable behavior, accuracy in typing, a sense of responsibility, and no perfume.

He blamed himself immediately.

Alice was only making a try. How could she know she was dull, prying, and inefficient; how could she know how she smelt? Vanderbilt knew himself well enough to recognize when his reactions were standard for his job and he knew Boyle was paid to have stronger reactions, to be more dogmatic. Boyle would consider the matter for a moment and say, "We'd better let her go, then."

"Well, I'll think about it," he said with an unpromising smile; then he managed to see himself from the other side of the desk for a moment. "I'll try. Let me put it up to Mr. Boyle in some relaxed mood. He's often very automatic about such requests."

She was just half satisfied, but there was only one reply. "Thank you, Mr. Vanderbilt," she said. "Here's hoping." She crossed two thick fingers ostentatiously and held them up for him to see, then followed her bosom out of the room.

He stared at the door resentfully. In a few minutes she had

managed to make things awkward for him and precarious for herself. Worse than that, his unconscious habits of good nature, all his allowances for her, had boiled away in the talk. All that was left was the residue of her inaptitude and her mistakes.

He looked at his desk clock and noticed that it was now eleven-thirty. He got up and opened the window, flapping the curtain for a minute hopefully and trying to remember what it was—the one pleasant thing that had happened this morning. He looked down to the street and saw a hatless man stopping at the newsstand. He had a bald head. Kleinecke. He recovered it now—this forgotten friend was returning $700 to him after ten years.

He had answered the telephone at eight-thirty this morning and a voice had told him it was a lawyer named Clifford. "Now I'm calling for a client of ours, a Mr. Kleinecke. Personal matter, remember it? We have a letter from Kleinecke saying that he owes you $700 from some years back. Do you recall?"

"Yes, I believe so," Vanderbilt had said uncertainly.

"Anyway," the voice said, "Kleinecke has directed us to pay you and has transmitted the money. I sent it to your home address this morning. Okay? Thank you very much."

Vanderbilt put the receiver back slowly. He was beginning to remember Kleinecke now and, vaguely, the $700 debt. The reason he had forgotten was that he had long ago lost track of the man and given up the money. They had come back from the Philippines on the same troop ship in 1945; during the voyage they had played cards, traded war stories, and counted the days. Kleinecke said he was broke, cleaned out in Manila. Vanderbilt had saved some $1,300 from his captain's pay. Kleinecke, whom he remembered as a short balding man with honest pretensions, had some scheme for starting a business of his own. Vending machines? Mail order? Vanderbilt couldn't remember. A sure thing, anyway, Kleinecke had said. The night before they landed, in a spirit of new starts and war-end comradeship, Vanderbilt had lent Kleinecke the $700. He had seen him once more—on the dock in the morning, long enough to shake hands before Kleinecke was rushed and kissed by a blonde woman in a fur coat. Now he felt amazed and justified.

It seemed a little strange and—Vanderbilt thought—sentimental of the man to want to pay back the money after all this time. It was something that could affect Kleinecke's life in no practical way and an old-fashioned phrase came back to Vanderbilt—a "debt of honor." Honor: a reputation for behavior that is becoming or worthy. It was not sentimental. Just rarely he had caught some instance of outdated pride like this, which he could add to some imaginary museum.

This seemed to him to invalidate the debt far more than the money, which seemed useless by comparison, although Vanderbilt had a son in college and a daughter just about to enter; it could be spent. Then it struck him that he would rather not spend it—or at least until some natural need for it arose. He thought of a small neglected savings account he had started some time ago. He would put the money quietly away for the time being and not mention it at home.

He took his hat and went to lunch. In the elevator he met Waley and they ate together in a small restaurant two blocks down the street. He always found Waley's out-of-office conversation relaxing. He provoked no thought and no arguments: it was the batting averages of big-league ballplayers.

"I've made something of a study of it," he sometimes remarked modestly.

Waley worked hard during lunch. He juggled figures and
built up estimates to discover just how Ted Williams's lifetime averages would have worked out in comparison with
Ruth and Hornsby if he had not lost so many years in the
service. Vanderbilt was required only to say, "You've got a
point there," or, "I never thought of *that*." Waley, he reflected, batted a steady .200 both in life and in conversation.

Before going back to the office, they walked once around
the block, Waley still proving things with page after page
of fine print, delighted to have such a passive audience. The
sun felt good on Vanderbilt's face. Taggert and Alice, the
worries of the morning, fell back into the daily history and
he felt ready for work again.

He did work quite steadily during the afternoon. The firm
was handling a block of real estate on the west side of the city
and there were a number of problems connected with it. It
was proposed that the property be bought for business de-
velopment and Boyle had an ambitious building scheme in
mind. Everybody was enthusiastic about it. Nobody else, he
thought, had paused to notice how pleasant the unsym-
metrical old houses with their scrollwork trimming and
steamboat porches still looked, even though the old trees
were untrimmed and the wide lawns now smoke-stained and
frowsy. Vanderbilt had stopped in the high dark front hall
of one of them, looking at the carved newel post and thinking
of his grandfather's house, when Boyle came in, rubbing his
hands and saying, "There's a load of money in it, Bob, once
we get these old barns torn down."

At one moment in the afternoon something reminded him

briefly of the check the lawyer had sent him and he mentally countersigned his resolution. He would not mention it to anybody, but would take it to the office tomorrow and deposit it in the savings account. He thought that it might be used for some special occasion—Jerry's graduation or Ellen's wedding—when it would provide for something extra, something completely unexpected, something entirely frivolous. It ought to be something like a sacrifice of two white oxen, or a grand display of fireworks over the river.

He stopped work exactly at five, a small negative sign of independence which pleased him. Boyle and Waley and Becker were still, importantly, at their desks and he could see light from under their doors. This had become a mechanical game. Boyle stayed to set an example, and Waley stayed to outdo Boyle, and Becker would still be shuffling papers at six-thirty—all three of them crouching over their separate desks wearily waiting for the click of the others' door latches.

It was thus necessary to drive to work. The three of them lived within a mile of each other, but the after-hours rivalry made a car pool impossible. Vanderbilt, unmarked by small success, bought a newspaper and waited on the corner for his bus.

By the time he reached his street, the light had gone amber, a rich meerschaum color that briefly glorified wall and roof of the stodgy modern brick ramblers of the neighborhood. In the western sky, he noticed, a number of small clouds were scattered like worn gold coins and a plane's white contrail curved among them like a dissolving string.

He turned into his gate, entered the house, took off his topcoat and hat, looked automatically on the living-room table for the mail, and discovered the letter from Clifford, torn open.

The check, however, and a note from the lawyer had been stuffed back in again. He frowned at the loss of his small scheme. The note said nothing he had not been told over the phone and he threw it into the fireplace; the check was indeed for $700 and he put that away in his billfold. As he did this, he discovered signs of a new development—there was a blue sweater hanging on the lampshade in the corner and a small stack of notebooks and textbooks on the table.

Confirmation came from the dining room. "Is that you, Bob? Jerry came home for the week-end. He's taken the car."

"Since when do week-ends start on Thursday, Marcia?" he asked. "Amherst must've changed. They were Saturday to Monday when I was there."

"Oh, don't be gouty," she said, coming into the room. "It's a big dance. He's been looking forward to it for weeks."

"Somebody's been opening my mail," he said, trying to avoid an accusatory tone.

"Yes, your check came. I have big plans for it."

He evaded. "You're all dressed up. What's this?"

"Oh God," she said with theatrical weariness, "don't tell me you've forgotten we're going out to dinner with the Morgans tonight?"

"Of course I have," he said. "Dinner with the Morgans is a natural-born subject for forgetting. In fact it may still become a classic example in psychology textbooks. With hardly any effort at all, I—"

"They'll be here in an hour. You'd better get dressed."

"It's possible I'll begin to remember," he said, "—with a little more help from you."

They heard the sound of the Pontiac in the driveway, slewing gravel. "Jerry and Ellen," she said. "I'll fix you a drink while you change. Why don't you get started?"

"O.K., O.K.," he said, "but I want to see Jerry first." He went out into the hall to meet them coming in and stood for a few moments exchanging father-son commonplaces. Jerry looked even taller than he had a month ago; he needed a haircut, acknowledged it saying, "They'll shoot me for a buffalo," and laughed when his father said it was good to see that the old school clung to its traditions, that the jokes hadn't changed since he was there. Otherwise, the only difference seemed to be a hideous green-striped sports jacket.

Jerry put his hand on Vanderbilt's shoulder and said, "I want to speak to you, Dad."

"While I'm dressing then. Your mother decided to have dinner with the Morgans at the last minute."

"Deepest sympathies," Jerry said, following him up the stairs.

While he was taking his shower, Vanderbilt had various pieces of information shouted in to him. Something about "Home Thursday . . . so week-end to study . . . exam." An open lie.

Something about "Roomate . . . lamp post . . . half a dozen cops." An unintelligible anecdote.

Then quite an animated message he lost while soaping his head. It ended up . . . "Elizabeth Jane . . . wonderful." An estimate no longer news.

When Vanderbilt came out of the bathroom and began to dress, Jerry was lying in a chair sketching a beard on the face of the cabinet member on the cover of *Time*.

"You have talent, I see."

Jerry cocked his head and squinted at the picture. "I'm not bad," he said. "I can't do moustaches, though."

"What was it you wanted to see me about?"

"It won't be a big surprise."

"I just sent you forty dollars at the beginning of the week."

"No, Dad," Jerry said impatiently. "It's not anything pressing like that. This is long-range, part of my education, you might call it."

"Well?"

"Well, Dad, I happen to know you got an unexpected check in the mail today. As a matter of fact, it's a wide-open secret. I've been thinking about it this afternoon and it looks like just the answer to my prayers."

Vanderbilt looked at his son, but saw that he was completely in earnest. As usual, he was working along some exclusive line of thought that ruled out everything else. Vanderbilt paid especial attention to buttoning his shirt and said only, "Your prayers?"

"M-huh. You see, I've got this wonderful opportunity for the summer. I was talking it over with Manning and Lambeth —two of my best friends—and they said I'm welcome."

"Welcome to what?"

"Well, they're planning a trip to Europe in the summer. Just knocking around, sightseeing, hitting the famous cities, Paris and so on. They figure the whole thing won't cost more than $800 if we use bikes to get around and go over on a freighter. It's a wonderful chance, Dad," he said with his voice rising. "It'd practically be an education in itself."

"*Vous voulez perfectionner votre français?*"

"Oh, you know I can't understand that stuff. Manning says they all speak English, anyway."

"You have a great ambition to see the monuments of Western civilization? Mont St. Michel, the Uffizi, the Parthenon?"

"Well, if they're on the way, I guess. We had Paris and Monte Carlo down for a starter."

"Or is it research—the British Museum and the Bibliothèque Nationale?"

"Oh, *Jesus*, Dad, can't you be serious? We just want to knock around and see things."

Vanderbilt suddenly stopped putting on his jacket. With one sleeve dragging, he walked across the floor and looked directly into his son's face. "I would give you the money," he said slowly, "if I thought you had any use for it. I'd give it to you if I believed you'd come back with two thoughts to rub together in your head, if you came back speaking some bad French, if I knew you were going off your rocker about French cooking, or cathedrals, or Italian painting, or mountain climbing. I would probably even give it to you if I knew you were going to live in a working quarter and squander it in Paris whorehouses." Jerry threw back his head and stared.

"But I won't give it to you for the way you'd undoubtedly spend it—a stupid little bicycle trip with your buddies, a little beer drinking, souvenir buying, and youth-hostel parties with girls from Wellesley." He hadn't realized he was going to be so vehement, but the words came suddenly.

"You're slack and self-indulgent and self-satisfied. I'm not going to tell you how you ought to be, because you ought to know without my saying it."

Jerry got to his feet, turning pale, with a band of red like sunburn across his pale chunky face. He looked as if he wanted to speak, but found that he couldn't. With damaged dignity, he clumped out of the room.

Vanderbilt felt tired and sat down in the chair. He thought that he had done an admirable job of avoiding the truth all day long and now, probably in the wrong place and for the wrong reasons, it had got the best of him. Still, they were probably words that had to be said sometime. Perversely he hoped that they had left a scar. He hoped that Jerry would not simply hold a shallow and temporary resentment over the loss of the trip. He needed some anger to motivate him—the boy lived in a feather bed.

He stood up again and finished dressing. As he hung his jacket up, he noticed the letter and the check in its pocket. The check was already turning out to be a bad catalyst. He reflected, "This is a family that goes to pieces at the first sign of good fortune."

Immediately he got another reminder when he heard Ellen's voice calling to him from the foot of the stairs. "Are you dressed yet, Daddy?" she said. "Could I talk to you for a minute?"

"I am," he said, coming down, "but I'm afraid we don't have much time. Your mother and I are going out to dinner in a few minutes."

"Mother's on the telephone," she said, taking his arm and guiding him into the living room. "It looks like a long session, too, inasmuch as Mrs. Kennedy isn't one to hide the details and inasmuch as the Kennedys' house got robbed last night."

He sighed. She had stopped being just female and almost in the course of a night and a day had become feminine. Such new charm was a parent's worst snare. It was so awkward, obvious, just-tried-on, tender, it destroyed good sense. He never knew when she was just practicing her powers, but this time he resolved to be firm.

"I heard about the check you got today, Daddy," she said, "and I thought we could save some money by getting some of my school clothes and my luggage and my record player—"

But he had been prepared. He made himself talk at length, reasonably, discouragingly, and dully, referring to family finances, promising she wouldn't be disappointed next fall. "However—" He used a number of "howevers" and managed to make the windfall diminish to nothing in the course of them. She lost interest as he went on and lay back in the chair with a petulant but resigned expression. He knew that she never listened to logical explanations, but on the other hand was likely to take all long explanations as logical. She would go away with a feeling of slight restless resentment and the next time she wanted something would argue that it was owed to her because she had been refused before.

Just as he was beginning to repeat himself, Marcia ended her telephone call and came into the room. She was carrying two drinks in which the ice had melted. She said, "Imagine being stupid enough to leave your pearl necklace in a dresser drawer."

Ellen got up and went out of the room without saying anything. "What's the matter with her?" Marcia asked.

"Nothing much," he said. "They each wanted some money for special projects."

"Oh, the $700," she said. "Well, they can't have it. I saw it first."

"I'm planning to keep it."

"What would *you* use it for?"

"I didn't say I was going to use it; I said I'm going to keep it."

She was beginning to answer this when they were interrupted by the door knocker and the Morgans. Marcia went and in a moment he could hear Roy's bass drum in the hall and Carrie's penny whistle.

He went to fix the Martinis they both asked for when they came into the room. He found Marcia in the midst of the robbery by the time he returned. She seemed to be expressing her greater sympathy for the burglars and noted the impossibility of "trying to find *anything* the way she keeps that house." The Morgans were more interested in the way the entry was made; they lived only three blocks from the Kennedys and they seemed to be mentally checking their windows and estimating the reliability of the baby-sitter.

The drinks smoothed Vanderbilt's nerves and he began to resign himself to the evening. He knew it all: dinner, then bridge with plenty of Roy's stories and plenty of local talk. He got up and made another round of drinks and then it was time to go to dinner.

The restaurant was a new one, a north side place called the Charles V for some reason, and for some reason now popular. It was hard to discover what the place was trying to be, though there was a noticeable effort in the way of mirrors, carpets, vases, and pseudo-French cooking. As they were going to the table, Vanderbilt said that it should be named after King Charles II, who was known as "Charles the Bad," but no one seemed interested in this slightly scholarly joke.

While they were waiting for dinner, Marcia had her eye on him and in her eye he saw the matter of money. She referred to it indirectly once or twice. Then she said, "We're celebrating tonight. Bob got a mysterious check in the mail for $700."

The Morgans said expected things.

"Well, I don't know whether it's wonderful or not," she said. "What would you think of a man who gets mysterious pay-offs in the mail? Especially when he won't tell his nearest and dearest how he spends them?" she asked, making a whole history out of it. "I think it's time to make your motives clear, old boy." Vanderbilt recognized the usual signs. Marcia ought to learn to stop at one. The second zoomed to her head and God knew what she would become. Bully, tragic actress, kind-hearted mother, everybody's former mistress—he never could tell what part she would play. The Morgans looked at him with smug little smiles.

"I wish you wouldn't talk about it now," he said as stuffily as he could.

"But Bob, I'm *interested*," she said as the waiter brought her another highball. "Don't you think it's a fascinating subject we all ought to speculate on? For instance, when I saw that pretty pink check I began to think about some new drapes and furniture for you and a new winter coat for me. Just a few things like that I've wanted for the last five years."

"You're boring Roy and Carrie," he said, being stuffy without any effort.

The Morgans tried to change the subject and Marcia waited patiently until they were through. "I'm tired of the mystery," she said. "The fact is some lawyer named Kleinickel sent him $700 in the mail today. All he does when I ask him about it is say that it's none of my business." She called the waiter and made quite an affair of ordering another

Bourbon and soda. "Just a little *slosh* of soda," she said. "Now—"

"I'll give you a complete financial statement in the morning," he said sharply. It seemed to him that the whole day had been like this, full of demanding, oppressive conversations. He had begun to feel a slow anger that was more like a chill than a fever. "Marcia, for God's sake, forget the money for this evening. The Morgans didn't ask us in order to hear a review of our finances."

"If there's nothing to hide, a simple explanation in a few well-chosen words ought to do it," she said unpleasantly. It was her evening to be compulsive. In a mood like this, she never simply attacked a subject; she conquered it. She sat down on it like an army of occupation. She requisitioned every aspect, razed all the possibilities, and finally sowed salt in the ruins. "Let's hear about it," she demanded, waving her glass at him.

He suddenly felt frozen to the bone. He knew that he could either hit or run. He looked in agitation around the noisy restaurant, where smiling people were being ushered to tables by smiling waiters. He had a glimpse of his taut face in one of the mirrors. Then he got up quickly and began to edge his way through the people toward the cloak counter. When he reached it, he asked for his hat and coat and, looking back once, saw Morgan coming after him and gesturing. But Morgan was caught in a small crowd of elderly men and women intent on getting to their table. He opened the door and went out into the street, where he found that it had begun to rain.

He walked furiously for a few blocks, then turned onto a narrow side street that led generally in the direction of the river. He was in too much of a rage to notice just where he was going. All he could think about was grabbing Marcia by the shoulders and shaking her, then throwing her drink in her face to sober her up. She had done it too many times in the last year or so, almost always on subjects like this one.

The rain stung like shot against his back and the back of his neck and that was what finally slowed him up. Gradually he began to walk at an easier pace and to think a little more clearly. He came to a little grocery store with a light in the window. Somebody had forgotten to put up the awning and he stopped under it for a moment as the rain came down in a blast of wind.

He was staring into the window at a huge glass jar full of brown beads. Then he realized they weren't beads, but coffee beans, because there were pyramids of cans labeled "Cafe Latino Coffee" on either side. Down below he noticed a sign, hand-lettered with some pains and reading, "Guess how many beans in the jar and win ten pounds of this good-tasting coffee. Entry blanks inside." The last line said, "This is a riddle." The wind died down and he began to walk again.

"A riddle," he thought. "This is a riddle." Something round, hard, bright, oblong, soft, dull-colored; received in great amounts without effort, won in little amounts with labor and pain; blamed wrongly for great crimes, but not in itself guilty; guilty on the other hand of a million small treasons, quarrels, bitterness, small lies, bad discoveries, faults, rejections, pretenses, accusations, disappointments, revelations, deceptions, the ills of man; good for turning into fat, revenge, laziness, vanity, bragging, contempt, unfairness, ineptitude, a little power, especially good for wasting; not very helpful to change yourself for the better, but highly useful for adding to old leaves, making yourself more of what you already are; perishable but immortal; always with you, but you can't take it; found in the ruins of nations whose ideas have all vanished; not the root—we are that—but the flowery branch.

A tiresome, repetitious, platitudinous, obvious, old riddle, he thought. But true.

As he walked on, more deliberately now, down the dark and deserted street, he began to have a feeling of going somewhere. He looked at the street signs and tried to locate himself in relation to the place he had come from, but at first he couldn't. Then he began to notice the houses. They were big, ramshackle old houses, set quite a distance back from the street. It was, in fact, the district that Boyle and Company had decided on for redevelopment, but that couldn't be the reason his feet had led him here. He went on down the street as if he knew it. The rain was lessening, but the wind still worked in the branches of the trees and he got sudden showers now and then.

He began to think about a story his father had told him once about an old friend. This man, he remembered hearing, had lived with his wife for a number of years in France, where he had a clerk's job in a travel agency and earned next to nothing. In the summer the two of them took a week's cut-rate vacation at a Swiss mountain town, where they lived in the smallest and dingiest pension. They always saved their money carefully during the year, but when the trip began, it was always spoiled by the rigid watch they had to keep over every sou. Each suspected the other of wanting to buy something not in the budget. They sat in their room and quarreled sourly for fear that going outside would cost them something.

One summer, just before the first war, they arrived at their pension and the weather turned cold and rainy. The landlady charged them extra for fireplace wood. They decided never to come again. Then, a few days before they had to go back, the warm sun came out and the mountains looked beautiful through the window. They decided, as a special luxury, to take a trip on one of those scenic railways—they had always planned to go, but always recoiled at the cost.

After a little while what did they see floating past them in the air but a five-franc note! They made a grab for it and even laughed when they missed. But soon another one came dipping along and they caught that—money out of the air! They were glad they had come; they felt rich and intoxicated. In a little while, everybody around them was trying to grab the notes as they came along. Successful two or three times, the woman even gave one to a little girl who had missed out. There were quite a few jokes about the eccentric millionaire who must be at the head of the train throwing away money.

All at once the man remembered that his wife's handbag, with the rest of their vacation money, was lying on the seat up ahead. She had forgotten to close it, or it had come open. He turned around in horror to tell her, but she was laughing happily for the first time in years.

A long time ago when he had heard this story, it had seemed too plain to be interesting—people so stingy deserved to lose their money. But now it recurred to him out of the past as a well-drawn illustration for his side of things. He wished he had thought of it earlier in the day.

He looked around him now and could not tell where he was. He was on a street of tall brick houses with ugly two-story bays. Most of the houses were dark and the only sound was the creak and swish of branches moving overhead. The rain had stopped and the moon came out quite suddenly. He thought he would have to find a way to get home; he looked at his watch and saw that it was almost ten and at the same moment he realized that he was very hungry.

He walked on to the corner and looking down the street saw —like a marvel—a pale electric sign reading, "Napoli Grill." As he walked toward it, he thought he recalled some vague coincidence about the words. It seemed to him that he had once eaten in a Napoli Grill before, perhaps when he had come to look at some of the houses in this section. His main hope, though, was that the place would still be open.

As he entered the door, it did indeed look familiar but of course, he thought, there is nothing in the world more familiar than those linoleum floors, counters with catsup bottles, and small scarred plywood booths. He stood dripping in the middle of the floor for a moment.

"You'll catch cold, mister," said a small dark man with a moustache who stood behind the counter. "Hang it up ovva ta radiator." And he looked familiar, too, with his long nose and blunt head like a bear's.

Vanderbilt hung it up and sat down in the first booth. "Paolo!" the man yelled. Paolo came from the back room, a thin old man in an apron with suds on it, holding his hands outstretched in front of him. "Paolo will take your order," said the dark man curtly, as if annoyed that he must give *all* the instructions around here. Vanderbilt said he'd like a large glass of red wine and a plate of spaghetti. "Pasta?" asked Paolo stupidly. "O.K., pasta, then," Vanderbilt said.

The waiter went away and left the place to silence except for the noise of the coat dripping on the radiator. Finally the man behind the counter shifted his weight a little and yelled, "Has Joey called yet?" Vanderbilt looked up, startled.

But evidently there was communication because Paolo's muffled "No, no," came from the kitchen.

The man yelled again, "I expect Joey to call. He shoulda called." It was clearly a hope and a worry. Paolo stuck his head out of the kitchen and said, "No, not yet."

The place was silent again. Then Paolo came back with a big tumbler of red wine. He smiled apologetically at Vanderbilt, wiped his lips, and said, "Pasta in a minute. *Subito*." Then he went to sit on a low stool at the far end of the counter near the kitchen door.

The telephone rang. The dark man did not move or smile. In this place the owner did not hear bells ring, Vanderbilt decided. He was properly informed that a bell had rung.

Paolo came to his feet and got around the counter; he seemed to be happening rather than walking across the floor. He was very slow and the telephone rang twice more while he was at it, but all this time the owner moved only his moustache in a small, nervous, up-and-down motion.

Paolo grasped the receiver and peered into the phone. "Hello?" he said, looking. "Joey! Joey! Hello, boy." He turned around and said, "It's Joey."

"Is it?" said the owner and gave a broad smile. He came out from behind the counter and almost ran to where Paolo was holding the receiver out to him at the full length of the cord.

"Joey!" he shouted into the phone. "It's Papa. Can you hear me, Joey? I can hear you fine. What have you been doing? How's everything? When you coming home?"

As he listened, his white teeth appeared under his black moustache; he nodded his head; he cast up his eyes. "Joey, it's good to hear your voice. What are you doing up there? You get a job?"

He listened again intently, then he laughed and slapped Paolo on the back, bending his knees and shaking his head at something almost incredibly humorous. He straightened up and stretched out his neck toward the telephone on the wall. "Listen, Joey, you got a job yet?" he said fiercely.

His face began to grow serious as he listened longer; finally all his upper face was pulled together in a frown. He raised his eyes to the ceiling, then he frowned again. He began to crowd the telephone. Finally he shook his head violently. He grabbed the mouthpiece with one hand and put his face directly up to it. "No, no, no, no," he said, waited a minute, then "*No!*" He yelled into the phone, "No more money. *No more money, Joey.*"

Vanderbilt was looking through the plate-glass window into the dark and he saw Joey. Joey was sitting hunched in a pay phone booth with a cigarette-littered floor. Vanderbilt could see by the dim overhead light the change—dimes and nickels spread out on the small metal shelf in case the old man proved stubborn—and the boy's dark head—a junior bear's head—the anxious face close to the black mouthpiece, could see the slight shine of perspiration on the boy's temples, could hear the short quick breathing.

"*Stupido,*" said his father. "What did I tell you last time, *Babbione?* Can't you understand nothing?" His whole face sank with a dramatic look of disgust. He shook his head and stooped, as if his flesh had suddenly become too heavy for him. He dropped the receiver from a lax hand and let it swing to the wall, where it bumped hard once, then gently three or four times. He waved aimlessly with an upturned hand and walked back into the kitchen.

Vanderbilt finished his wine while he waited for him to

come back. He heard a few creaks from the pendulous receiver, but still the man did not return. Vanderbilt began to feel nervous. It may have been the wine, which was warming him, or it may have been something else, but he decided that he ought to act somehow. Somebody ought to say goodbye, at least.

He walked slowly over to the telephone and picked up the receiver and for a moment he didn't know what to say. Then he said, "Listen, Joey, this is a friend of your father's talking. What's the trouble?"

Paolo came into the room with a plate of spaghetti and stood stock still in the doorway.

"Who's that? Where did my Dad go?" It was a very young voice.

"It's all right. Maybe I can help you. What's the story, Joey?"

"I got trouble, that's all. I need money. I gotta have money for rent and clothes, that's all."

Paolo shrugged his shoulders and put the spaghetti down on the counter.

"I'm going to hang up if you won't tell me the truth."

"Hey, wait a minute. Just a minute." Vanderbilt waited. "Don't tell him this for Chrissake. It'd tear him apart. But I got a girl knocked up over here. I figure we need about a hundred fifty to fix things up, the doctor who'll do it and all. Maybe two hundred's better. Don't tell him what it is. Tell him something in a kinda general way, you know. Tell him it's very important."

Vanderbilt thought for a little while. "What if you got more than that? What if I fixed it up to send, say, about seven hundred to you? Would that change the situation any?" Paolo looked startled, then suspicious and began to edge toward the kitchen door.

"Who the hell *is* this? Man, you're crazy. I couldn't pay no seven hundred back."

"That doesn't matter. Don't worry about that. Would you marry her?" Vanderbilt waited tensely, staring at the wall.

"Oh, Christ, I couldn't. She's a nice kid and I'm a son of a bitch." It was a lonesome wail of self-truth. It was a sound Vanderbilt had been listening for for a long time. He smiled with gratitude and relief.

"Okay, Joey, that's right. You're honest. But I won't give you the money for an abortion."

"Hey, wait a minute," said the boy's voice. "I got an idea. Seven hundred would fix it up wonderful. There's a guy would marry her if he had that for a backstop. He don't care about the other thing; he still goes to see her. A good steady guy like Bonfiglio would treat her right." He slowed down. "Hey, who'm I talking to, anyway?" He stopped for a moment. "Ah, crap, I don't want your money. I can get it somehow."

"Joey, my name is Vanderbilt. You've heard that name? Vanderbilt. I've got money. I'm an old friend of your father's and I've just been doing some business with him—buying something."

"Yes, Mr. Vanderbilt," Joey said.

"Now listen, I have a check here for seven hundred dollars. I'm going to endorse it over to your father. I want you to guarantee that you're going to do what you say you'll do with it. In a minute I'm going to call him back to the phone."

"Holy Christ," said the boy. "Thanks, Mr. Vanderbilt."

LEGEND OF THE
TWO SWIMMERS

EVERYONE must have a worthless uncle; it is a part of life.

At ten I knew all there was to know about remittance men and black-sheep younger sons shipped off to Australia. It seemed significant that no one in the family ever mentioned such a thing and I was certain that, if I watched carefully enough, one morning I would find a letter dropped through the slot onto the faded blue of the hall carpet, addressed in an unfamiliar hand and carrying a foreign postmark.

I was certain then that I would discern a strained look on my grandmother's face, or a trace of tears. My father would upset his coffee cup at the table and shout for no reason. I had begun to read the indecent language of signs, a child's first corruption.

There would be tense consultations behind closed doors. One day I would come across a picture in an album, the face cut out, or a silk hat in the attic, marked with unknown initials.

The months passed and letters with a foreign postmark

came—but only from a friend of my father's vacationing in England. I never found the picture in the album nor the silk hat in the attic. The front door never opened to the sudden sight of a tall man in dark clothes with a wicked familiar-unfamiliar face. By the end of that year I had finished the shelf of old paperback novels in the basement and had begun to forget all about that uncle.

In dull truth I did have an uncle—he lived only four blocks away and owned half interest in a small, failing dry-goods store in a bad neighborhood. Under the shadeless bulbs hanging from the tin ceiling, he fussed around among the counters piled with Big Yank and Oshkosh B'Gosh boys' corduroy knickers, caps stuffed with tissue paper— marked down from $1.98—and canvas gloves. The air in that place was a weight on the lungs, loaded with the smell of cheap new cloth. The shadows in the rear hid only bare-ness and a roll-top desk, for everything Mr. Rood and my uncle had in stock was piled on the front counters. "Come in out of the rain, boy," Uncle would say as I stood reluc-tantly in the doorway on my way home from school on a Friday afternoon.

My mother was dead three years; my father was, most likely, on one of his business trips; and Mrs. Fahey, my grand-mother's iron nurse, had said at least three times this morn-ing, "I won't have them kids underfoot around the house this week-end." My grandmother ruled, but Mrs. Fahey made the common law in the house.

It was not so much that I would be bored and lonely. As I opened the door to the jangle of the brass bell above it, I knew that I entered the world of worn linoleum on kitchen floors, sooty front porches, smells of cabbage cooking, back

yards full of washing, darned socks, pinched pennies, over-
due rent, angry protests and angry silences—the gravelly
downhill slide of the poor.

In my grandmother's house I felt rich and good. In the
cold persistent mist of my aunt and uncle's company, I felt
sad and pauperized. I had begun to divide things clearly not
so much between good and evil, but between good and bad.

A year or two ago I would have gone along willingly
enough, squabbled with the Polish neighbor's two boys, con-
tentedly mooned over an old picture book in the living room
while the clock hands slowly drifted towards Sunday night.
Going there now seemed like the act of becoming my uncle's
son. What was it like to be dumpy, ineffective, getting bald,
needing money? I knew. I felt it already in myself.

My mother had lain complaining and bedridden in the
little house on Jefferson Street for over two years. When she
was gone, my sister and I cried at the funeral, but it was
more of an exorcism than a death. We moved in with my
grandmother—with her temper and her money. My father
seemed to work longer and was away more often. We seldom
saw him and when we did it was like too much candy all at
once. "He is becoming a very successful man," my grandmother told us. "Like your grandfather. You should be proud
of him." We sensed a secret reproach to my mother and our
fading loyalty stiffened for a moment. But Mother had always
been a reproach to *us*—she suffered so much and we were
so selfish. It was often brought home to us how selfish we
were. Her painful smile had seemed to live in the room long
after she disappeared.

My grandmother was the colonel of the family; she assumed we had a regimental duty to live up to, not unpayable

debts of tears. She was the drillmaster of our ideas; our silly feelings she conceded us and left alone. One Sunday a few months after we had come to live in her house, she made my father take me to the "upstairs parlor" to explain, in a way, what she meant.

It was by far the pleasantest room in the house and, though dusted daily, almost never used. Long windows the whole length of the north wall made it a reservoir of sunlight. Beneath them were oblong wicker baskets of ferns, a tame jungle two feet high. To the left of the hearth was the glass showcase with all its trophies.

On its shelves silver divers poised gracefully for the double jackknife that would never follow. Crossed oars that would never touch the water lay on polished plaques; medals of different shapes and sizes glinted at my eyes out of silk-lined boxes. Obscurer mementos filled the lower shelf—a copper pocket-piece, a pipe and pouch, seashells, a leather-bound picture album, a framed sketch of gulls, a box with a silver dolphin on the lid. To me it was an undistinguished hoard. On the center shelf there was a black silk object of some kind, lying there like a small discolored puddle.

Abruptly my father said, "Over here. Come look at them." The spirits of the room, the two champions life-sized and piratical, posed above the fireplace.

Their bare arms were folded on their chests, like great oars momentarily shipped. There was an impressive curve of chest muscle under the short-sleeved swimming jerseys. Their heads were tipped back at the same slightly scornful angle and their black eyes, even through the dull filter of time and the lens, showed total confidence, like a lost trait of man, the sense of absolute monarchy. It persisted for a few moments.

Then, like one of those trick geometrical drawings that will change before the eye, the picture would change and you saw only two young men in striped swimming suits staring dourly.

They had identical moustaches like startling pairs of wings, thick eyebrows, my grandmother's heavy cheekbones and her Welsh head; they were, I heard, her dead brothers, Owen and Lloyd.

My father shuffled reverently through the pile of picture postcards from the table drawer. Tebb's Beach, Florida, 1902. A million dollars has changed the name and the landscape since then. A ramshackle boarding house-hotel on a fine beach, backed by scrub jungle. A *splendid place*, my father said, quoting, *a mite lonesome. Just fishermen and a few boarders. Wonderful sunshine.*

Yesterday we saw an Indian ninety-eight years old. Still smokes seven cigars a day—he fought in the Seminole war and they left him for dead in the swamp. Big pink shells here, most beautiful you ever saw. We gathered some, are sending a basketful. Is it snowing in Michigan? We hear there is ice and snow. Sometimes we go out with the fishermen. Owen is getting wonderfully good at the Trudgen stroke. Yesterday we swam for three hours. We had our picture made and we shall send it to you. Give our love to Nettie and Mama.

There wasn't much more to the story, just a glimpse in a letter of the two sunburnt young men on the beach one morning, taking off shoes and robes and preparing to go into the water. Owen, who was the younger, must have tired after a while, it said, and came in to sit on the beach. Someone saw him there for a moment, wringing out the little black silk skullcap he always wore while swimming. Evidently

Lloyd stayed out in the water and evidently after a little while Owen looked up to see a shark-blade cutting near him and then his brother must have been gone.

Owen must not have waited, my father said. When the man from the hotel happened along the beach a half hour or so later, the beach was empty and the sea was empty too. Owen must not have hesitated for a moment.

That was not quite the end, he said, because they found the skullcap. It was lying in the sand in the afternoon sun, quite dry by this time.

My father said I was always to remember how Owen had never paused or waited. It may not seem like anything very much to you at your age because you are so young. And it may sound very simple, but it isn't at all simple and you should think about what I'm telling you. There will be times when you yourself will be called just as Uncle Owen was and then you must remember him. When you are older you will understand.

In his voice there was a terrible undertow of pride and I felt it dragging me down. I tried to think of just what it was that had happened and I thought that two young men had gone swimming in the ocean twenty-five years ago and had disappeared. My father stood in the sunlight in his gray suit and tried to tell me about sharks and oceans in a place where he had never been. But I could hear the urgency in his voice and I felt that he was really talking about something that had to be paid back, a strange debt not of money which would keep us poor all of our lives.

"Do you understand?" he demanded, unsatisfied.

I felt shameful and small because, try as I would, I could think of no answer. What kept coming into my head was a warning sign that said, "Watch out for sharks!" and finally I just hung my head and lied, "Yes."

As time went on I began to understand, or thought I did, and I strove to make up for my failure by covering the swimmers in imagination with doubled glory. I would spend hours in the room, lying on the windowseat in the sun reading or idly examining the souvenirs.

"Come in out of the rain, boy," my live uncle said again and I stopped in the doorway. It was not raining. The late afternoon sun, half-tangled in long rags of clouds, shone momentarily down on the street. With his poor joke dropping from his lips, my uncle stood in the middle of his shop and life gathered dust around him.

One day he had confessed why he made jokes like this. "I found out in the army I wasn't strong enough to fight and I was too fat to run, so I took up telling jokes." It was the truth; I had never heard a grown man say anything so spineless. When he was nineteen, he said, he ran away and joined the army. First they taught him to take care of horses and then they taught him to cook. The World War was just one pan of hash after the other. He came home, borrowed money from my grandmother, lost it, borrowed again to go halves in the shop, was losing it again.

Grandmother's soldierly kindness was qualified by her high blood pressure and occasional tempers that glowed and smoked like a coal fire and sent off poisonous fumes. There were times when she could not bear the thought of children in her house; her own had betrayed her so. Annette, her daughter, a beautiful girl by family standards, had turned traitor at the age of nine and died. My father's older brother Will, a pale figure not easily recalled, had got himself killed at Belleau Wood. My Uncle Clinton turned money into dry goods and dry goods into debts, and there it was. My father, who was at least getting somewhere, went completely out of her mind. On those days my sister had to stay in her room and not make any noise and I was sent off to my uncle with $1.75 for board.

I played with the Wisnewski boys down the street until we fought bitterly. Thereafter I moped around the house. My aunt urged me to read the Bible and my uncle took me for walks in the woods. We walked along the river road, which began on the other side of the railway tracks, and he showed me how to make a willow whistle. I said, "What good's a willow whistle? That's for little kids." He told me some army stories and I took interest; then I was bored. They had no gunpowder in them. They were all about what the first sergeant said to the chief cook about the stew. He liked to potter around the woods, with a city man's interest in birds' eggs that had fallen out of trees and the sight of a rabbit. He had a noisy little dog named Butch who sometimes went with us.

The one thing I liked to do was to go fishing with him and during the summer, when I was pawned off on Aunt and Uncle for weeks at a time, we would often go out for an afternoon on the river. We used bamboo poles and angleworms for bait. He dropped things in the water, rocked the boat, then went to sleep while his line slowly wound around an oar. Still he had marvelous luck. He caught many fish— mostly bullheads and catfish that had to be thrown back again.

I liked those somnolent afternoons when I had nothing at all to live up to. I could see French cliffs rise up on the far side of the river as I lay with my arms over the gunwale. I thought we drifted past the estuary of the Tagus and there was Africa on the horizon. I dozed and saw a blue sea with a black fin splitting the water a long way out and came to myself with a shock, asking myself if I wouldn't hesitate, wouldn't wait a minute until it was too late.

The trouble was, I felt, that this very instant was traveling in me like an air bubble in a vein and I could never foretell the moment it would reach the heart. When my father had talked to me, for the first time in my life I had doubted him and thus had doubted myself. I wondered if when Owen was a boy my great-grandfather had told him one day he would see a fin in the water and that he mustn't hesitate or wait even a second. I tried to imagine him telling Owen that. Boys die young and become their fathers.

I looked at my uncle, asleep on the back seat of the row-boat, his face sagging peacefully under his sagging hat. I wondered if he had ever heard the story, or if it meant anything to him.

Then one day I brought the subject up. He fixed the angle-worm carefully on the hook and yawned. "Mother never did get over the death of those two darn fools," he said.

"Fools?" I said, shocked. "They were as brave as anybody can be and Owen went to save . . ."

"I know, I know," he said. "That's the way people talked. I say it was lack of good sense. Hadn't got brains enough to stay on dry land or a boat at least. Then go swimming around in shark waters. One got himself eat up, then the other one got himself eat up, too. Darn fools, I say."

At first I was too angry to speak, then when I looked again I saw it was only sluggish Uncle Clint bending over his bait pail and I realized it wasn't even necessary to forgive him.

When the cold water in the bottom of the boat would reach his foot, he would wake up. "Bail for dear life, men," he would say, "the ship is going down." The boat was an old one, paintless and splintery. He had found it one day half submerged in some rocky shallows down the river. He had dragged it ashore, nailed tin strips over the most obvious holes, caulked it, had given the bottom a coat of tar. He loved it in the same way he loved my aunt, who sustained him on the muddy waters of day to day, but who might sometime disappear and leave him to drown.

He was very much afraid of deep water. It must have been the earliest thing that set him apart from the rest of the family, of which Owen and Lloyd had been natural products. Almost all of the men had been skillful swimmers. My father, who never let me have such a dangerous thing as a bicycle, would point out the deepest part of the lake and dare me to swim to it. When I told my uncle about the swimming lessons I was taking from a professional, he pinched his nose and cast his eyes up, as if he were sinking hopelessly among the fish.

Our slow leak he regarded as a monster of the deep. Sometimes he would give up an hour's fishing and drifting because of an extra inch in the bottom of the boat.

"I couldn't be expected to save you," he would say, rowing for the shore.

"*I* can swim pretty well," I would say defiantly. The phlegmatic old Grand River seemed safe as a sidewalk—safer.

He had no very good place to tie the boat and so we just

pulled it up on a sandy strip where he had put down a stake with a chain. Then we took our basket and our poles and started back along the river road.

The most agreeable spot in the world, I thought, with woods on one hand and an outpost line of huge trees along the waterside, a great green arcade in summer, it had been claimed by squatters and their shacks. Once it was fashionable to have a boat and a cottage down here, but now people went north or west to the lakes. Bristly mongrel dogs stood by the doors of mimic chalets with sinking roofs and crumbling lines of gingerbread. Four—five—six children's faces were piled in a pyramid inside a window. A man in a ragged leather jacket refused to answer hello, just took another swing with his axe. Some of the places were recently built huts, actually projecting over the riverside slope and supported there by a crazywork of long poles. Underneath them, like the droppings of a tethered animal, were tin cans, newspapers, ash piles, old tires, broken bottles.

Darkness dropped out of the air; it had already dimmed the city by the time we reached our street. My uncle hummed a tune. I walked pigeon-toed and lagged behind, nursing a wish like a bruise. A hundred seventeen steps from the corner, ten steps down the walk, four steps up to the porch; he reached for the knob.

I hung back, kicking the risers. The thought of that house with its long bare hours between bed and bed stunned me. In the hall, my uncle gave a three-note whistle and Butch came running. "Angel, we're home!" he shouted.

At dinner—fried mush and boiled cabbage were nearly inevitable—he talked about our afternoon as if remembering the striking events of history—"Just then a grand trout jumped in the air about fifteen feet away from us. Oh, it was a thrilling moment." He discussed manners and morals —"Six kids, a hound dog and an old car. No curtains on the windows, no running water but the river and still enough money to buy gas for an old car . . ."

Mute and unimpressed, Aunt finished her food and poured the coffee. When he had drunk his cup dry, my uncle began to rise, but it was only a poor habitual try. My aunt raised her eyes and stared at him. Saturday night meant prayers and bath for all good Christians. We bowed our heads.

"Forgive us for what we have left undone . . . guide our steps in the right pathways . . . make us better and stronger to withstand temptation in the week to come . . ." As she worked into the substance of her appeal, she became more fervent, more obscure, more biting. She referred obliquely to those who, though not unblessed by the hand of the Lord and having plenty of the goods of this earth—though how they expected to get through the eye of the needle she wouldn't presume to say—refused to help others needier than themselves and acted as if water was just as thick as blood. She worked around to those who sometimes through pure chuckle-headedness neglected to do certain unspecified things they ought to do while their nearest and dearest suffered as a result. My uncle dozed.

Ordinarily she did not scold or complain but went silently on with her work, her mouth like a seam; she was a different woman when she prayed. I listened and was scared at her tone. It came from a hollow distance. Even though its mixture of sarcasm, anger, bitterness, and sorrow confused me, I could recognize it. It was low and muffled through the thickness of many walls, but it came unmistakably from the torture chamber itself.

When she was silent again, Uncle raised his head, yawned, and said, "That was fine, Angel." He went into the living room and she began gathering up the plates.

That summer, the summer of which I am speaking, approached. My sister in a white dress played in the piano recital in the school auditorium and all remarked that she didn't make one mistake. I practiced my curve at the playground and pinned a picture of Lefty Grove over my dresser. My father went to Kansas City on business. My grandmother began to feel the heat approaching and predicted it would be the worst summer on record. School let out. I was banished to my uncle's. Uncle came home at night, slumped, and my aunt put a dishpan full of cool water next to his chair for him to soak his feet. He stared at the water and said, "We can't do it, Angel. It's no use." A man came to see him in the evening and they sat out on the porch for a long time. When I was in bed, I could hear their voices rise occasionally above the ziz-ziz-ziz of the tree toads and I heard my uncle ask, "Foreclosure?"

The summer clouds piled high over the river like marble monuments. I tried my crawl stroke in the river (this was forbidden) and watched the grainy water slide over my arms. On the bank one of the river kids, a solemn child in a patched dress, stood and stared.

My uncle hadn't the heart to go fishing much. Aunt's Saturday-night prayers increased in violence and developed in mystery. June turned into July. The lawns burned brown and crisp like shredded breakfast food. My friends were away at camps or cottages and I no longer wanted to go down to the river alone. From the swing on my uncle's porch I watched the clouds transform themselves and move away. I longed for fall, school, a disaster, anything.

In the course of time, it became Sunday morning of the first week in August. My father was home again, my grandmother was in a fit of well-being, and my exile was over. I was to go back to the other house the same day. Belly down, among the comic strips, I lay in squalid comfort on the worn rug. There was, thank God, no Sunday school in summer. My uncle lolled in his plump chair and surveyed the world as it came, printed, before his eyes. He muttered comments on it. The clock struck nine, shortly ten.

Aunt came home from church with a queer look. We heard her feet on the porch and then she came into the room and stood looking at us. "I'm going to see Mrs. Banning this afternoon," she finally said, but it wasn't what she was thinking.

Slowly she began to pull off one of her gloves, staring in apparent pain at her hand, exactly as if she were in the process of stripping the whole skin from it.

"You must ask today," she said in the voice of her prayers.

Uncle was alarmed. He looked up at her with a deserter's look. His glance roved to the window; he tried to raise the newspaper in front of his face again, but the inexorable skinning stopped him.

The glove came off at last with a final little snap and he jumped—it was as if we had all expected to see white bone. He said hurriedly, "I'll try. Yes, today's the day and I certainly will consider going to ask. They can't refuse me, can they, Angel?" He sighed. The newspaper began to cut him off again. Aunt stood quietly and began on the left hand. For some long-drawn minutes we could hear the same soft stripping sound. Only her fingers worked.

At last my uncle jumped out of his chair and yelled, "Stop!" He was breathing heavily and his thready hair was flying. He yelled, "Don't get so excited!" and rushed upstairs where we could hear him crashing his dresser drawers. He reappeared in a coat and tie and hooked his straw hat off the hall rack as he hit the bottom of the stairs. "Come on, son," he said, grabbing my arm and pulling me protesting to the door. As we went stumbling down the steps, I looked back and saw my aunt sitting in a chair with wet eyes and her hands buried in her dress. She looked beaten.

On the way over we marched and did not speak. When we came into the cool living room, I saw my father and shouted, "Dad!" In a cold voice he said, "Go upstairs and play. We've got business." Then I noticed my grandmother, Mr. Rood, and a stranger in a dark suit. The men were sitting in the shadow on the far side of the room while my grandmother, all by herself, garrisoned the nearer end. Her hand opened and closed on a little ivory stick.

I resented it, but my only choice was to go through the glass doors into the parlor—a room overfurnished with a stupefying taste. I went upstairs, wandered in and out of rooms and finally found myself in the swimmers' room. I stood before the fireplace looking up at them. Nothing had changed. "Play the game! Keep the faith! Grasp the nettle!" they said silently. It was all very easy, all very well, I thought. It was in their bones and muscles. It was only in my head. I was frightened. Then I thought—times change. For all I knew sharks were killed by some kind of machine nowadays. It didn't help. I stood in despair for a long time.

When I heard a clock striking in the hall, I finally went slowly downstairs. I crept through the parlor, up to the glass doors and looked in. They were still talking. My father stood in front of the fireplace, his arms half extended in his usual gesture of irritation. My grandmother's face had petrified—the horrible calm before she opened her mouth. She must have said something to Mr. Rood already because he sat heaped in his chair like a pile of worn-out clothes. Only the stranger seemed detached. With one eye in a squint, he calmly looked across the room at a china figurine of a camel perched on the whatnot. He looked as if he might be ready to take a shot at it.

My uncle looked as if he had been boiled. His face was red and puffed with his eyes bubbled, his mouth sunken. On the other side of the glass, my grandmother was saying, "Last time was really the last time, Clinton; you know it."

"Mother, just think what you're saying," Uncle pled.

"We have thought," said my father harshly. "We have thought and we can't do it." I saw him turn his back.

And he was right to do so because my uncle was crying. In his horrible little fat-man way he was crying and tears ran down his cheeks. It was unbearable for me and I had to go into the room to distract their attention, even though it might make my grandmother angry. I had to stop the beating. But I would never be seen with my uncle again. I would run away and get a job as a cabin boy on a ship.

"Well," said my father pleasantly, "you're back. Now why don't you go for a walk with your Uncle Clint? He hasn't been feeling well, you see. He'll bring you back in time for dinner." It was the last thing I had expected.

"I won't go with him," I said.

My father came over and took me by the shoulder with a strong hand. "You will go," he said abruptly. "We've had enough trouble for one day." He did not say this as if it were meant for me, but to all in general. As we were going out, I heard him say to my uncle in a confidential tone, "Don't worry, Clint. I'll do the best I can." I couldn't understand what was happening.

When we were outside, Uncle stood on the walk and looked back at the front windows of the house while words seemed to thaw in his throat. "So that's the way the land lies, hm? So that's it? For your own good, they say. Well, if you ask me . . ." I didn't know what to expect. I stood and listened to him mutter.

He looked down at me and said, "You got some better place to go?"

I shook my head. He looked queer and choked and we walked along with very slow steps.

Finally he laughed and said, "Let's go down by the river. Yes, the river's the place for me today." He suddenly started to stride and I had to half run to keep up with him.

The streets were quiet; in the heat of Sunday afternoon the houses dozed behind their screens of trees. We crossed the railroad tracks and finally got to the river road, which was cool and deserted. The sun through the leaves made yellow sketches and signatures in the dust of it. My uncle looked anxiously around and I felt his desperation. He broke off a willow twig and made a few random slashes at it with his knife, looked at me, dropped it.

We walked some more. Abruptly he said, "Do you want to take the boat out on the river?"

I nodded. He said in the same voice, "It may be the last time."

"Why is it the last time?" I said. "Why the last time, Uncle Clint?" but he didn't answer. We turned around the bend in the road by the big willow and started down the little track that led to our mooring place.

When we had gone about twenty yards, we began to hear a woman's voice in shrill ups and downs beyond the bushes. We could not hear what she was saying. I ran ahead to see what it was. In a minute I burst through the bushes and saw her. She was calmly sitting on the middle thwart of *our* boat.

Worse than that, she was holding an oar and awkwardly trying to pole the boat away from shore while a girl about my age, but small, like a skinny monkey, had just finished untying the rope. My uncle gasped behind me. "Robbers!" I said. "Look, Uncle Clint."

The woman turned quickly; she had long rusty hair and a rusty face with chipped features—like notches in an axe blade. She was wearing some plaid thing that looked as if it had been torn off a table and hastily stitched around her. The girl swiftly hopped around, twisted over the side into the boat, crouched behind the gunwale and gave us a look out of the same face, though younger, more furtive, and even more ignorant.

My uncle stood gaping as his ship was stolen. I could have counted ten. I yelled, "That's our boat. Come back here, you." I knew I would have to do it myself. I jumped for the trailing rope at the bow. He came along behind me with undecided steps.

As I reached, I saw something happening. Slowly, out of six inches of mushy bottom, out of the shallow water, high into the air in a great trailing slimy arc, the oar was rising. The wide-eyed woman seemed to be clinging to it rather than propelling it. I scrambled sidewise as fast as I could.

Such ponderous soggy haymakers are too futile to hit anything in this world—except Uncle, who was fated. He had come up behind me; I said, "Duck," but as always, he did not fail to fail.

The end of the oar smacked him squarely on the chin, filled the air with a great burst of slime, pitched him backward three feet into a clump of rushes, and buried itself with a spout in the river bottom again. He put his hand up experimentally to his eyes.

I was scrabbling for a stone; "A fast one low and inside, just like Lefty's," I prayed as it left my hand. Not very fast, low and outside, it merely hit a tin plate we'd nailed over a leak in the side of the boat. It hit with a loud *clack!*

They were out in the stream already gathering a sluggish momentum from the current. My uncle said feebly, "That's enough. Stop." Reluctantly I gave up the idea of clearing the decks with my high hard one, and went over to him. It occurred to me then that he was probably badly wounded.

He groaned and got to his knees, while I splashed some water over his face, which ran in red and black ribbons down his white shirt front. "Oh God," he said. "Is my nose still there?" It was. "Count my eyes," he directed.

"You've only got some blood on your chin," I said. "The rest is just mud. Open your mouth. You've got one, no, I think two front teeth out." He groaned again. I put my hands under his arm and tried to help him as he got to his feet. "You're all right," I said anxiously. "It's only one or two teeth."

"One," he said grimly, and spat it out.

While he was splashing some more water on his face, I recovered the oar and hid it in the bushes. I was already beginning to think about pursuit, recovery, revenge. They couldn't get far with one oar. If we worked carefully along the shore—but just beyond us the trees came right down to the river and it was beyond them that the boat had now disappeared. Uncle responded to my schemes with a weak "Ehh, uh," and attended to his face. He was holding his jaw and his lower lip had begun to rise into a purplish sausage.

He followed me aimlessly as I made a way through the bushes. Over my shoulder, I kept saying things to make him come on—"If you'd only pulled back just half a foot . . . they can't row, they can't get far . . ." He didn't answer.

We went on for about twenty or thirty minutes and it seemed hopeless. There was nobody in the woods and the river was empty; the bushes tore at my trouser legs. At last I knew that we had lost them. Uncle came up alongside me, nursing his hurt mouth in his handkerchief. "I'm going home and put some ice on this. We'll have to give up." He said it almost pleadingly.

"But the boat," I said. "We'll never get it back again, you know that." I was perfectly detached and not selfish. I had just decided that I was through with him and the boat and the river forever, but I was trying to save something abstract. I could not see him ruined completely in one short day. I could not stand to think of him sitting at the table tonight while my aunt was praying and he thought, The boat is gone for good. He shook his head feebly at me and I knew I had lost.

So we trudged back up to the road again while I thought bitterly of running ahead and leaving him alone. Just as I was deciding, we came opposite the place where the old pilings from a former landing dock stuck up in the river. I heard a yell and a sound of splashing. I knew and I began to run.

I cut through the bushes quickly and got down to the river bank again. When I got there, I saw what I knew I was going to see—it was the unexpectedness of the completely expected. Out from the shore about fifteen feet was our boat with the rusty woman and the girl in it. They had evidently hit against one of the stumps and, as Uncle had always predicted, the boat was at last stubbornly sinking.

She was thrashing around frantically in her wet tablecloth, trying to scoop water over the side, trying to push with the remaining oar, slapping at the girl, screaming directions. When she saw me, she wailed, "We can't swim!" Then she yelled, "Your damn boat's full of leaks."

I was so winded I could only stand and watch with a feeling that this contemptible day had finally justified itself. I *had* wanted something terrible to happen. Everybody who involved himself with Uncle, even to steal from him, was going to suffer. I was getting out.

The boat lurched; the woman screamed again; Uncle arrived, running like a car on two cylinders.

He didn't ask anything, but pushed by me to see better. The next thing I saw was his clumsy lunge into the river, knees pumping, heels skidding on the slippery mud; then brown sprays of water shooting up over his pants legs. His mind had gone—I knew it, but what could I do?

"Come back! Come back! Where're you going?" I said, but

he sloshed on with surprising speed. He caught the nearest black pier stump in the crook of his arm and grabbed for the next one further out; he was doing a comic swim, half out of the water. He sank to the level of his belt, then to his shoulders and the water bounced furiously around him. Then all at once I was thoroughly frightened—because he was not frightened. "Come back!" I yelled frantically. "Uncle, *you can't swim.*"

He had his arm hooked around the last old piling and he was reaching out to grab the gunwale of the boat. It lurched just then and he caught it; he managed to drag it towards him a few inches. His chin dipped under water and he let go of the boat as he reared his head backwards. I saw his eyes open, white and wide, and I knew that I was wrong. He was strangling with fear.

I started forward alarmed, but at the same moment Uncle had succeeded in grasping the woman's wrist in one hand and pulling her toward him. She was holding the girl in one arm and Uncle inched them over the side of the boat as they weakly fought against each other and him. They hung for a moment on the slanting gunwale, then disappeared together in a great spew of water and plaid cloth.

But in a moment his head emerged, an uncertain island around which they wrapped their arms. But underneath the panicky mess of grasping hands, wet hair, muddy faces, and cloth, a slow dogged engine was bringing them in to shore.

There was a slopping sound from behind them and I looked up. The boat gave a last pitch in the lazy current, slid sideways, and vanished.

And here my uncle, too, vanishes from my recollections. He had ceased to take any place in my memory the moment he stepped on shore, as if my mind has let him sink at the exact moment of his success. I do not remember if he was triumphant or cast down. We must have walked home together, but I cannot remember it and we must have said something or other about what had happened, but nothing remains.

Nothing remains of him except a few hearsay memories— I walked by his shop some weeks later and saw the windows plastered with signs advertising a sale. A fat man with curly black hair stood in the doorway cleaning out his ear with his little finger. My father did speak of his brother Clint sometimes and, I believe, sent him money after he had moved away.

That is all, or would have been all if it had not been for my father, who never lost his taste for moral fancies and noble illustrations.

Years later, in October, 1943, to be exact, I was a member of a regiment specially trained for amphibious operations. We were waiting at an east coast port of embarkation. The bleak barracks town lay under a gray sky and the days went by in a routine of preparation, apprehension and boredom.

There was nothing to do except line up for inoculations, play cards, check your equipment over again, lie on your bunk for hours tracing the water stains on the beaverboard ceiling. The water stains on those ceilings are remarkable because many of them look like drawings of ships going down, men struggling in the water, or figures suddenly disemboweled. All of the worst deaths known to the world are painted there.

On the Saturday before we were to leave, our last mail

arrived, forwarded from our former camp. All I had was a letter from my father and a small package.

The letter began with his usual cheerful sententiousness. On the second page, it went on to say ". . . now I am sending you a memento of your uncle, who, as you remember, was a most courageous man. You might wish to have it with you both as a kind of family souvenir and as a reminder of someone who . . ." I stopped reading and the day came back.

I saw vividly the brown sluggish waters of the river with my uncle's terrified face bucking up and down in them, just as he reached for the gunwale of the foundering rowboat, the ridiculous sputtering, swollen face that against all the probabilities of nature was going forward.

But as far as I knew, my father had never known much of anything about this, or, if he had known, would have dismissed it. It seemed impossible that he could have found anything he could call a "memento." I knew that I now had the only memento of that day. I spent some time recalling it.

At last I opened the package he had sent. In it there lay a small half circle of faded black silk. I took it out and handled it and for a long time I sat turning it over in my fingers, unable to connect it with anything. It was only after some minutes that I recognized it as a small, faded silk skullcap, of course.

THE CHEVIGNY MAN

"THE last of the Renaissance men," said Paul Teeling, tipping the bottle uncertainly at the jigger as if trying to salt the tail of some elusive bird. "Poet, art critic, novelist, playwright, traveler, officer—he was in the British navy during the war, you know—editor and a dozen other things. Veritably an *uomo universale*." This sounded a little pedantic. "A man of parts. He's had a dozen distinguished careers." That made it better. He now noticed that in his excitement he had given Marian, his wife, a double shot of the good Bourbon and the Dean a single one of the imitation Scotch.

"But will he *live*?" asked Watters from the sofa.

Poor Watters. Paul looked at him and almost smiled. Still sniping from the bushes even after he'd been completely outmaneuvered. Watters' man was Samuel Daniel, who died in 1619—no chance of *his* ever coming to the campus to lecture.

"Not a doubt," said Paul pointedly. "His *Collected Poems* alone make him one of the outstanding figures of the twentieth century." This was cruel, but deserved. Watters blinked behind his spectacles and nervously dipped up a handful of cheese crackers. For the past year or so his greatest apprehension had been that Daniel was fading. He had almost disappeared from PMLA altogether, the Oxford Press man had shown only the mildest interest in Watters' manuscript of the *Life* and a library talk on "Several Themes in the *Civil Wars*," had been saved at the last minute only by the compulsory attendance of Sophomore English classes.

"Do you know Mr. Chevigny?" asked the Dean. "Personally, I mean."

"The crucial question," Paul thought. The question that had galled him so often in the past. He deftly switched the little straw glass holders with their identifying colors between Marian's glass and the Dean's before he answered. "No," he said with just a tinge of smugness. "Not *yet*."

How often he'd seen the look of interest fade. The old lady who approached him after his lecture in Dayton two years ago. The bright students in his modern literature course. The young writer from Chicago who'd called on him. "Do you know . . . personally, I mean?" they'd all asked at various times and, trying to choke back that sense of insufficiency, he'd had to answer, "I must admit . . ." And they had all stared at his apology in the same way: He got it all out of books. The talk ebbing, the questions dying off, people turning away. "Well, nevertheless, it was a very informative discussion." He'd never felt the magic touch, seen the face that appeared so often in the *Times* Sunday book section, couldn't quote a single anecdote that began, "I remember Geoffrey saying to me once, 'Now Paul, I'm astonished at your perception when you say . . .'" Letters to Chevigny had drawn only a brief reply from a secretary.

"Not *yet*," he said again.

"Now aren't we fortunate," Martha Baker, the Dean's wife, said, "to have the greatest authority on Geoffrey Chevigny right here just at the time he decided to make an American lecture tour? I think it's a wonderful coincidence." Martha always babbled on.

"Thank you, Martha," he said with a smile a little broader than genuine and handed her the glass of sherry he had just refilled. "The man and his work have always fascinated me— ever since I discovered one of his plays when I was a junior in college. *The Exiled*—it's about the old age of Prince Charles Stuart. A wealth of material about the Stuart character in it."

"I heard he'll be passed over for the laureateship—that is, when Masefield dies," said Watters rudely.

Didn't the man know when he was demolished? There were so many answers to this that he hardly knew which weapon to choose—or whether it wouldn't be more damning just to keep silent. He wondered if the thought weren't passing through the Dean's mind that a man who had never heard of *The Exiled* and who still thought of the poet laureateship as a great distinction ought not to be teaching English on the college level. Then he suddenly realized that he was mistaken to attribute these fine distinctions of his own to Baker. As a matter of fact, the Dean *did* love Masefield. He remembered hearing him say so.

Confused by the wide range of possibilities, he suddenly realized that they were all coming out in one sentence. "Surely after its history—after Shadwell, Cibber and Austin —you can't take that thing seriously and so Chevigny stands with Milton, Pope, Byron, Yeats . . . he has nothing to do with such faded official honors, or can you imagine the author of *The British Consul* ever *wanting* it and anyway he's quite old, you know, rarely ever stirs from his house in Rome—can you imagine what satire there'd be in Chevigny's 'Ode to the Youngest Princess on the Occasion of Her Ninth Birthday'?" Seeing that he was going wrong, he stopped. They were looking at him in a slightly puzzled way, he thought. He'd meant to be a load of bricks on Watters, but he'd only succeeded in burying himself.

From his seat in the corner Dr. Dunmeade chuckled at him. For years the head of the English Department had practiced and cultivated that sound until now it was rich, rattly and, more than any other sound in the world, fitted the word "chuckle." It sounded like a pair of oversized dice being rattled around in his throat.

"Teeling, my boy," he said. Whenever Dr. Dunmeade called him that, Paul felt confusedly that it had some reference to his disappearing hairline. Dr. Dunmeade still had an ugly black shock on his head. "Teeling, we understand your natural warmth of interest in Chevigny. Admirable. But I don't think Watters meant anything by his remark. After all, it's an academic question, isn't it, with Masefield still hale and hearty?" Dunmeade was a Wordsworth man—therefore unassailable. Paul was often irritated with his absolute neutrality; as a matter of fact, when the Donne man in the department had been nominated for the headship in opposition to the Shelley man, Dunmeade had finally come out as the compromise choice; Wordsworth was felt to be safe and middle-of-the-road.

"No offense meant," Watters said offensively. "How old *is* this Chevigny? He must be up in his eighties, isn't he?"

He didn't die at the beginning of the seventeenth Century—but Paul thought better of saying this.

"He's sixty-nine," said the Dean, "born in 1871." The Dean must have been looking him up in *Who's Who*, or perhaps he had been reading one of Paul's own articles in *The Northeast Review* or *The Journal of Modern Literary Scholarship*.

"I think he owes a debt of gratitude to Paul," Marian said loyally. "In spite of his reputation, he's never had the serious consideration he deserves—outside of Europe, at least. Why, do you know Paul's book will be the first biography to appear in English?" She *had* been listening to him these past ten years, in spite of her distracted looks and frequent interruptions to ask if he'd paid the grocery bill. Good girl.

"I'm dying to meet him," said Mrs. Dunmeade. "I enjoyed his *Brief Encounter* so much." Here was support. Let Watters notice that even Mrs. Dunmeade, who read almost nothing but Lloyd Douglas—even *she* knew something of Chevigny.

"*The Curt Reply*," he said.

"Why, I didn't mean to be," said Mrs. Dunmeade.

"No—that's the name of the play. *The Curt Reply*."

"Of *course*. I *knew* the other was by Bernard Shaw the moment I said it."

He thought Watters was looking sly. Wasn't there some way of reminding him how the conscripted sophomores had hawked and shuffled during his interminable droning about the *Civil Wars*? Teeling had refreshed the last of the drinks and now he sat down again.

"Well, now, tell us something more about Chevigny," said the Dean, who always threw a good deal of heartiness as a kind of makeweight into his most banal remarks. "I know him by his popular reputation, of course [*Who's Who*, Teeling thought again] but I'm not too well acquainted with the details."

Leaning back in his chair, Paul Teeling said, "Geoffrey Chevigny was born of an old family of Norman descent in York, England, in 1871."

"The Dean already gave us that," said Watters.

"I'm sorry, George," Teeling said mildly. Watters looked sheepish.

"No, *I'm* sorry," said Watters. "Shouldn't have interrupted you. It was a very good beginning."

"His father, Sir Manfred Chevigny—named for Byron's hero, by the way—was high in the councils of the Tory party during his lifetime . . ." This oft-told story had now become a part of his life and it was with a sense of satisfaction that he realized while shaving in the morning that he had been thinking of Geoffrey Chevigny ever since he had arisen— that period between 1885 and '87. Weren't there any letters still in existence to account for Chevigny's whereabouts and, more important, his thoughts at that period? In the department store a pretty girl waited on him and he had some trouble in describing the curtains that Marian wanted. He wondered what Chevigny would have thought of the girl. Wasn't she rather like "the sinuous girl with the ivory face" in *Ucalegon*? Perhaps the same one mentioned in the journal as "the jade-and-ivory Jeanette." He read the war headlines in the paper and thought, "Chevigny said that historians have misunderstood the Battle of Jutland. It was actually more than decisive." He had read and mastered every maneuver of that conflict, finding, to his disappointment, however, no mention of Chevigny in the official report and very little mention of his ship, *The Indispensable*, which had, it appeared, arrived a little late and had returned to drydock before the battle was completely over.

What epigram would Chevigny have coined to dispose of Watters at lunch? What was the reason for Chevigny's great attraction to ballet dancers in that 1895 period? Was it that the movement of the classical ballet was very much akin to the kind of movement of his plays and poetry? Teeling had waited anxiously for the appearance of the Ballet Russe in town and then, to his mortification, had fallen asleep in the middle of the second ballet.

As he walked to the bus stop, he wondered what Geoffrey Chevigny had been doing on this sunlit morning thirty years ago. Let's see—he had been living in Venice at the time, working over *The Three Roisterers*. Had he, at this exact time, been walking along the Grand Canal (he had lived two houses away from the one in which Browning had died and Teeling had a map of the neighborhood) signaling for a gondola, just as Teeling, on this fine May morning thirty years later, was signaling for the King Power Co. Trolley Car? What had Chevigny been thinking? Undoubtedly the theme of self-destruction that runs so brilliantly and gloomily through *The Three Roisterers* was more connected with the suicide of his friend Caldwell than himself. Chevigny had always been in favor of life.

And so Chevigny had become almost a part of him. Paul knew considerably more about the man, he reflected, than most of Chevigny's closest friends. It was really amazing how much could be learned—to the minutest detail—about the life of a man who had never come within a thousand miles of you. In fact it was probably true that Paul knew many things that Chevigny had forgotten or had never realized about himself. It would be amazing when they met. He imagined the two of them in his study late at night. "Do you realize," Paul was saying, "that at the same time you were working on *Dead Mansions* a very good friend of yours was writing a poetic drama with the identical idea—stemming from the anecdote about General Burgoyne and the children that you told one evening—June 1, 1905, I believe—at a dinner party at the Byerleys' house in Paris?" "No!" Chevigny would say, starting from his seat, "I never suspected. Not . . . ?" Paul would nod gravely. "I'm afraid so. A brilliant man, but he outlived his genius, don't you agree?"

That recalled a delicate problem, a problem that was actually more one of introduction than accomplishment. How was he going to get Chevigny aside for a long session of tactful questioning that would serve to fill in those baffling gaps in the biography? The truth had to be known, for instance, about that two months in 1907 that Chevigny had spent on an island in the Cyclades. Teeling was absolutely convinced that it had been neither Lady Judith Perrigeau nor the "Turkish girl with odd tastes" that malicious gossips had hinted at—but a long poem on a classical subject that had apparently never been printed. He had a clue to that. And the six months in the Swiss hospital that ensued? And the mysterious Dane with whom Geoffrey had taken that walking trip in North Africa? His opinion of Winston Churchill? The famous quarrel with Yeats? Had he actually called Pound a "damned, dirty, stinking—" as Widdicomb had reported or had he actually been referring to Widdicomb?

But all this had to be approached with the greatest smoothness—it all had to be in context. For the last two months, ever since he had heard from the agent that Chevigny would accept the lecture engagement, he had been wondering about a setting that would induce the reminiscent mood. Nothing seemed to help very much here. At Cambridge, he knew, Chevigny had been known as a "four-bottle man." The encyclopedia was unfortunately blank on this term. Dunmeade, who had been at Oxford, wasn't much help. He had said, "Might be Vichy water. That's all I drank when *I* was there. Couldn't stand English beer." Then, Chevigny liked long walking trips and mountain climbing—almost out of the question here in Indiana. Brilliant women were supposed to stimulate his conversation—then Paul thought of the faculty wives, a great many of whom, unhappily, seemed to be pregnant just at this moment, and the college girls, most of whom were trying to look like Lana Turner just now and—what was worse—succeeding. There was one pretty girl in the English Department, but, Paul reflected, she was a Swinburne man—in the middle of her thesis about Swinburne. Nothing would enrage Chevigny more than to hear all about *that*.

". . . and so," Paul began to wind up, "at the outbreak of the war he was forced to remove from his house in Rome whence he traveled to Majorca, where he now lives. It's a delightful place, I understand. He has a study overlooking the 'wine-dark waters' of the Mediterranean where he sits every morning from nine to twelve and writes on his work-in-progress, which is to be a grand critical study of all his literary contemporaries."

There was a brief silence. "It's snowing outside," Watters remarked.

But he had lost the patience of the group. "Illuminating.

Most illuminating," said the Dean. "I shall look forward to your biography with the greatest pleasure."

"*Very* interesting. I'm dying to meet him," said Mrs. Dunmeade.

"I hope he won't be too—well, you know how some of those writers are," said Mrs. Baker.

"Please try to be here at six-thirty for a drink or two before dinner. you remember that the lecture is at eight-thirty," said Marian.

They went out into the hall, putting on coats and rubbers. Watters lingered a little behind the others and Paul saw a forlorn look on his face. With a sudden warmth of forgiveness, he helped him on with his coat.

With his hand at the knob, Watters turned and leaned towards him, the wretched look magnified behind the show-windows of his large spectacles. In a low voice he said, "I envy you, Paul. I wish *my* man were alive."

To Paul the next two days were intense but hazy. They spent a lot of their time doing what Marian called "stocking up." At the liquor store Paul took an annoying half hour trying to get several wines he had never tasted, wines famous to literature but nearly unknown in the Dandy-Corner Liquor Store. Claret, Port, Bristol Cream Sherry and sack—no, sack was Falstaff—it must be hock.

"Have you any good hock?" he asked.

"This ain't a pawnshop, mister," said the fat man, laughing heavily.

He laid in an extravagant stock of Benson and Hedges cigarettes and pipe tobacco and Marian made two heavy hauls at the delicatessen. The house was cleaned and their part-time maid was engaged full time for the next three days. After some debate, Marian even bought her a uniform.

Coming into his study the evening before the arrival, Paul saw how thoroughly it had been cleaned—and even rearranged, a bit ostentatiously, he thought. All of the Chevigny books, for instance, (his collection was complete) were now on the top shelf of the bookcase along with the magazines containing Paul's articles. *The Manchester Guardians* for the last six months had been brought out of the closet and laid in a neat overlapping file on the lamp table. His big book of newspaper clippings relating to Chevigny, his friends and the places where he had lived for the past twenty years, had been placed on the top of the desk. Over the desk, Paul noticed something missing. On one side always hung the greatly enlarged photograph of Chevigny that Paul had had made from a publisher's publicity picture and on the other side hung a reproduction of a portrait of Landor—an old love from Ph.D days, now forsaken. Landor had been stored away. A small feeling of guilt prickled in his mind and he wondered if Chevigny hadn't taken somewhat of an advantage with him over Landor—a rather unfair advantage simply by being alive.

Watters had made that point, but Paul still wasn't sure of all the ins and outs of it. Until recently he had hardly ever thought of Chevigny as actually being alive; he was still breathing somewhere, of course, and still furnishing material for the last chapter but, in a sense, not really living. He moved the Chevigny picture over to the Landor hook, judging that there it could be seen a little better on first entrance into the room.

He slept badly that night and Marian accused him of mumbling. The next morning in his ten o'clock class he felt a little tired and on edge. He talked about Chevigny's life and read a selection of his poems. There were ten minutes left then and he called for comments or questions. A discouraging silence followed. Finally a boy in the last row raised his hand. "Yes?"

"Did Robert Frost know him?" he asked.

"I doubt if Chevigny would have noticed Frost," Paul snapped, being unfair and knowing it. "Any other questions?"

"You said *Ucalegon* is one of the greatest modern poems," one of the girls said. "It isn't in our textbook and . . ."

"Simply ignorance on the part of the editors," Paul said grimly. "These questions are all pretty frivolous, it seems to me."

Perry Reynolds, a great smoother-over, trying to nurse his athletic scholarship along for another year, said, "Sir, I understand that some critics place it above *The Wasteland* in importance. Isn't that true?"

So the class ended on a sweeter note and after a good lunch, Teeling felt somewhat better. It was just nerves, he told himself as he sat in his office going over the typescript of his little introductory speech. "A modern Odysseus on a voyage of intellectual discovery through . . ." Didn't that phrase sound a little too rhetorical? And the reference to his own work on Chevigny? However modest it might seem here in the quiet of his office, wasn't it possible that it might have another ring when spoken into the microphone in the auditorium? Finally he drew a light pencil line through several sentences, leaving them optional, to be decided on later. From time to time he had glanced out of the window and at last with a feeling of displeasure he went and stood at it, looking out on the snowy campus. It was only three o'clock and already it was becoming alarmingly dark. A sweeping wind coming out of the west kept the deserted walks bare but cast up odd drifts around the bases of the tree boles and at the edges of buildings. One moment, when the wind died, the air seemed salted with granular snow and the next moment was cleared with a vicious new blast. Standing there, Paul had an odd, almost portentous feeling, a half wish that Chevigny wouldn't come or that he had already gone.

But he had to leave; it was already only a half hour before train time. He muffled up and went out to the lot for his car. The streets seemed tortuous with slowly moving traffic, cars looking like monstrous buns with a layer of frosting. As he drove down the long street of gloomy warehouses and whole-sale establishments that led to the railway station, he thought how dreary this must be and how strange to a man accustomed to the bright air and colors of the Mediterranean. But he censored that thought quickly; it had no bearing whatsoever, he told himself.

At the station he found that he still had fifteen minutes to wait and so he walked around aimlessly, peering at the magazines on the stand, stopping for a moment to call Marian to let her know everything was all right, getting caught in the middle of two embracing families who were about to be parted.

Five minutes early he got out on the platform in the vicious wind. The light down the tracks was green but the train seemed to take a long time coming into the yards even after its whistle. But finally it was slowing up alongside.

The porters were jumping down and beginning to haul bags off. Passengers stood waiting on the steps with money showing between the fingers of their gloves. A great crowd had appeared from somewhere and he was shoved in the legs with suitcases and sideswiped by children, caught in a sudden steambath from beneath the train. How in the world was he going to find Chevigny in this mess? He started down the platform.

Then he suddenly discovered that he had been gazing at the face of an old man without understanding who he was. It was partly the overpowering familiarity of his looks that made him unrecognizable. It was partly that Paul, almost unconsciously, had been hearing the long physical description with which he had begun chapter five: "those eagle eyes beneath the sharp-cut brows . . . the military moustache . . . the clean angle of the cheekbone . . . the clear, reddish tone of the skin." Chevigny was taller than he had imagined, broader in the shoulders. With a gulp, Paul rushed up and spoke to him.

"Eh?" he answered. "No—CHIVingee, CHIVingee. Yes. You're the boy sent down from the school?"

It was a terrible blast for Paul. For years he had been calling him SheVEENye and everybody in college knew it. No time to worry about that now.

"I'm *Paul Teeling*," he said, waiting for the fierce face to soften into a recognitory smile.

It didn't. "Howjado."

"Paul Teeling," he said again with despair, but Chevigny was already getting his bags away from the redcap. "Now, sir, here is my luggage," he said brusquely.

On the ramp, Paul couldn't help staggering under the

weight of the three fat bags. Chevigny strode ahead of him like a brigadier leading a charge into the thick-packed but demoralized natives.

Paul finally caught up with him in the middle of the station and panted directions to the car. Once they got there, Paul nearly dropped the luggage. His muscles felt like broken threads. He leaned against the fender and caught his breath. Then he raised the cover of the trunk and slowly and carefully stowed the bags away.

When he turned he saw that Chevigny was still waiting for him to open the car door, though it wasn't locked.

"Inevitable awkwardness at first," Paul thought as they went down the street. "There's a kind of genuine hauteur that surrounds a truly great man." He'd decided that by no means would he ask Chevigny what he thought of America or Indiana—he'd have only scorn for such a hackneyed opening. Better let him speak first.

"Damned depressing place," Chevigny said. "Reminds me of Manchester and the Naples slums scrambled together at the North Pole."

"Yes, it does, rather," said Paul, weakly, trying to accommodate himself.

"I'm used to the bright colors of the Mediterranean, y'know," Chevigny remarked again.

CHIVingee. CHIVingee. CHIVingee. He must drill himself and remember to say it that way. "Mr. CHIVingee, your talk has been much anticipated. I think you'll find that your work is well known and appreciated here."

Wait until he saw the study—he'd tumble then. In the excitement at the station he probably hadn't connected the name with Paul's writing.

"Mph?"

"The weather *is* nasty but I think we can offer you a little bit of compensation at least with a warm fire and a good glass of Scotch."

"Bawph."

Paul tried once or twice more, but got nothing. When they came to a stoplight he took a quick sideglance at the author. "You look a little pale, Mr. Chevigny. Are you tired?"

"Oh. Quite. That is, not really." He put a fine carved hand to his forehead. "I was a bit dizzy in the train, you know. I had a fall. Nothing, really. I'll soon be right as rain." He seemed to slump even as he said this.

"Some sleep and all's well," he said. Paul thought of the people coming for cocktails, the dinner, the lecture, the Dean's reception after the lecture, and began to pass cars recklessly on the slippery pavement. It would have to be a quick nap. Marian would be firm about that.

At last he turned into the driveway and stopped at the walk. Chevigny seemed to waken from a slight doze. He looked out of the window. "Where are we?" he asked.

"Right here at our house," Paul said heartily, "and only a minute away from a good drink."

"But, my good fellow," Chevigny said abruptly, "those people at the school are expecting me. You'd better take me there at once. I do appreciate your offer, but . . ."

"I should have explained," Paul said in a rush. "You're staying with us. We have the honor . . ."

Chevigny got out of the car somewhat doubtfully, opening the door by himself this time. He followed Paul, who carried the bags. Marian had been waiting. She threw the front door open before he could touch the knob. "Mr.

SheVEENye!" she exclaimed. But it was only Paul and the luggage. Chevigny was standing several yards back, looking uncertainly down the street as if wondering whether any rescue was in sight.

They bundled him inside and got his hat and coat away from him. Marian was brisk and forceful and full of bright conversational bits. Chevigny was marched upstairs with the maid to be shown his room. He was given five minutes to wash and then marched down again—this time to the study where Paul had a fantastic battalion of bottles arranged on a silver tray in preparation for "a little drink before they all get here." Chevigny, to Paul's alarm, looked paler than ever and he saw him sink into the easy chair with a feeling of relief—even though his eye had passed blankly over the photograph and the books.

"A Scotch and soda, sir?" Paul asked.

"No. Just a little Martini. Very dry."

Horrors! Englishmen *never* drank cocktails if they could help it, never Martinis.

"Just a moment. I thought my wife called," said Paul, turning whiter than Chevigny.

Ten minutes later it turned out that the Claphams next door had just half a pint of gin left and a nearly full bottle of American vermouth they had intended to throw away because of its unexpected sweetness.

"He wants to take a nap before dinner," Paul whispered to Marian.

"Out of the question!" she hissed, dropping an olive into the glass.

Back in the study, Paul wondered how to begin the friendship, how to get Chevigny around to literary matters. "I suppose you realize, Mr. Chevigny, that American critics have been increasingly absorbed in your work? A great deal has been written about you over here during the past few years."

Chevigny tested his Martini and set it down. "Oh? 'tso? Somebody sent me a copy of a piece by some damned fool. Didn't read it. On a frightful juvenile thing of mine called *Ucalegon*. I daresay there're better, though."

The insufferable old—! This was getting impossible. It was not only insulting to Paul but it was insulting to Chevigny as well! Then he remembered that this *was* Chevigny. He almost said, "Sir, I happen to be the damned fool . . ." but he thought better of it and after he had taken a long draught from his glass, another thought crept in. It might be just as well that Chevigny *hadn't* connected him. But oh, the moment when he did.

The situation had to be straightened out somehow, sooner or later. Paul tried again. "I think you're being too modest, Mr. Chevigny," he said in a slightly strained voice. "It seems to me that *Ucalegon* is one of the few modern poems that successfully exploits the thematic and ideational conflicts of our times—in the very cacophony of the language and dichotomy of the structure. In a time when poetry is growing increasingly hieratic . . ."

"Heard of it, eh?" Chevigny asked and relapsed into silence.

The clock on the wall ticked and Marian and the maid knocked and rattled things in a subdued way in the kitchen. At last Paul began. "Mr. Chevigny, I wanted to ask . . ."

"Better go up if I'm to have that sleep," said Chevigny, rising.

Paul went along with him and followed up the stairs, not knowing quite how he was going to put it. At the door of the bedroom, just as Chevigny was going in, he finally managed to get something out. "Mr. Chevigny, I'm afraid it's a little late for a nap right now. We have guests coming in for cocktails—all of whom want especially to meet you—and then we're having dinner. The lecture is at eight-thirty, you know, and after that"—it began to sound worse—"the Dean, Dean Baker, is giving a reception at his house." Chevigny had turned around in the doorway and his pale face seemed to darken. Paul stumbled on, "Of course, you'll have a chance to get a nice long sleep in the morning—er—your train doesn't leave until ten-thirty . . ."

Chevigny's sharp eyebrows, pulled down, seemed to stab at him. "Well!" he barked. "Such awful damned bloody nonsense!" He shut the door.

Paul went slowly down the stairs again and sat in a chair in his study. He tried to think of every rationalization. The man was very old and used to a different kind of living. Besides that, he was evidently tired and out of sorts. Perhaps after a few drinks he would begin to be a little more convivial and the rudeness would wear off. Paul had often smiled at the anecdotes about Chevigny's sharp replies and Johnsonian squelches, but this—this was just plain—he looked at Chevigny's chair and saw the full Martini on the table beside it.

Paul tried not to think of what Watters would say or how the Dean would look at him and all he could hope for was a miracle that would change Chevigny. He sat there with his head in his hands for nearly half an hour, hearing Marian's voice occasionally and dreading to look at the clock.

He couldn't avoid it finally and he saw that people would be arriving any minute now. Then he heard a car stop in the street outside. He pulled himself to his feet and he realized that all his muscles felt strained and sore from the heavy bags. He went slowly to the stairs and began to climb them.

He hesitated outside Chevigny's door, not knowing what to say again. Then he heard the knocker at the front door and so he rapped twice. "Mr. Chevigny? I don't want to hurry you, but I wonder if there's anything you need before you come down?" No answer.

"Mr. Chevigny?" He knocked again. No answer. "Mr. Chevigny!"

He *had* gone to sleep, the old fool. Paul tried the door quietly and found that it wasn't locked. He began to push it open slowly.

Just as he had expected, Chevigny was lying stretched out on the bed with his eyes closed. He had, however, started to change and he wore evening trousers and a dress shirt. Paul stopped a moment when he saw that he was barefooted. The surprisingly narrow long feet were very white with dark blue veins, like queer outcrops of water-eroded rock. Teeling halted, then heard the Dean's voice downstairs in the hall, which urged him on.

He touched Chevigny gently on the shoulder. "I'm sorry, sir, but I'm afraid you'll have to wake up." There was no response. "The guests are coming and we're about ready to begin. If I can help you in any way . . . ? *Wake up*, Mr. Chevigny."

But Mr. Chevigny would never begin again or wake up again and he no longer needed any help. It took Paul quite a long time to realize this and to believe it. With increasing hurry and confusion, he discovered first that the hands were cold, that there was no heartbeat at all, that no breath came from the thin nostrils. He knelt down and put his ear to Chevigny's stiff shirt front. There was nothing.

He stood up slowly, feeling sick. He felt as if he were in a whirlpool and about to go down the drain. He steadied himself against the wall and looked down at Chevigny. Already the man seemed to be looking better. Paul began to think of his face as "benign," perhaps "noble." The hard sarcastic lines had all been eased out of it and the lips seemed to be smiling gently at him. "A certain calmness and greatness of spirit shone through . . ." Paul wrote in his mind. "The white hair still neat, the classic brow unruffled, the magnificent eyes now closed in . . ."

He turned away and walked slowly out of the room, closing the door behind him gently. The noise of arrival had increased and he stepped softly along the hall to his own bedroom. When he was there, he walked up and down from window to dresser several times with no particular object but with the thought that he must gather all his ideas, must synthesize all the aspects.

He had been walking for several minutes when he stopped before the mirror. He saw a smile on the face of the man there and realized that he was rubbing his hands together. Only then did he know that the miracle had happened. He began to walk again, hardly able to contain himself.

He would not have to face everybody with Chevigny— but that was only an added blessing. The important thing was like a kind of grand legacy. Already the last chapter of the book had begun to take form in his mind and, magnificently, he himself was a part of it. He had shaken the hand, he had looked into the face, he had shared the last moments of the great man! For all practical purposes, he had been at the bedside in the last extremity *and* without a doubt he had heard his last words. "Paul Teeling, his biographer and close friend, describes in his book the fortitude and resignation with which Chevigny . . ."

"Did you . . . I mean, personally?" What an answer he could give to that question now! He was almost too full of it to think what the answer would be—perhaps simply a bowed head and a mournful "Yes."

He began to wonder about this evening. Perhaps a little elegy-like speech, dignified, touching, simple—in the tradition of the French *oraison funèbre*? And that too would go in the last chapter, would be quoted in future studies.

One idea glowed in his mind after another and he paced up and down the bedroom for a long time, the titles for articles occurring to him, the name "Paul Teeling" in various kinds of type on various bindings coming before his eyes, a vision of the photographs and the long reviews in the Sunday book sections.

At last he was aware that there had been a tapping at the door for two or three minutes. It opened and Marian stood there.

"*Paul!*" You're not dressed! Everybody's been waiting for just hours. For God's sake, hurry up."

"Oh! Yes, yes. Sorry," he said and began to go to the closet for his tuxedo.

"And listen," she said, "what's happened to your man? He hasn't come downstairs either."

Reminded, he turned around exultantly. "Oh, Marian. He's dead! He's dead! At last he's dead!"

About the Author

Since 1947 Robie Macauley has been contributing stories to the best American Literary magazines. Some of them have been reprinted in the *O. Henry Prize Stories* and *Best American Short Stories* volumes. He wrote the critical introduction for the reissue of Ford Madox Ford's *Parade's End* and in 1949 won the *Furioso* fiction award. His novel, *The Disguises of Love,* which was published in 1952, received wide critical acclaim.

Mr. Macauley is married and is the father of one son. At present, he lives in Washington, D. C., and works for an organization doing educational research.